ISBN 978-1-5262-1044-9

To all those with growing pains

ONE

Umbra's hand brushed the thorn of a weed nestled in the rice plants. It left a gash in her skin. Her blood dripped into the paddy's water, staining the soil below. She took her rusty knife from its holster, quietly cursing the pain in her hand, and hacked away at the weed before picking the rice again.

She worked in her little patch of the nursery paddy, where the rice plants had grown from seeds into small spuds over the past month. Her sack was nearly full of infant rice plants. Huffs and yawns drifted through the humid air and mingled with the stirrings of nocturnal creatures, while her people worked under the fast-setting sun. Umbra yawned the loudest—under-rested and thoroughly exhausted as she was.

The horn finally sounded to signal the end of another day of hard labour. The workers each threw their sacks of rice onto the wooden cart, one after the other, and left the fields. All were eager to go home for their second meal of the day. Adorjan, the overseer of the paddies, stood by the cart as they did so, and he was the only one with any zeal left to show. He offered praise and received only grunts or feeble thanks in return.

'Are you trying to break the cart with this much rice?' he said when he took Umbra's sack and threw it over his shoulder with exaggerated effort.

'Do you need me tomorrow?' Umbra asked.

'Nope. We should be getting our fish tomorrow, so no one will be working. I'll get this cart to the main paddy, and we can start planting there the day after. Get some food and sleep. No offence, but you look like you need it.'

'Goodnight, then,' Umbra mumbled, then she turned to take her leave.

'Hold it,' Adorjan called after her. He held a small pile of rice from her sack, sprinkled with red. 'I wasn't aware that rice could bleed.'

Umbra shrugged. 'It was just a weed. I hacked it up.'

Adorjan smiled again. 'Then justice was served. Let me see your hand.'

The wound was dark, and the bleeding had already subsided. 'It was only a thorn,' Umbra said. 'It hurt a little, but it's fine now.'

'Let Vada see it all the same,' Adorjan said, tossing the blood-splattered rice back into Umbra's arms. 'The last thing I need is for one of my best workers to get infected right before we plant in the main paddy.'

Umbra made her way in the general direction of her

home. She walked toward the island's western shore, down a hill overlooking the sunset and the sea. She already felt a chill in the evening air, though it was not yet dark. This was her favourite time of day—the hour of sunset when the stars began to appear. It was the time when she was left alone, and most of her kin were already home for their fish and rice. For a little while, until she was expected back home too, she had the little world of her island for herself.

She wandered, letting her feet decide the way. She didn't feel like climbing the cliff faces today or straying too far from home. She was growing hungry and didn't want to make a long trek for dinner. This evening called for some relaxation in sweet solitude while watching the orange sky turn black.

The beach called out to her this time. She clambered across rocks peeking out of the sea to sit in her favourite spot. It was on a shore covered by the shadow of Burial Hill, where she was watched over by the wooden burial figures at its peak. She sometimes pretended they were watching the sky with her, or that she was eavesdropping on a secret conversation of theirs. She was too young to have met any of the people the figures immortalised, for most had died long before she was born, so she made up her own personalities for them. One always slept, one always argued, and one always laughed. As she grew older, it dawned on her that she had based some of them on islanders she knew. It was a fun game to play sometimes, but today she only wanted to relish the ocean's salty breeze on her face and the tickle of the sand on her skin.

Not much time passed watching the ripples of the

dying sun on the waves until she realised she still had bloodied rice plants in her hand. She tossed them as far into the water as she could, which was barely far enough for the waves to grab them and slowly carry them away. She watched it float away on the sea's calm ripples until it vanished into the deep, washing her bloody hand in the water as she did so. It stung, but it stopped bleeding quickly.

Only when the sun fully set did Umbra pry herself away from her perfect peace and carry herself home. Umbra had salted mackerel and seaweed for dinner that she fried in her stone cooking pot atop an open fire. The scent was alluring and always lingered in her home long after the meal had been eaten. Umbra could smell lemongrass as the mackerel roasted on the fire, which Adorjan must have picked and added to the day's rations. That little touch added some novelty to the otherwise ordinary meal. She filled two wooden bowls with rice, seaweed and mackerel, then filled two cups with water from an almost empty bucket.

'It's ready,' she said.

'Hm. So am I.' Varyis, her father, lay on his floor-bed with his long and unkempt hair flailing out around him. He sat up with effort and accepted the portion she offered. The bowl shook in his hands a little more gently than the night before. Umbra thought he had more strength than most evenings, for he could sit up and eat unaided. His mood seemed better for it. She left the cup of water by Varyis' feet.

'Adorjan gave us some lemongrass,' she said.

Varyis grunted through his first mouthful, his lip trembling each time he swallowed. 'Working tomorrow too?'

'No, the day after. We'll be planting the rice in the main paddy.'

Varyis grunted again, battling with the chopsticks shaking in his fingers. 'Your hand,' he said.

Umbra looked down at her palm. The gash looked far worse than it felt. 'Just a cut from a thorn.'

'Clean it in the sea after you eat.'

'I already did.'

Umbra ate a mouthful of food and watched her father sitting on his floor-bed with his head bowed and his long, locked hair hiding his face. She had almost forgotten the sound of his voice. She was used to hearing his grunts or groans of pain on the bad days. His skin had become pale after so many years spent in the shadows of their tiny hut with only candlelight to warm him. Umbra took another bite. The mackerel was rich in flavour, and the salt in the rice was heavy, making it hard to swallow. She heard a clattering sound beside her. Her father's cup had fallen and spilt its contents on the ground. Varyis' fingers shook as he watched the cup roll by his feet. Umbra quickly finished the water in her own cup.

'I need more too,' she said. She took the empty cup from the ground and reached for the almost-empty bucket of water. But there was another clattering sound—her father's bowl fell from his fingers too and hit the ground with a hollow ring, spilling out its contents. Both his hands shook violently. Umbra sighed as she saw her father's head drop.

'You can have some of—'

'Just...' her father said. 'Just get out.'

'Father, I can—'

'Get out. Get out.'

Varyis kicked the bowl with what might have been all his strength. It slid along the ground with a chime and tapped Umbra's foot. She didn't hesitate. She filled her father's cup with water, placed it at his feet, and left the hut. She took the rest of her meal with her.

The sky had turned into a blend of black and deep violet since Umbra had gotten home. She walked along the calm sea tide outside her home until she found a spot on the beach where her hut was out of sight. She quietly finished her meal. She looked out over the sea at the pale white moonlight rippling on it and the islands in the distance. Every moment alone was peaceful, playful, or whatever she wanted it to be. Nothing ever imposed on her little world. Not until tonight.

Umbra noticed a subtle change in the sky after she ate her last bite—there was a crack of vibrant green light far above, as though part of the sky were torn in two. It grew brighter and brighter, but never more than a subtle glow. It might have gone unnoticed if not for how alien the tone of green was. Umbra was enthralled and utterly baffled. It looked lonely, like a solitary flame in the dark. It flickered and pulsed like an unsteady heartbeat and cast a subtle green reflection upon the sea. The longer she looked at it, the more she realised how colossal this crack in the sky was. Umbra watched in a trance of awe. It was utterly captivating for the brief time it shone.

The light soon dissolved into darkness. It left nothing in its wake but the normality of a clear night. Umbra waited a while longer, keeping her eyes keenly on the sky, but the light never appeared again. The rest of the night passed like many others—Umbra watched the sea until it became too cold on the beach to stay out, and then dragged herself home again.

Her home was dark and quiet. Her father sighed in deep sleep. The smell of mackerel still lingered, and only remnants of the spilt meal were left on the floor. Her father's bowl was empty, and the spoils of fish oil and seaweed were still on his fingers. Umbra felt guilty as she realised he had eaten his spilt meal from the floor. *He had to do that because I left him hungry, and I didn't give him my bowl.* Umbra decided to apologise in the morning if her father were awake before she left.

Umbra quietly lay on the bare floor as far from her father's mat as she could. Sleep did not find her swiftly that night, as a mixture of guilt for her father and fascination for the strange green glow kept her awake. That same light eventually led her to a sound sleep and followed her into her dreams. She dreamed of fishing on the open sea under the light of a bright green moon.

Umbra woke up to a bright orange sun piercing her eyelids and heat on her skin. It was close to midday, and she had already made good use of her day of rest. She heard music being expertly played outside. She rose from the floor and changed from her sweat-drenched rags into her other tattered garments while her father still slept. Umbra drank half of the lukewarm water left in their bucket and then stepped out of the hut with an empty woven food sack in her hands.

Some of the islanders sat on the beach where Cadeo stood playing his t'rung. His long, locked white hair clung to his back in a woven sack as he played to the sea and smiled. It was the same unnamed melody he played every day that the fishermen had a haul to share. Umbra named it The Wandering of Fishermen, since its purpose was to guide the fishermen back to the island shore. Umbra used to imagine herself as the one at sea for whom the song was played. She imagined being out there, filling fishing nets, sweating under the hot sun, and sailing back ashore to a beautiful song welcoming her home. That romantic daydream lasted only until she was old enough to learn the song's purpose. Then it became only another practical facet of her weekly routine.

Umbra had also learned why the song was created from Vada, the herbalist. She had shared a story with Umbra that the oldest islanders had told her—about a dense fog on the island and sea that caused the fishermen to lose their way back home. Some stayed lost and were never found again, and were immortalised in songs and wooden figures on Burial Hill. Umbra had heard many stories about what may have happened to those fishermen lost at sea and about old islanders who wandered too far from the shore, only to be caught in an angry wave or to lose sight of land. The song Cadeo played was now for little more than tradition maintained for decades, as there had been no fog in years and no one had been witless enough to sail or swim ahead of an impending storm. The fishermen could find their way back home fine now, with or without the song to guide them. It was especially pointless now that Cadeo had only begun playing The Wandering of Fishermen when the boats were already in sight of the shore. But, Umbra was glad that the song was still played, as it was pleasant to her ears and nostalgic even still as a youth.

Two boats presently floated far out on the sea. Umbra joined her islanders on the shore and quietly waited for the fishermen to return home from their voyage once more.

TWO

Cadeo's arms ached with each note he played. The two sticks felt heavier in his hands every time duty called upon him to play this melody, and he had lost count of the years he had persevered in playing through the exhaustion of an ageing body. Even still, the sight of the fishermen drawing closer to his people in the morning made up for it. A smile never failed to touch his lips as he played, and it only got brighter whenever the young fishermen's feet touched the sand.

The boats carrying the fishermen were close enough to the shore for Cadeo's ageing eyes to see the fishing nets aboard. They held fish, but the nets weren't as full as usual. He kept playing the song until their boats touched the sand and the fishermen dropped their anchors. His people's silence was broken as they got up and gathered around the boats with their empty food sacks in hand, while Nghi coated their fish in salt. But this morning, they were far more aggressive than usual. They shoved each other to get their share of fish first, and some demanded bigger servings. Adorjan jumped onto a boat's bow, calling out instructions and bringing some semblance of order to the people. He and the two fishermen gave the islanders each their fair share of the spoils. *We will soon be coming to the end of our rice reserves,* Cadeo reflected. *And the people are conscious of it.*

One fisherman named Quy argued with Ruhan, the man Cadeo considered to be as close as a son.

'It'll be a miracle if this thing sails again without the whole hull falling out,' Ruhan said. He was a stern and harsh-looking man with an unkempt beard and thick, locked hair. His body was tanned and muscular, and he had eyes that effortlessly uneased anyone they were set on. 'You can't neglect it much longer until you go sinking to the depths with it.'

'If that happens, so be it,' Quy said. He was a comparatively small and slight young man and did not speak as measurably as Ruhan did. Everything about him was the antithesis of Ruhan—even Quy's locked hair was thinner than his. Quy was not an imposing man, but was well respected on the island for his work ethic and undying optimism. 'Regardless, you're not laying one finger on her, Ru.'

Quy left Ruhan to grumble and look over the state of his boat with disapproval. Cadeo thought that he could hardly be blamed. Cadeo had given the boat to Quy years ago, long after he had given up on sailing himself and shortly after Quy had come of age to learn the art. Quy clearly hadn't let Ru touch it since his first sail. That was especially evident beside Ashan's boat, which was practically immaculate and looked able to sail easily amid any storm.

Quy bowed his head to Cadeo and rose with an expression that was at odds with his usual relaxed demeanour. He was young and always full of vigour. Cadeo had much affection for him, perhaps more than any besides Ruhan and Gratus, though he would never admit that he had favouritism among his people. Quy had a slim, tanned body, and most of his skin had been covered with beautiful and vibrant tattoos. Cadeo's tattoos had become duller with age, and seeing Quy's reminded him of his youth. It made Cadeo's heart glad to know that there were still those who took traditions like tattoos to heart and that they would likely remain with his people long after Cadeo was gone.

'A word, please?' Quy said to Cadeo, dispensing with his usual courtesies.

'Something the matter, child?'

'I fear so.'

'Well, carry the t'rung for me, if you'd be so kind. We can talk on the way to my hut.' Quy's steps beside Cadeo were slow, and the wooden instrument weighed heavily on his back. He had the look of a man whom sleep had been eluding.

Cadeo tightened the sling around his torso and cradled his share of fish in one hand. His long, locked hair was held in a bundle on his back. It was another burden he was proud to bear, as his hair was the longest and heaviest among his people—a worthy reflection of his many years of life and the wisdom it afforded him.

'So, what's the problem?' Cadeo asked once they were away from the others.

'Something strange happened at sea,' Quy said. 'Very strange. Perhaps a bad omen. I fear that hard times may soon come upon us.'

'An *omen*?' Cadeo felt a chill. The word omen hadn't passed his lips or ears in decades, and he hadn't missed its absence.

'Yes, out on the sea at dawn,' Quy continued. 'The fish were plentiful when we arrived and set the net in the water. But the fish fled from us when the sun fully rose. Every one of them dove into the depths at once and left our nets half empty. There were hundreds on the surface at first, Cadeo. But all of them fled together as though they were of one mind.

'We waited a while for them to surface again, but they didn't. We ended up waiting together for the whole morning for even a single one to resurface. But there was no movement in the water at all. When it was close to midday, we saw them all rise to the surface—dead fish. Dozens of them. Maybe hundreds. Just floating beneath our hulls. We first thought it may have been a predator in the water, and so we made back for land. But actually, the fish were left whole and uneaten, so I doubt it. We have no idea how or why they died.'

Cadeo was quiet in thought as he listened, as was his way. 'They vanished together and died together,' he reflected. 'And you saw no other living fish on your way back?'

'No, not the one. I thought to let you know now because this worries me. At best, we now have fewer fish than usual for the next few days. We didn't take the fish that were already dead—it may have been some kind of disease that killed them. Maybe the next time we set sail, the fish will be alive and as keen for our bait as usual. But at worst...I'm not sure. A sign that a famine is soon to come, perhaps? Maybe the fish had starved to death themselves. That would bode ill for us too.'

Cadeo smiled despite himself. 'So extreme an assumption from just one bizarre event, Quy.'

'Like I said, there were *hundreds*, Cadeo,' Quy said. 'Hundreds of fish just dead on the surface, and those were only the ones we could see. That's more than just *bizarre*.'

Cadeo frowned. 'What did Ashan think?' he asked while suspecting he already knew the answer.

'About what you'd expect. He said that Ru must have been bathing in the sea again, and every fish for miles would surely die after that. He said they probably died from the stench alone.'

'Meaning he does not take this seriously.'

'Does he ever take anything seriously? I'm going out on the water again this evening. I'll go when everyone else is settling for dinner. Then we can see if my assumptions are too extreme or not.'

Cadeo suddenly felt dread in his heart. He spoke before he could think. 'No, do not. You're not to sail after sundown, and not with the fish...' Cadeo's words trailed off as he realised the randomness of his outburst.

Quy looked at him with an eyebrow raised. 'Well, I wasn't asking,' Quy said—firm, but not unkind.

Cadeo nodded. 'I...I understand,' he said with the dread still in his heart. 'But I will stay awake to play music for you on the shore. And for now, it would be best that we keep this to ourselves. No use causing alarm with talks of famines. I'll only play if you are gone for more than a couple of hours, so as not to wake the others.'

'Of course. I'll leave quietly at sunset.'

Quy made the climb with Cadeo up to his hut, which was set in the face of a hill that overlooked the sea. He set the t'rung down and politely bid Gratus a good morning before taking his leave. Cadeo sat on his floor-bed, quite exhausted and quietly anxious. He had forgotten the unease that came with nature's deviation from routine. This routine had been one which he had enjoyed for decades.

Omen. Famine. These were words that had no place in this land of tranquillity and hard labour anymore, and Cadeo refused to believe that they would ever have a place here again. A mere few decades without either word being uttered was not nearly long enough.

Adorjan wiped sweat from his brow as he stood in the heat of the soon-setting sun. He stood in the main paddy as workers planted the rice that would soon grow tall for harvest. The soil was healthy, and the rice had been planted well. Adorjan was satisfied with the assurance that hard work would soon be rewarded. He blew his horn to mark the day's end, then walked the rows to thank the weary workers. He started with the eldest of them. He praised her work in his usual way with a warm smile.

'Your sack is practically empty, Gratus. Thank you for your hard work.'

Adorjan only received a smile in return. Gratus recently looked far older than her years. All the years she had spent toiling in the sun had not been kind to her skin. She bowed and hobbled away from the paddy with the long hair bundled on her back, weighing her down and slowing her steps. Adorjan wished, as he did every day, that she would stop coming to the fields and take the deserved rest that befits a woman of her age. But he knew better than to suggest it out loud, as she would only berate him for it. So, he chose instead to be grateful for the work she stubbornly persisted in. Though he couldn't help seeing that her sack of rice plants was far fuller than the others. Planting rice in the paddy was gruelling work at any age, and this was the most Adorjan could hope for from Gratus in a day. He set the sack by the cart, out of view of the others. *Looks like I have a few more hours of work to do today.*

He watched over the fields where the last few workers were leaving with heavy feet. Lihn and Thi walked together as they always did. They were close friends, yet Adorjan very rarely saw them share a word, even while they worked beside each other. They were very different from each other to the eye—Thi had a smile that never left her face, whereas Lihn rarely smiled at all. She seemed like a miserable woman and, as Umbra had once told him, her mouth constantly hung open like a dead fish's. It was a wonder to him how they ever became so close. Kien had worked alone as usual and walked to the cart alone with a solemn vibe. Her straw hat covered most of her face. Adorjan wasn't even sure what colour Kien's eyes were, as she was never seen without that hat on her head.

Umbra's feet looked particularly heavy, and her head hung the lowest. Adorjan could see even from a distance that she was exhausted. She looked far worse up close— her eyes were dull and barely open.

'What's up with you?' Adorjan asked as he took a heavier-than-expected sack from Umbra's hands. She was usually the hardest worker with the most vigour in her youth.

'Not much,' she replied with a strained voice.

Adorjan pulled her closer and placed his hand on her forehead. She barely reacted and stared blankly at him. Her head didn't feel any warmer than it ought to after a day in the sun.

'You're not sick, are you? Did you see Vada about that cut on your hand?'

'It was just a scratch,' was all she said before she left the paddy. Adorjan decided to let her go and imagined her mood as normal for a girl her age who worked as hard as she did. It was a wonder she wasn't moodier more often.

Adorjan watched the rest of his kin leave until the paddy was empty and he was alone. His thoughts lingered on Umbra and her demeanour as he planted the rest of her and Gratus' plants. She was often quiet and reserved, but such moodiness was unlike her. *She must be hungry, just like everyone else*, he concluded. *It would be just like her to suffer quietly. How many fish did she get this morning in that rush on the shore?* He shook his head and sighed, frustrated at the thought that a little girl's hunger could have gone ignored.

Adorjan was exhausted after he finished planting the rest of Gratus and Umbra's rice. He sat on the ground beside the paddies, indulging in his daily solitude. This brief respite was the most calming part of his day. It was easier to find serenity in this place, with nothing to distract him from nature. He owed his understanding of the paddies and his sensitivity to their needs to years of this simple practice. The land, the water, the weeds, the changing weather—he understood their tireless labour for the young rice instinctively when he sat here to simply observe and feel. *The soil will be prone to weeds this time, with the soil so healthy,* he noted. *But this harvest will be a rich one.*

Adorjan eventually made his way home when the sun was almost set. The island was empty, as it always was at this time of the evening. He saw only Quy on his way back, who had his harpoon and a basket of bait in hand.

'You're going fishing again,' Adorjan stated more than he asked.

'Just to test the waters,' Quy replied. 'I told Cadeo about the dead fish. I'm gonna spend a few hours out there and see if anything's changed.'

'Right. Listen, yesterday morning was a complete mess on the shore. Some may not have gotten any fish, or not as much as others.'

'Yeah, I saw that too. We can figure that out when I'm back, which should be before sunrise. Any fish I get this time can be shared with whoever didn't get enough yesterday.'

With that, Adorjan returned to his messy home. His spare garments were in a pile on his floor-bed. The remains of last night's roasted cockroaches were in his only bowl, and the hut reeked of their stubborn, heavy stench. Bugs made for a more tasteless meal than one would expect for such a potent smell. Adorjan yearned for the taste—and the smell—of fresh fish in his hut again.

He decided not to stay a moment longer than necessary. He would be back soon for another uncomfortable night, as his empty stomach was keen to remind him. He opened a sack hanging beside his still-dirty utensils. Two small fish stared back at him from inside, which were his share from the day before. It was enough for three small meals at most. He took the sack and headed for Umbra's hut.

It was quiet when he arrived. The sun was fully set, and their hut was lit by a small fire. Adorjan called inside, but there was no answer. He entered to find Varyis lying on his floor-bed, asleep as usual, and Umbra lying on the floor next to him, hugging her stomach. Two empty bowls contained the remains of what looked like mushy, discoloured seaweed. A cup of water was spilt under Varyis' hand. *It was indeed hunger that put her in that mood,* Adorjan bitterly reflected. *Poor girl.*

He gently shook Umbra's shoulder. 'Umbra?'

She groaned in response, and her eyes half-opened.

'I've brought some fish for us,' Adorjan whispered. 'Come, get up.'

She groaned again. Adorjan's heart sank at the sight of her. She was frail and utterly helpless. Her shallow breathing and pale skin were stark even in the fire's warm glow. He let his hand rest on her shoulder for a moment of sympathy, but had to turn away from her to resist shedding tears. Firewood was still burning in the room under a pot of boiling water. He added the small fish and a couple of handfuls of seaweed from their bucket. A pleasant aroma swiftly filled the hut.

'What're you doing?' Varyis asked, still lying down with his back to Adorjan.

'Oh, you're awake,' Adorjan replied. 'I'm boiling fish.'

'Whose fish?'

'Yours now.'

Varyis grunted. 'That's your share of fish for a reason. You mustn't go hungry on our account.'

'Not to worry, I've had my fill already.'

'No one has their fill here. I doubt you've even had a bite.'

Adorjan smiled at Varyis' back. 'You shouldn't live on seaweed and rice alone, not when there's fish to spare,' he said.

'It's no wonder that we must, when a little girl can't fight her way through a crowd of hungry adults to earn her share of fish.'

Adorjan's smile quickly faded. 'I'm sorry,' he said. 'We'll make sure everyone has their share without having to fight for it, I promise.'

Varyis grunted again. 'Nothing to apologise to *me* about.'

Adorjan looked at Umbra, who slept curled up with her face to the floor and her hair tied around her shoulders. It dawned on him that this was the first time he had seen her sleep since she was old enough to walk. She looked restless, even while dormant. He shook her shoulder again with a bowl of fish and seaweed in hand. 'Umbra?'

'She's overworked,' Varyis said. He looked relatively well tonight. He was not visibly shaking, and he spoke relatively clearly. 'Maybe let her sleep again tomorrow?'

'Of course. She need not keep coming every day. You'll have your share of fish and rice regardless.'

'She wouldn't accept a morsel that hasn't been earned. You know this.' Varyis managed to sit up on his floor-bed and held out his hand. 'I'll make sure she eats this.'

Adorjan handed him the bowl. 'She's worked hard enough for a lifetime of fish already, I'd say.'

Varyis said nothing in response. He took hold of his daughter and hauled her up with great effort to lean on him. Umbra's eyes slowly opened. Varyis began to shake as he took the boiled fish in his hands.

Adorjan took that as his cue to respectfully leave. His heart was still heavy with sympathy as he did. *Two fish. That's all we can do for them after all her labour. Two tiny fish and two more empty stomachs in the morning.* He felt sick at the thought.

Adorjan returned home and made a small meal out of rice, roasted cockroaches, and lemongrass. As he anticipated, it was another uncomfortable night spent hungry and exhausted until sleep eventually found him.

THREE

No clouds blemished an enchanting sunset. The wind was tame, and the sea was dormant. It was as perfect an evening for setting sail as one could hope for.

Cadeo washed his hair and tattooed body in the sea. His hair grew heavier with water, flowed down his back and rested on the sea's surface. Yet, it was not as heavy as it had once been, much to Cadeo's sadness. Age had caused much of his hair to shed, and he was left with far fewer locks from his youth, though his hair remained long and full. The art on his skin shone with the setting sun glowing on him. Cadeo was quite self-indulgent and proud while bathing, admiring the colours and patterns on his flesh. Some of the more recent tattoos had retained their form well, but what were once beautiful depictions of nature had become abstract streaks of pink, purple, and green over the years. Even the faded art still had a beauty to it that befitted a man of seventy-six.

Cadeo sat alone on the sand after his wash and watched Quy sail further away in his ageing fishing boat. Cadeo rarely saw lone boats on dark waters—there was little reason to sail after sunset. He rubbed his sticks in his hand, already preparing to guide Quy home once more. His t'rung stood before him in the sand. It was a strange-looking instrument made of hollow bamboo poles lined along a curved bamboo spine, which arched to a tip like a bony finger pointing to the sky. Cadeo had heard its chimes and felt its vibrations through his bones for so many years that the music he played held little novelty for him.

The instrument was almost as old as he was. Yet, it had admittedly aged far more gracefully than he had. It had been made for Cadeo as a child by his father's hands, and Cadeo's hands had been the only ones ever to make it sing. Cadeo had chosen to use his talent to guide fishermen back to the island amid the famine. He remembered feeling, not joy, but burdened with responsibility and scared to hold the lives of his people in his hands. Cadeo later realised, with the benefit of age and wisdom, that it never mattered what melody he played, nor how skillfully he played, as long as it was loud enough to reach the boats on the water. He also realised that that role had served to distract him in a time of famine, fear, and helplessness. Only after his father's passing did he become grateful for this t'rung and resolved to keep this responsibility in his heart forever.

Cadeo presently waited by the shore until the time came to play again, even after Quy insisted that he could find his way back well enough. But Cadeo soon felt the burden of old age wearing on him as he waited. He caught his head nodding a few times and felt his eyelids closing before Quy's boat was fully out of sight. The last thing Cadeo saw that night was the boat drifting away on the water toward the dark orange sky. Then sleep caught up to him. He spent the rest of that night looking out to sea with his eyes closed.

His sleep on the beach felt short and restless. His dreams were abstract and cruel, creating a warped vision of memories with his offspring. It was a familiar dream in which the sea was harsh, the sky was black, and the horizon was empty. He rowed with two small children on board in the dead of the night. The dream progressed much the same way as it always did. A strong wave rocked their boat when their island home was almost out of sight. The children fell overboard. The name Adra fell from Cadeo's lips, over and over, as he reached out to the sea. It ended with Cadeo's hand holding the child's as she barely stayed afloat. But he was always too weak to hold onto her. He had to watch as the dark waters swallowed her.

Cadeo woke up soaked in sweat as though he had been the one drowning. *Adra.* It was always Adra in his dream. His memory had become hazy over the decades that had passed, like a dream itself, but he refused to accept that he had not screamed out Amado's name as he had drowned too.

Cadeo felt his eyes close again, this time in contemplation and painful recollection. They both would have been adults now. They would have had many tattoos, and their hair would have been long enough to carry in a sling on their backs. They would have been seasoned fishermen. They had a love for the sea, which Cadeo had encouraged them to indulge in one too many times. Such were the thoughts that stayed with Cadeo long after he woke from this dream. He instinctively rubbed the lotus tattoo on his arm while lost in thought. He often thought that his twin children might have been saved from that wretched storm as he had been, if only they had been old enough for tattoos. He wondered if such wards were truly a blessing to have saved him on that day, or a cruel curse that had allowed him to survive longer than his offspring. Cadeo had never decided.

Cadeo now saw a calm sea before him from the safety of the beach. His playing sticks were still gripped tightly in his hands. He had woken up alone for the first time in years and was disoriented for it. He soon recalled how the sky had been orange before he slept, and he now saw how the moon was preparing to set and mark the end of the night. Cadeo anxiously looked out to the sea for Quy's boat. A curtain of white hovered in the distance over the sea, as though a rain cloud clung to it. Cadeo almost passed out from overwhelming terror.

It was fog.

It floated over the water, hiding the neighbouring islands in the distance. So foreign and distantly nostalgic was the sight that Cadeo thought he might still be dreaming. He felt immense dread as the fog brought more and more memories to him, and his waking dream felt more like a nightmare. *Omens. Famine.* The words crept into Cadeo's mind again, and he trembled.

Cadeo realised then how foolish he had been to allow Quy to go back on the water and to so quickly dismiss his unease. He kept watch, but the fog refused to fade. Rather, it spread further and turned into a vivid shade of white as the moon continued setting. Cadeo felt sick to his stomach with fear.

The wait dragged on, and it was torturous. He looked out over the coast again, at the fog and the setting moon. He saw the first tone of orange in the sky to signal dawn. He had waited for far too long already. He stood with his sticks in hand and began playing the t'rung. The song came to his hands instinctively and rang through the air with perfect clarity. Playing on the edge of the shore in the face of a passing fog, the significance of the occasion was not lost on him—the song was once again serving its intended purpose in guiding his people home. Cadeo hoped and prayed that it would be for the last time, and that the t'rung would never be needed for more than tradition again. He prayed that this fog would be one that would pass swiftly and never again linger.

'Who is it?' Cadeo heard. Ruhan and Ashan stood behind him, both of whom had surely been drawn by the music. He must have been playing for longer than he realised, as he thought he was still alone on the beach. 'Someone is fishing at such an hour?'

'Is that fog?' Ashan asked. 'Who's out there?'

'Quy...he set out a while ago,' Cadeo said, in the calmest voice he could manage and with a forced smile. He saw Ashan's face become grave and tense. *Of course, you were out at sea and saw the dead fish with him.*

'For what?' Ruhan asked.

'Just for some more fishing. He was worried that this morning's haul wouldn't last very long.'

Ruhan frowned. 'In the middle of the night?'

Cadeo said nothing and turned his back on them. He

carried on playing the melody. The fog was growing thicker still and drew closer to the shore.

Vada, Thi and Lihn eventually were drawn by the music as Ashan and Ru had been. His people sat together on the sand to overlook the sea. Cadeo felt something on his skin as the fog kissed the sand—cold air that sank into his bones. The chill came with light rainfall. A new cloud had formed overhead that was as grey as ancient stone, stark against a pale blue morning sky.

He felt another drop. Then another. The soft raindrops on the sand soon became plentiful. Cadeo's worry only deepened. He knew that no one else had cause to fear mere rainfall, for rain would be welcomed for the health of the rice paddies. But he and Quy had checked the skies before Quy took to sea. Quy had even climbed atop Burial Hill first to look out for any approaching clouds as far as he could see. There were none. Yet Cadeo now felt rain on his skin from a cloud that had come as if from nowhere.

Just a rain cloud, Cadeo resolved in himself. *You are looking for peril where there is none.* It was probably the talk of famine, coupled with his haunting recurring dream, that put Cadeo's mind in such a state. But he could not deny the bizarre events unfolding before his eyes. Cadeo felt fear in his ageing heart. Voices called to him—his people, worried and anxious. They no doubt needed his reassurance, but he could not answer. He couldn't even turn to face them. He was lost in his own fears and prayers.

The island was soon consumed by fog, and the air felt colder for it. It sheltered the hills and hid the sea. The fog, paired with the dull colour of dawn, rendered him almost blind to all but what was right before his face. The soft clapping of sea waves sounded like thunder to his ears. His hands still played the song on the t'rung even as they ached and his fingers began to shake. Cadeo played the melody badly, with the clarity of the song gone from his mind. His breath was heavy and laboured. There were still stars in the sky even as dawn began to break. The sea waves were still tame even as the wind became riled up. Every aspect of this dawn felt unnatural.

Something finally emerged from the fog before Cadeo. His people stood in bafflement and stunned silence at the sight of it. It was the large and familiar body of Quy's fishing boat. It drifted toward the shore by the strength of the wind and waves alone, gently swaying to and fro and casting a small shadow on the water.

Cadeo's sticks slipped from his fingers. The song ended. The boat drifted closer and closer until it met the rain-soaked sand of the shore and burrowed itself in it. Only a pool of seawater and Quy's harpoon floated inside. No one was there to hold the oars that hung from its edges, and no one was aboard to hold its rudder.

FOUR

Umbra woke up to *The Wandering Fishermen* being played outside on the coast. It was only dawn. She wondered if the music was for another fishing boat's return and whether there was another lot of fish to come. But she didn't allow the thought to excite her. She had had a helping of fish that night and did not want to be greedy in wishing for more. Umbra did not bother to check outside or even sit up from her floor bed. She did not have the energy to fight her people over food portions again. She hoped that her father was not awake to hear the music, for she did not want him to know about any more missed opportunities for food. She heard his soft breathing as he slept behind her and was relieved by it.

She drifted back to sleep once the music ended, waking again later in the morning. She sometimes wished she didn't have to work as hard, or as often, as she did. There were no other children close to her age on the island to compare to, but she couldn't imagine that a childhood spent in labour on behalf of her parent was a normal one. She longed to be left alone most days, to relish the twilight before sunset for longer, and to sleep while the sun was still up once in a while. As with most days, Umbra ate cold rice and seaweed for breakfast and left her father behind to sleep.

But the morning that greeted Umbra outside was unlike any other—the air was white like a cloud had descended onto the shore and spread across the island, and her lungs felt cold each time she breathed. Umbra was equal parts confused and fascinated by the spectacle. She could barely see the coast from her hut and could see even less of the sea beyond it. She saw a lone figure standing beside his t'rung in the sand. Umbra imagined Cadeo was enthralled by the mist just as she was. She decided to leave him to his wonderment to instead savour the brief time she had alone again.

Umbra was drawn once more to a quiet beach, which was fine by her. The fog made the walk there disorienting, as though her home now resided in another world. Her home felt cold. Though the island huts were in the same places as always and the same people would soon eat their breakfasts in them, the fog made the island feel far less like home. It was all the same, yet slightly different.

Umbra heard more voices on her way. She recognised Ashan's voice. He spoke sternly to someone whom she couldn't make out. She quietly walked passed them and went unnoticed. There were others scattered about along her walk. This was a bizarre change from routine, for so many to be awake in the morning but not working, and Umbra knew something had surely happened to cause it. She only hoped this meant she could stay at the beach longer without anyone noticing her absence. Perhaps she would not need to work on that day at all.

The beach was lonely and untouched. The fog was not as thick here as it had been on her way, but there was a sole blemish on the otherwise perfect sheet of pale sand—a fish. It was small and lay just out of reach of the tide. Umbra looked at it for a moment. Her stomach grumbled. She reached down and took the fish into her hands. Life returned to the fish like a miracle the moment her fingers touched its scales, and it flapped in a frenzy. Umbra glared at the fish with spite for a meal now missed.

'You're lucky,' she said to it. She never could stomach the thought of killing a fish herself, nor of killing anything else. Working in the paddies suited her fine for that reason. She threw the fish back into the sea as far as she could, and it disappeared into the depths with a soft splash. A strange sound then filled the air. It was long and coarse, gentle yet powerful. It flowed into Umbra's ears and through her blood like a cold and imposing whisper. It came from beyond the cliff faces, from Umbra's favourite beach at the foot of Burial Hill.

The sound came again, as soft yet imposing as before. Umbra was enamoured by its foreign nature. It was like she was being called from a hundred miles away by something omnipresent. Umbra's feet moved of their own accord, and soon her hands were upon the cliff face. The climb to the beach was slow and difficult. Sharp rocks peeked out from the sea below her, and moss tickled Umbra's hands as she moved. The sound came once more, louder than before.

Umbra soon could see the beach. It was small, with many pebbles scattered to break up the sand. The haze here was thick and clung to the beach like an odour. Umbra could barely see more than a few steps ahead of her. She stepped onto the sand. The air fell silent. She realised that she was scared. She didn't know what madness took hold of her to press on, yet she could not stop herself.

Umbra saw something through the fog, something immense lying in the sand, something dark as a shadow. It barely moved, but Umbra saw its body rise and fall as it breathed. The fear abandoned Umbra as she realised what lay before her. She reached out and gently placed her hand on the whale's skin. The whale's eye opened and fixed on Umbra. Its gaze was vacant as it resided in a limbo of sleep.

The whale hummed at her touch.

Gratus' hand had never felt so cold to Cadeo's touch. There was an unnatural bite in the wind at the top of Burial Hill. It was a strange view from the island's peak — the typical blue afternoon sea was now a sheet of grey. Cadeo stood amid his people and looked over the tiny wooden idols at the hill's peak. They all watched Nota set a new addition in the soil. Her long hair flowed in a steady sea breeze. Some of her locks were dyed a subtle tone of red that only showed when hit by sunlight, and she looked distinctive for it. She seemed to have more red in her hair after each burial, though Cadeo could not be sure of that. Nota was rarely seen outside her home unless her skills were called upon, and so her appearance was always striking. She had never marked any of her own skin with tattoos despite the duty of her talent. Cadeo was conscious that she and Ashan often spent time together, and he wondered if it wasn't his influence that dissuaded her from joining in that tradition. *He's absent today, too,* Cadeo noted as he looked around at his people. *He's become predictable in his negligence of tradition.*

Nota had worked on Quy's idol with impressive detail, even carving lines resembling tattoos into his would-be flesh. Though tattooing was her craft, Nota had a talent for other art forms too. The idol was firmly set in the soil. Cadeo heard his heartbeat in his ears amid the silence of mourning that followed. So many times had he stood in this place, and for so many years had he watched the idols grow in number, yet there had not been an idol made under these circumstances for many years. It had been a long time since anyone had been lost at sea.

The idols stood together in the grass, surrounded by beautiful red and pink flowers. Each was familiar to Cadeo, and each brought back unique memories of tragedy and death. He remembered the day Priscus was lost at sea when she was just a girl. Her death had turned cultural superstitions into a very real fear. He remembered when the village learned that Acta had starved in the famine. He remembered how Saepe had fallen into despair and jumped from the cliff where Cadeo now stood. He remembered sitting beside Son for his last breath and thinking that he was one of the lucky few who died in the grace of old age in his own home. He remembered all of their faces, their tattoos, and their personalities through the incredible likeness of these wooden idols. He could never bear to look upon Amado and Adra's idols, and today was no different. Nor did he need to ever look upon them with the faces of children carved into his waking and sleeping mind forever.

Nota set Quy's idol in the grass beside the idol of his father. It was uncanny and even reflected his likeness—from the sombre expression on its face to the unkempt hair he always let flow freely, almost perfectly. The silent mourning was a loud and deliberate silence to Cadeo's ears—one of sadness and dread. It voiced an accepted truth that there had been a change on their island home. Lihn's tears broke the silence, and she quietly wept into Thi's arms.

Nota was the first to leave the hill after the silence was broken, and others soon followed. Thi left hand in hand with Lihn while she still wept. Adorjan was the last to leave. His eyes met Cadeo's for a moment before he did. He looked dejected and exhausted. Cadeo had no words for him, nor did he believe he should have. Adorjan had the look of a man who needed time to grieve for a lost friend alone. Only Cadeo and Gratus remained on Burial after Adorjan was out of sight.

'Your hand is shaking,' Gratus quietly said after a long time had passed. Cadeo felt how his palm sweated in hers. He looked at the ground—at the flowers that swayed in the wind.

'I'm scared,' he admitted out loud. It was perhaps the first time since the famine that he had said those words. 'Actually, I think I might be terrified, Gratus.'

If Gratus was surprised, she did not show it. 'Of course,

you are,' she said. 'It would be far stranger if you weren't after this.'

'Stranger, but better. With fear, one is too easily prone to inaction and despair. I can see danger all around us. I see something on the horizon coming for us, something I know all too well, but I am powerless to stop it. We are to see history repeated, and I do not know what can be done to even ease the days that are to come.'

'You are not their leader or chief, Cadeo,' Gratus said in her soft yet firm tone of voice. 'The earth, the skies and the sea will always have their way with us. There is nothing to be done. It is not your responsibility to fight that which cannot be fought.'

'Oh, Gratus,' Cadeo sighed, holding her face with his free hand. 'It is. It has to be. I must be a shepherd to all that I call my kin. These memories and nightmares do not plague me for no cause. Surely it is so that I may prevent the past from being repeated. If it is not my responsibility, then whose?'

'There is no responsibility, Cadeo. Only the natural way of things.'

'The natural way,' Cadeo echoed. 'There is nothing natural about this fog or the nightmare it brings along with it.'

Gratus said nothing in return. She instead laid her head on Cadeo's shoulder. The simple touch was like a warm embrace for Cadeo during hardship, and she knew it. Cadeo allowed the reminder of her love to ease the dread in his heart as they stood there together until the sky started to turn dark. The walk back down from Burial Hill took more effort than the last, and more than the time before that. Cadeo wondered on the way down how many days they had left with enough vigour to make this climb at all. It dawned on him that the day would come when—whether through the weakness of their bodies or their lives ending—they would never be able to see the idols for themselves again. A part of Cadeo hoped that they would be immortalised as idols beside their people before their bodies gave out, as no part of him wanted to abandon that duty as a shepherd, despite the sadness it brought with it.

Cadeo and Gratus were exhausted and hungry by the time they reached their home.

The wooden idols watched over the island of fog and grey sea in their wake.

Umbra finally made her way back home in the dead of night. The fog had made the flow from day to night harder to see, and Umbra had only realised it was nighttime when she saw dull moonlight seeping through it. She rushed home in a panic. She would surely be berated for missing an entire day of work, and she would have no excuse for it. But Umbra's father was thankfully fast asleep when she got home. She spent the rest of that night with her eyes open, reflecting on a bizarre day and an even more bizarre evening. She thought about the whale and how she had left it lying on that beach alone. She was ashamed of a thought that had crept into her head—a creature like that could feed her village for many days, and no one would even have to fight for a fair share. Yet, the creature was still alive. It had beckoned her to the beach with a hum that ran through her blood. It had hummed again at her touch. Umbra felt sick at the thought of having that creature killed, and she could not imagine bringing its cooked flesh to her lips for any amount of hunger. That, to her, seemed better than slaughter at the hands of Quy or Ashan.

Umbra decided that she did not want to tell anyone about the whale. Not yet. She wanted the whale to live a little while longer. She wanted to hear its hum again and to spend another day beside it. The whale was already living on borrowed time as it was stranded out of the water. Its death was inevitable, and Umbra understood this. She just wanted to be with it as much as possible before that moment came. Umbra decided she would go to the whale again the next evening after her work in the fields. She hoped no one else would find it before then, though Umbra had never known anyone to bother making the climb to the beach where it lay but herself.

She rose from her sleepless rest in the early morning. She bade her father a good morning and quickly ate a breakfast of seaweed and cold, mushy rice with him. Umbra had one mouthful with her father's piercing eyes on her. Then it dawned on her—she was eating leftovers from the night before, from a meal her father must have made. He had had to cook for himself because Umbra had not been there to feed him. She saw food and water spilt on the floor—signs of the ordeal he must have faced cooking for himself.

'You seem better,' Varyis eventually said between mouthfuls.

Umbra kept her face to the floor. 'A little.'

Those were the only words shared between them until their bowls were empty. Soon after, Vada entered the hut and broke the heavy silence. She gave Umbra a courteous bow of her head and knelt by Varyis' floor bed. She smelled of herbs and flowers, as she always did.

'You know what to do, pops,' Vada said to Varyis. She opened up her sack of strange tools and utensils. The smell of herbs increased tenfold when she did so.

Varyis lifted his arm and held it at shoulder height, as straight as he could manage. Vada placed her arm atop his.

'You're oddly quiet, old man,' Vada said.

Varyis grunted. Vada smiled and gave Umbra a wink. 'Walked in on a fight, did I? Face the roof.'

Varyis leaned his head back with some difficulty. He coughed raspily. 'Fathers don't fight their children.'

'Mm-hmm. Show me your hands.'

Varyis opened and closed his fingers as quickly as he could manage, which was not quickly at all. They shook as he did so. 'Work, Umbra,' he grunted, glaring at his daughter.

Umbra gladly stood up and took her leave.

'That would be why she fights you,' she heard Vada say.

Umbra made her way to the fields for another day of labour. It was raining that morning. The fog still covered part of the shore in front of her hut and hid much of the morning sky. It was a grey and miserable day. It was also a day that quickly distinguished itself from her usual routine —soft raindrops on the sand and grass, along with the insects' morning songs, were all that Umbra could hear. Cadeo was nowhere to be seen, absent from his usual morning spot on the shore. Gratus sat outside her hut rather than toiling at the paddies. She gave Umbra one of her rare smiles when their eyes met. *She's finally taking a break*, Umbra thought as she hurried past. Gratus never complained about her work, but it was clear for all to see how demanding it was on her old and frail body. Umbra quietly hoped that she would see Gratus on the paddies less and less.

The paddy was unattended when Umbra arrived. There was nothing there but the freshly set rice plants standing in a shallow body of water. Adorjan was nowhere to be seen, nor were her fellow workers. Umbra was unsure of what to do with herself. She waited for a while, but no one else came. She checked the rice for weeds in the meantime, and had checked almost half of the paddy before she gave up waiting. Of course, something was amiss, and it seemed to Umbra that the bizarre weather was the likely culprit. Perhaps the fog and chill in the air kept the others huddled in their homes, and they would wait for it to pass before they worked again.

Umbra didn't mind the cold, and she certainly didn't mind this bizarre fog. It was a new phenomenon for her eyes that had come about, and was likely to leave swiftly. Umbra didn't want to waste a second of it stuck indoors. She made for the beach beneath Burial Hill, drawn once again by curiosity and concern. There was no sound to beckon her this time, and she feared the whale might have already died. The cliffs were harder to climb than the day before, as the fog had moistened the rocks. She got some cuts on her hands and feet for her effort, but she didn't mind much. She washed them in the sea once her feet touched the sand.

The whale lay before her in the same spot as the day before. It glistened from the rainwater falling on its hide. The sand it rested on was caving in to the whale's weight and embraced part of its body. The whale breathed. It lived. Umbra marvelled at it, glad yet incredulous at its survival. She thought perhaps the rain had helped preserve the whale for a while longer. Yet, she wondered if such light rainfall was enough of a substitute for the sea itself, even for a single day. Regardless, Umbra was glad it had not been absent for its final moments, which were surely fast approaching.

She laid her hand on its skin again. Its immense eye opened. It was buried among layers of hard skin, and it was as dull as the morning sky, yet as alluring with its depth as the sea. It was stunning and terrifying to behold. The whale seemed to speak with its gaze. The fear and longing it emitted were almost tangible to Umbra and were suffocating. Umbra found she could not break its gaze. She spent her day on the beach in the soft rainfall, listening intently to the whale's silent voice.

Umbra could not remember a day when she had felt so at peace.

FIVE

Adorjan lay on his back, fighting off the sleep he would usually yearn for on any other night. He stared up through the hole in his roof that he never found time to repair, and never got around to asking Ru to repair. Ru could have had it done in less than half a day, yet Adorjan always forgot about the damage until he was back home and staring at it again as he now was. The orange glow of the setting sun shone dimly through the fog and into his hut.

Adorjan put his wooden pipe to his lips and inhaled. He was retaining too much of his thinking faculties for too long, and the relief the smoke usually brought would not be hurried, no matter how deeply he breathed or how long he held it in his lungs. He was desperate for the relief, for it had been a day full of grief, anxiety, and bafflement. *Just to test the waters*, Adorjan recalled in Quy's voice—his friend's final words to him. It was such a simple, innocent, noble errand that had led to such tragedy. No one had said the words out loud, but Adorjan didn't doubt that everyone knew Quy would never be seen again. *So fleeting and random, life is.*

Adorjan wiped his damp eyes and hung his head. He breathed through the burning wooden pipe again and felt the warm sensation in his stomach as his mind drew closer to the relief he longed for. It came in waves as it always did —his thoughts would grow hazy and be gradually washed away by indifference, like a morning tide washing sand from a shore. He would see ripples of that metaphorical tide in his mind's eye and feel them lift his spirit. His dull, dishevelled hut would be elevated by the new vibrancy of twilight. His home would be raised to the clouds, far above his tiny island.

But tonight, these were not the white and beautiful clouds he was accustomed to—they were black, stormy, and heavy with rain. His hut soon reflected not the vibrancy of early twilight, but the darkest part of a midnight sky where even moonlight could not reach. Adorjan's mood was not raised. Instead, he was dragged down deeper into the same mourning that he yearned to be free from for a while.

Tears flowed easily down his face. Something left his lips—perhaps a scream—that echoed long in his ears after his breath was spent. He was dragged deeper and deeper still, until his consciousness became a mess of dark thoughts and inexplicable sensations. Adorjan was embraced by the black cloud seeping into his room. It melded with him until he became as intangible as mist.

In this moment, Adorjan ceased to exist, and the relief finally hit him with full force.

Adorjan smoked again.

Adorjan watched the moon rise along with his fellow black clouds.

Adorjan's relief ended with dreams of him and his people drowning in morning tides.

Gratus' warm skin was a pleasant sensation against Cadeo's. They lay together side by side on their floor bed. Cadeo's mind was intently on the feel of Gratus' fingers intertwined with his own while she slept. It was an incredible sensation—such a yearning for Gratus' company, such strong reassurance in her presence and such a feeling of home being with her. Cadeo needed this moment tonight—a reminder that he was far from alone and that the world had not yet fallen apart.

Cadeo's eyes were closed, but he was far from asleep. He was riddled with a foul blend of guilt and fear. He was absorbed in bizarre memories after a day of mourning, of a time no one else was old enough to have known—a time defined by great distress and pain, which too had been prefaced with strange happenings. He lost himself in old memories of the mist, the lives lost at sea, and the madness that spread among his people. The fear in his heart refused to stop growing. He thought about Quy—the source of his crippling guilt. He cursed himself for dismissing the unease he felt from the moment the word *omen* touched his ears again. *I fear that hard times may soon come upon us* was what Quy had said. Cadeo prayed those words would never come true, but he feared he was proving himself to be naïve in his old age.

Sleep eluded Cadeo still. He lay with his eyes closed until he felt a hand on his shoulder. He opened his eyes and saw someone kneeling beside him. He recognised the unkempt hair of Ashan, even in the dark. Ashan pointed to the outdoors when their eyes met, then stood and left. *Blunt as ever*, Cadeo sighed. *This must be about Quy. What else could he want to discuss at such an hour? Perhaps even Ashan needs comfort from time to time.*

Cadeo knew little about Ashan's friendship with Quy, but he, Ruhan and Nota were the only people Ashan seemed to spend any time with. He also realised that Ashan would have no source of comfort right now, for neither Ruhan nor Nota were the types to be leaned upon. Nota had many virtues, but Cadeo could think of no one worse to mourn with, given her eccentric nature and...philosophies regarding death. Ruhan was instrumental to the well-being of all, but he was not one for emotional support or even kind words. Ashan certainly wouldn't call Cadeo a friend, so it showed a certain desperation he must have felt to go to Cadeo that night. Cadeo pulled his hand away from Gratus' and followed Ashan outside.

Ashan stood in the sand at the foot of Cadeo's hill home with the calm and retreated shore behind him in the fog. His hair was short for his age, as he insisted on cutting it every so often and keeping it only a little longer than shoulder length. So often did he cut it that not all of it was locked, and many loose strands fluttered around his face in the wind. His face was as stern as ever.

'Better to talk now, while the village sleeps,' he said.

'Were you unable to sleep too?' Cadeo asked.

'Why was Quy at sea?' Ashan asked with his usual bluntness. His voice was never easy on the ears or soothing for the spirit. It was always harsh and stabbing, even now as he spoke in an undertone. An air of sureness and coldness clung to the man wherever he went, attacking whoever he conversed with and repelling those who didn't. Cadeo sighed to himself. *As if it would be any different today. As if Ashan would seek out anyone for comfort, least of all me. I truly am becoming naïve.*

Cadeo drew closer to Ashan and sat in the sand by his feet. He still felt yesterday's trek up Burial Hill in his legs, and even standing was exhausting. 'He told me what you saw out there,' Cadeo said. 'How the fish had vanished and died, with no clear reason. He told me he was concerned it could be an omen. He wanted to fish again in case these were signs of a coming famine. He set out at night to avoid any concern among—'

'That's not what I'm asking,' Ashan said, staying on his feet and looking down at Cadeo. 'Why was Quy at sea, from your perspective?'

Cadeo looked up at Ashan and furrowed his brow. 'I do not understand.'

'We all know about Quy's superstitions,' Ashan said. 'It's clear to see with all those tattoos covering every part of his body. For most of us, hearing Quy talk of omens over some dead fish would hardly be surprising, but it gave you pause. It resonated with you enough to entertain a solo voyage at night and to wait out on the shore all night for his return.

'Then there is this fog. I've never seen so much in my lifetime, nor have most of us. We're all curious, yes, but you were afraid. Your manner changed the moment the fog came here. I've never heard you play the t'rung so loudly and so badly. Something about that fog and that talk of omens has frightened you. So, Quy was not just out there to bring home another meal for us, was he?'

Ashan let the statement hang, with the question left unspoken but implied—*what are you hiding?* He looked down at Cadeo expectantly. Cadeo could not meet his gaze for long and looked instead at his feet. The silence soon grew too heavy for him.

'Perhaps...it's just superstition,' he murmured at last.

'Tell me regardless.'

'Then you need to know what happened during the famine.'

There was a subtle change in Ashan's face. 'What more is there to know?'

Cadeo breathed in deeply and closed his eyes. 'There was more happening than hunger and fog,' he began. 'We grew hungry, yes, and the fish died for months. But we still had rice and herbs to eat. The fog lifted, and the fish returned before many of us starved. Worse was that... oppressive feeling that came with the fog. It was even thicker than it is now and lasted for months. Imagine— months of feeling blind and helpless, with fog so thick we could not tell if it was day or night. Some of us turned against one another, quite quickly after the fish died. The few fish that were caught would be fought over, and some were hurt over them. Then, when our strength left us, we became thieves instead, stealing fish while others slept.

'Then there were certain sightings: cracks of light in the sky beyond the fog, shadows rising from the sea as tall as mountains, whispers in our people's heads that they said were loud as thunder. I saw and heard none of this myself, and I could never even be sure whether our people spoke truly or if it was the madness that took hold of their senses, too. But after Priscus disappeared at sea, those sightings suddenly felt a lot more real to all of us. After she died, we became paranoid of one another. I believed we were all going to kill each other if we didn't starve first. For those months that the fog lingered, and for a while after that, life was utter misery and terror.' Cadeo opened his eyes once more and met Ashan's. 'Those months of famine all began with a few dead fish in the sea.'

'So, it *was* the fog yesterday that scared you,' Ashan said, not missing a beat. 'Why have we never heard about the fog or the sightings?'

'Even memories like that fade over time, and you come to question your recollections. You weren't even born when the famine came, so it may be difficult to imagine how reality and imagination can come to feel like one and the same. Nothing can be said to be true or certain about what happened back then. What was certain was the hunger, the fog, and those who were lost to the sea. All else was superstition and paranoia born of despair.'

'*Was* superstition,' Ashan echoed. 'So, it isn't just more superstition to you anymore.'

Cadeo stared at the sand again. 'I am not certain yet.'

'If you're not certain after almost forty years, you never will be.'

Those words made Cadeo smile at how hard they hit his heart. Cadeo felt somewhat bitter toward Ashan for the harshness and truth those words held. He was right, and Cadeo could not turn away from this fact. Cadeo was still plagued by uncertainty and doubt, and was perhaps too old now to ever change that.

'How did the famine end?' Ashan asked, breaking Cadeo's introspective trance.

Cadeo met his eyes again, taken aback. '*How*?'

'The fog just disappeared one day, and the fish all came back to life?'

Cadeo dropped his gaze to the sand and gave a slow nod.

'Then tell me—does that sound like some curse? Or just nature doing what it does? Surely omens don't just fade away when they tire of tormenting us.'

Though Ashan was mocking with his tone, Cadeo couldn't deny the question's weight.

'It matters not, Ashan,' he said. 'Because the madness, the violence and their hysteria were all very real, whether it was natural or not. Should history repeat itself, *that* is what we face.'

Ashan paused for a moment, then said, 'Or the madness never went away,' with an even harsher tone. 'You all just put it to rest and gave it a new face.'

He looked deliberately at the tattoos covering Cadeo's arms. Cadeo followed his gaze and looked at himself. Not much of his natural skin tone was visible anymore with the tattoos and their vibrant colours covering most of his body. Wards and charms, his people had long called them—a protection against whatever even nature may be powerless against.

'It's self-inflicted madness,' Ashan continued. 'Inflicted by obsession with superstition and your fear of what you don't understand. The madness never left. It just slept— waiting for the time to wake up again.'

Ashan left Cadeo sitting in the sand after spitting out those final words. Cadeo stared blankly at the familiar horizon, his heart heavy with more painful memories than one should ever have to bear. He looked down at his wrinkled, weathered hand and the fading fish scale art on it. *Has it truly been forty years?*

SIX

Laziness and isolation at the time of day when the sun had just passed its peak were not common for Adorjan. It was unnatural for him to spend a full day away from the rice fields, especially when the plants had recently been moved from the nursery paddy. These were the days when the rice would need the most nurture to grow healthily — the seedlings were still fragile from being uprooted, and they would need to be well cared for while they grew new roots. They would also be prone to pests and disease in their infancy, and would demand constant attention. Yet Adorjan had decided to forsake that duty today.

He sometimes wished for more time like this, for more moments of isolation and quiet. He longed to spend his days a little less exhausted. He thought that some respite might be a good substitute for the herbs he relied on for relief. His bamboo pipe was currently ablaze again. It filled his hut with smoke and a pleasant, earthy aroma. He was unsure how long he had been lying there, staring through the hole in his roof. He could see nothing but haze.

Immense tendrils of fog slid through the roof hole. They spread along his ceiling and formed the shape of a colossal tree taking root within a new host. Adorjan spent hours in the tree's core, with the daytime never-ending and the tree's roots ever spreading until they encompassed his entire home. It was a serene, unblemished feeling that the herbs blessed him with this day.

A voice crept into Adorjan's mind, blemishing the perfect scene for a moment. 'Adorjan,' it said. 'Get up.'

'Soon,' Adorjan replied, smiling at his lie. He inhaled the smoke once more, and the voice left him to his respite for a time.

However, that respite came to a swift and abrupt end with the sensation of a cold slap to Adorjan's face. Consciousness hit him like a wave. He shot up from his floor-bed, gasping for air. Ashan stood above him with an empty bucket in hand, wearing his usual stern expression.

'That stuff is still rotting your brain,' he said. 'I dunno how you can even stand the smell.'

Adorjan looked up at the hole in his hut roof again. The fog had gone timid and recoiled its tendrils. The sky looked its usual tone of grey. He felt his clarity of mind returning all too quickly. 'You chased the tree away.'

'Sure.' Ashan filled a chipped cup with water from Adorjan's pot.

'You weren't at Burial Hill this morning,' Adorjan said, accepting the cup of water being offered.

'No, I wasn't at Burial Hill. I don't imagine he'd care that I wasn't there to see his doll set into the ground. He hated these rituals almost as much as I do.'

'But why weren't you there?'

'Listen,' Ashan said. 'Come out on the water with me tonight, right after sundown.'

Adorjan gulped down a mouthful of water. It was warm and felt like it slithered down his throat. 'On the water,' he echoed. 'Tonight? Why?'

'Why else? Something happened to Quy while he was at sea, and I don't like not knowing what. Do you?'

'You mean something dangerous.'

'Yes, obviously.'

'Obviously,' Adorjan echoed. He took another mouthful of water. He only now realised how thirsty he was. He hadn't drunk a thing since last night, before he started smoking. 'So, you're telling me you want to go out on the water and risk us disappearing too?'

'Quy had no reason to be cautious, other than some dead fish. We'll be more prepared than he was.'

'Prepared for what? We have no idea what happened out there. We would be leaving our people in peril if anything were to happen to us—the rice fields would have no overseer, and there'd be no other fishermen.'

'And what's the alternative?' Ashan asked, without missing a beat. 'How long do we wait before we sail again? Since I'm the only fisherman left, we won't get any more fish unless I sail. If for nothing else, we'll be going just to catch more of it. Now, are you coming or not?'

Adorjan rubbed his temple. Thinking was proving mountainous with the herbs coursing through his veins. 'Why both of us? Just you would be enough.'

'One wasn't enough for Quy. We'll go after sundown.' Ashan snatched the bamboo pipe out of Adorjan's hands. 'That should be enough time to get your head right.'

'Why not tomorrow?' Adorjan asked, lying back onto his floor-bed. 'Why the rush?'

'Quy sailed at night, so we can't expect to see what he did if we wait until morning. Be on the west shore at sundown.' Ashan tossed the pipe to the ground and left Adorjan to ponder.

It would be stupid of us, he thought. *To risk leaving our people without a means to fish or to harvest rice. We would be condemning them to starve were we not to return. Yet, Ashan will set sail with or without me. If I abandoned him, am I just condemning him to die instead?*

Adorjan truthfully knew what he was going to do that night already. He maintained that Ashan was about to act recklessly and without regard for those who depended on him, whether he would admit it or not. But Ashan had also been right—Adorjan needed to understand what happened to Quy, and he could attribute part of his grief today to not knowing. *Besides, Nota paints these tattoos on us for times like this,* Adorjan reasoned. *Tonight is the time to put faith in them.*

Sleep found him quickly as he tired of waiting for the herbs' effects to fade. He dreamt about being a bird, living a simple life in a tree on the burial hill overlooking the sea.

Cadeo was restless, yet his day was unproductive. He sat by the entrance to his hut with the smell of Gratus' seaweed and fish stew in his nostrils, watching the pale-skied world pass by. He watched what little he could see of the waves through the fog. The grey sea was calm but relentless, stroking the sand almost silently. It was all so quiet. Cadeo was lost in the flow of whatever time passed while he sat there and pondered over nothing in particular.

Gratus appeared before him with a steaming bowl in hand. Cadeo saw her face in a truly new light—she looked old and tired, for her greying hair and the wrinkles under her eyes were more pronounced than ever. She looked down at him with a knowing expression of sympathy.

'Another portion already?' Cadeo asked.

'Someone will be hungry right now,' Gratus said. 'Find them and give it to them.'

Cadeo's heart sank. He stared at the bowl in Gratus's hands and felt ashamed. *Such inaction and restlessness are unlike me,* he thought, though he was unsure if he believed it himself as of late. The bowl was half full of rice and bean soup. He slowly found his feet. 'Thank you,' he said and kissed Gratus on the cheek. Her skin was still soft and welcoming after all these years.

'You're very welcome,' she said with a wry smile.

Cadeo did as he was bidden and began another walk around the island as though it were a brand-new day. It was a short-lived walk, as he made for the first person he saw. It was Vada whom he saw first. She walked toward him with a fresh batch of seaweed in her hands.

'Good morning, doctor,' bade Cadeo.

'It's afternoon, Cadeo,' Vada said. 'And I'm certain it's not a good one.'

Cadeo furrowed his brow, then sighed with the realisation that he had been sitting by his hut longer than he realised. 'You are right, of course,' he said. 'It is hardly a good day for mourning.'

'Never a good day for that, I'm sure. But my craft demands that I be familiar with death and do all I can to make the way to it painless. I'm not so sure I could mourn in the traditional sense if I tried. It is not the loss of Quy that plagues me on this day.'

'What, then?' Cadeo asked, perhaps with too much eagerness. Hearing so many words from the typically reserved Vada was rare indeed. Rarer still were her saying anything about her own feelings rather than the well-being of others.

'*Fear*, most likely,' she said. 'Look around, Cadeo. Can you not see it? Or feel it? The air has changed, and the people have changed for it, too. Even you have. Maybe this fog is to blame. We haven't seen the sky for days now, and it's natural for one to feel trapped without it. A death among us just makes the snare feel tighter.'

Cadeo swallowed. 'We mourn his *absence*, doctor. It would be premature to mourn his--'

'Oh? Is that despite his boat returning home without him? Even after Nota carved his idol and set it on Burial Hill already? Don't think us naïve, Cadeo. I have accepted that he is *lost*, and it seems to me that everyone else is in the process of doing so. Don't go disrupting their grief by giving them false hopes.'

Vada left Cadeo alone with the sting of her words. Perhaps it was due to the surprise at Vada's self-reflection, or perhaps it was her rejection of his attempt to comfort, as he'd been growing accustomed to lately. But he felt a nameless and formless weight lifting from his shoulders after hearing Vada's harsh words. He felt more prepared to face the day and to help his people in the ways he was able. *Our people have many shoulders to lean on, not just my own.*

He walked on through his island with slow and shaky steps. The bowl of rice soup in his hands had already turned cold.

Adorjan woke up from another bizarre dream. His dreams were often particularly vivid after he had been smoking, and usually involved being lost in some abstract depictions of nature or floating where the clouds reside. They were often memorable and had a way of relaxing him for a while after he awoke.

He had slept in and out of strange dreams since Ashan had visited, and it was only after the last dream that he realised that there was no sense to be made of them at all. He remembered some sparse details of it—he was stumbling about in the dark, floating around a dark and endless plane like a leaf in a breeze. He felt no purpose as he moved in that place—only the acceptance that he was lost and that that darkness was *home.* He was relieved when he woke, and his eyes were blessed with light falling through the hole in his roof, but the uneasy feeling in that dream stayed with him still. Adorjan became afraid of sleep, finding himself scared of what other dreams he might have had. That fear was enough to have him leave his floor-bed and his hut.

More light blessed his eyes outside. It was the middle of the afternoon, and he still had a few hours before he'd meet with Ashan. He had a fine view of the sea from up high in the hills, where his hut had been built. He was close to trees where birds had built their nests, which sang all day from the treetops. They would wake him early in the morning, and Adorjan had grown accustomed to using their songs as a cue to head for the fields.

Adorjan was usually exhausted by this time of day, as he would be near the end of his day's work on the paddies. He finally felt some remorse for leaving the rice untended today as the herbs wore off. He also needed something to distract him from this feeling that still plagued him from his dreams and keep him from sleeping again. *Maybe I'll work today, after all.*

As expected, the paddies were empty when he arrived. He wondered how well the rice would be cared for without him, if he were to have more days like this one, or if he were to be lost at sea as Quy was. He feared his people wouldn't keep the rice alive for long enough to make it to harvest. He took his duty seriously, more than most, and while his people depended on the rice to survive, these were *his* paddies. Whether they prospered or perished was on his shoulders, and he happily accepted that responsibility.

Adorjan realised he was already failing to be distracted as he had intended. He stepped into the paddy that was filled with infant plants. He often walked in the paddies when he was alone- partly to churn the soil and make it difficult for weeds to grow, to feel the health of the soil on his skin and glean the needs of the rice, and to feel clarity of thought in the place he loved so deeply. It had rained a lot in recent days, more than usual, and the paddy was fully flooded with calm water. The rice would be happy for it. Weeds were always the biggest danger to the rice's health and growth, particularly in the weeks after they had been carried over from the nursery paddy. Weeds thrived in dry soil and grew quickly. The recent heavy rain was therefore a blessing and a sign that nature intended to be kind for this harvest.

This fog was, however, a curse. Adorjan could only hope that it would pass as swiftly as it had appeared, or the rice would be starved of sunlight and their harvest would be less fruitful for it. There was little Adorjan could do to care for the rice in the nursery paddy on this day. None looked diseased, and all looked to have settled well into their new home. Adorjan was happy to let them be.

He sat beside the paddy and admired it. He listened to the birds singing their songs to greet the approaching evening. He felt how soft the mud was on his feet in the still water of the paddy. He saw the bright green tone of the young rice plants, even with the haze hiding the sun. He enjoyed his solitude here each day after his work was done, but the fields were especially beautiful and peaceful when there was little work left to do and nature laboured in his stead. Adorjan relaxed.

He watched a group of small frogs leaping through the grass, apparently in good cheer. Then saw a snake slithering in pursuit and realised the frogs were fleeing. The snake caught only one and ate it swiftly as the other frogs fled. Adorjan smiled at yet another sign of a blessing, for frogs came out in groups only when the weather was agreeable to them. Snakes also loved such weather because of how plentiful the frogs were for hunting.

The anxieties and unpleasant sensations from Adorjan's dreams faded while he sat there in silence. He closed his eyes, and he simply breathed.

And all that mattered as sunset approached was that he breathed.

SEVEN

Umbra sat against the whale's cold, firm body as the sun began to set. Her soaked clothes clung to her skin. The whale still lived. Its immense eye was closed, but its breath came strong and full. Umbra was astonished by how it clung to life without water to sustain it. Each breath sounded torturous. She wondered how it felt to lie here helplessly, with nothing to do but await death.

She wondered if leaving the whale in this state was crueller than letting her people have their way with it. She wondered if that was what *she* would have wanted, had *she* been lying in the sand. But she decided that she'd prefer to let death come when it was ready. Isolation spent under the stars on her favourite beach while looking over the sea would be a fine way to spend her final moments.

Umbra felt another drop of water on her already wet skin. She looked up to the sky, and more raindrops trickled down her face. She touched its hide. It didn't stir.

'It's getting dark,' she whispered. 'And it's raining again. I'll come back again tomorrow.' The whale did not respond to her voice, but sighed again in sleep. Umbra walked through the wet sand with renewed hope that the whale would see another day. Something would soon end its life, whether it be the elements, starvation, or the lack of water. But she left the beach this time ever more determined not to let the whale's final moments be spent alone. She was determined to spend every spare moment of her day by its side until its end came.

The climb up the rocks back home was difficult in the dark. Umbra was sure the fog had become thicker during her respite. It felt as though she breathed in smoke. The rain was thankfully light during her climb, but began to pour heavily as her feet touched the sand of the other shore, as though suddenly enraged.

She ran, the rain turning heavier with every step. The fog blinded her, and she found her way through instinct and memory alone. She could only see her hut when it was right before her. She stepped inside, thoroughly drenched and freezing.

There was a sole source of light and heat inside—a small fire under the stone cooking pot. There was an uninviting aroma—some blend of stale seaweed, beans and rice. Umbra's father sat on his floor-bed, hunched over an empty bowl in his hands. The look he aimed at Umbra halted her breath.

A wave of realisation and shame came over her. She

took a step inside—a step fuelled with a sense of dread she rarely felt. The words came easily and quickly to her lips.

'I'm sorry.'

'For what?' Varyis said. His voice was hoarse and harsh. 'For leaving me here until sunrise without a crumb to eat, *again*? As you can see, I ate without your help. Is that a surprise to you? Maybe you had intended for me to--?'

'Please,' Umbra said. The words flowed easily. 'Stop.'

Her father's glare turned venomous. '*Stop*?' he echoed.

'I already said I'm sorry.'

'You gave me words. Words won't feed me or bring you home at a decent hour, so save them.'

'What do you want, then?'

'Responsibility,' Varyis spat out.

Umbra felt something foreign and warm in her gut. She grew *angry*. '*Responsibility*? Like I give you every day?' Each word tasted quite sweet as it left her lips. 'I cook, I clean, I work on the fields, I bring our share of fish home. You just lie there all the time and tell me it's not enough. I've barely ever missed feeding—'

Umbra saw a bowl flying towards her face, but she had neither the energy nor the foresight to avoid it. She felt like she had blacked out for a moment when it struck her. The cut it left above her eye immediately stung and flowed with blood. She and her father met eyes. Blood forced her eye closed. Varyis became blurry before her as she held back tears. Her head ached so much that she felt sick. She did not suffer the silence for long. She ran back out into the rain. She made for the shore on weak legs and dropped to her knees. She washed the cut on her head in the water, and it stung viciously. The cut oozed blood down her face, and so she washed it again. And again. And she kept doing so until the pain became unbearable.

She fell onto her back. Raindrops pattered on her face from beyond the fog and cooled her skin. The sensation of lying alone in the alien white air fed some tranquillity back into her heart.

That was swiftly taken from her, however, as a most strange sight eclipsed her vision, and a strange sound seeped into her ears. A fissure of green light tore through the sky beyond the fog. Then there was an immense and hollow sound like the echo of a thousand crashing waves. It caused a tremor in the sand, which began and spread from within Umbra's own body. She sat up, her heart pounding in her chest. The rain poured ever heavier. The distant green glow loomed far overhead. She was confused and had a foreign sensation in her chest. Perhaps she was *afraid.*

Her instincts easily took hold of her, and she ran again through wet sand. She ran past huts that were lit with candles and cooking fires from inside, and ran along the barren coast. She looked up again. The glow seemed to look back at her and stalk her with a crooked smile. She climbed the rocks to her beach. She ignored the pain of sharp and wet rocks stabbing at her feet, driven as she was by a newfound fear.

She felt that terrible hollow sound inside her again, quieter than before. She could hear it with some degree of clarity. It spoke with a voice raw with desperation— furious, yet not wrathful. She knew not the meaning of its words, but they drove her still into a deeper fear.

She neared the end of her skilled and painful climb. The whale's glistening body appeared before her again, even through the dark, as the fog had now cleared from the beach. The rain battered the whale's body. Umbra could see that its eyes were open, even from a distance.

What Umbra saw along with it on that beach froze her on the rocks. It was unreal — a shape too massive to grasp and too vague to name, like an art piece birthed from the sea. It blended well into the darkness of the night. It was colossal. It was tall like the cliffs lording over the beach. There were two slits at what may have been its summit that glowed a vivid tone of deep green. From beneath them poured a vast amount of water, flowing like a waterfall onto the whale's body.

Umbra's strength failed the moment the creature's gaze met hers. She lost her grip on the slick stone and fell. Her vision darkened, and her consciousness faded as the waves embraced her. She sank to the sea's depths.

The shade of green looming in the sky was both beautiful and bizarre. It was an unnatural, inexplicable colour—both bright as sunlight and hollow. Adorjan was enamoured by it. It was as though he were in a waking dream with his every sense elevated. The raindrops on his skin felt like frozen shards, and he did not blink for the droplets falling into his eyes. There was a strange and fleeting sound which came with a flash of light in the sky. It may have been quiet as a whisper, but it sounded like a thousand crashing waves to his ears.

A state Adorjan knew well—a blend of sense and nonsense as the herb's effects wore off. He was aware of his waking state, yet the island seemed set on convincing him that he still slept with every colour far more vibrant and every sound clearer to him than in reality. This feeling was all the more vivid when experienced outside of his hut, particularly on a night with weather as bizarre as this.

The winds carried with them strong tides onto an unsettled shore and retreated. They washed against the sand with a harsh stroke, withdrew as if into a shell, and then stroked the shore again. The monotony of the motion drew Adorjan into a sense of calm and trepidation all at once. Though a sense of duty had led him onto the shore, he was afraid as he now stood on it. It dawned on him that by the grace of the herbs he smoked, it had been a long while since he had felt such fear.

Ashan prepared his boat, which was resting on the sand. He held his fishing net over his shoulders and tugged aggressively at the mast.

'We should wait until morning,' Adorjan called out to him as he timidly approached.

Ashan hooked his net onto his boat's aft, where his fishing harpoon hung. 'What?' he grunted.

'The storm might be gone by morning.'

'Quy didn't care to wait until morning.'

'There was no storm when--'

'There was when his boat came back to shore. It was much like this one. What, are you scared of rain? It's a wonder how you're such a good farmer.'

Adorjan flinched. *Always so harsh.* 'I'll wake Cadeo up, then.'

Ashan hauled up the rope, which rested in the sand. '*Cadeo?*'

'For the t'rung. If we must go, we should at least have a guide through the fog.'

'Cadeo would be our guide, and that's meant to be

comforting? Don't bother. We won't be going that far from the shore.'

'Then why are we going at all?'

'Quy didn't go far from shore either. Otherwise, his boat wouldn't have made its own way back here like it did. Now, hurry up and help me get her out to sea.'

Adorjan hesitated. He was hit with another rush of the herb's effects in the form of vertigo. He closed his eyes and may have blacked out for a moment. It was an effort to stay on his feet when his eyes opened again.

Ashan was looking down on him from the hull of his boat. 'If you're scared, don't worry,' he said. 'After all, you have those things to protect you.'

Adorjan looked at where Ashan pointed—at his arm covered with his lotus tattoos. Their vivid pink colour had never faded, just as Nota had promised they wouldn't. Beautiful as they were, their vibrancy stopped them from ever truly feeling a part of his skin. But they were often a comfort at sea, reminding him that he had a ward, of sorts, to bring him home.

He looked back at Ashan, taken aback by his harshness. Ashan had no love or respect for superstition, as his untouched skin proved, but never did he so openly mock it. Adorjan now wondered whether Quy's absence hadn't changed Ashan more than he realised. *He really needs this ride tonight. Even finding nothing at all out there might give him some closure.*

Adorjan did as he was told and pushed Ashan's boat out onto the water with him before climbing aboard. The boat rocked and took him off his feet. The sky swayed before him as he lay on his back and felt his stomach churning. The green light beyond the fog had faded, or the fog had grown denser.

He heard Ashan grunt. 'All those hours weren't enough to sober you up,' he said. 'Or did you just smoke again?'

'I'm fine.'

'That's not what I asked you. Forget it, I'll just have to take you as you are.'

Ashan rowed the boat away from the shore. The water sang an unpleasant song from beneath them to Adorjan's ears. The familiar sea breeze found his skin, cooler than usual in the night.

'Sit up and watch,' Ashan said.

Sitting up was an effort for Adorjan, and he felt dizzy when he did. 'Watch for what?'

'Anything you don't usually see.'

'We can't see anything in this fog.'

'Watch anyway.'

Adorjan did. The fog danced around the boat. Any familiarity with this voyage at sea was lost in the fog, as Adorjan soon realised. It killed any sense of awe by hiding the sky and only showing them the dark water right before their faces. Ashan's paddle echoed tenfold in the water, and it felt like his boat moved at a snail's pace.

Adorjan could see farther beyond the fog as the boat crept away from the shore and found its rhythm atop the waves. He saw stars appearing once more and taller waves taking form in the distance, with the moonlight shining on them as a single stream.

The water appeared blacker than it had in any night voyage Adorjan had taken. It looked like it was covered in a sheet of shadow. It felt completely lifeless, as though all life in its depths had been torn away. Adorjan became enamoured with the empty waves rippling against their boat amid the profound quiet surrounding them. It was an odd blend of tranquillity and fear that possessed him.

He reached his hand into the water out of pure impulse. A harsh cold seeped into his fingers and onto his bones. He hadn't felt such wonder setting sail since he was a child. Even with the dread he brought with him, amplified by the herb smoke still coursing through his body, this trip felt like a profound one.

The vessel passed the edge of the bay and approached deep waters. Adorjan felt something new brush against his fingers, and he gripped onto it. It had a familiar slimy texture. He lifted it from the water. It was a mackerel, his favourite fish to eat. It was newly dead, with its scales still fresh and glistening. A chill ran through Adorjan's spine.

'Ashan,' he said, holding the small fish tenderly with both hands.

Ashan stared at it with a blank expression. 'Just the one?' he asked.

Adorjan nodded. Ashan set down his paddle and dipped his arms into the water himself, exposing the horizon past him for Adorjan to see.

What Adorjan saw made him cry out with a sound between a shout and a scream. He saw something unfathomable, even to his own often tormented eyes. Not even the herbs had ever given him such a sight or cause for incredulity. He fell onto his back as he felt his heart sink into his stomach and his voice catch in his chest.

'What?' Ashan demanded, quickly finding his feet. He instinctively reached for his harpoon. Adorjan pointed to a now-empty and dark horizon. Only when he gasped did he realise he had been holding his breath. Ashan shot him a look of utter vitriol and dipped his arm back in the water.

'Of all nights for you to smoke those damn herbs,' he muttered.

'Ashan,' Adorjan managed to say, with a quavering voice. 'I-there was a shadow. I saw a shadow.'

'A shadow,' Ashan echoed contemptuously. But then his face changed once he heard the word in his own voice. He faced Adorjan again with a stern look. 'What do you mean *a shadow*? What shadow?'

'It…it looked like a man, but... A black body and a head came out of the water. But…it was colossal. It was as high as the sky. Its eyes were green…they were glowing. It was looking at us, Ashan. I…I think I heard it breathing.'

Ashan was quiet and looked at Adorjan with an intensity that was unlike him. He looked at the horizon again. It was still dark and empty, partly hidden by fog.

Adorjan held his spinning head in his hands. He cursed himself after the words had left his lips. *A tree was growing new roots in your hut just yesterday. Do you dare to trust your eyes now?*

Adorjan said: 'I…I know because I smoked--'

Ashan ignored his words, took up his paddle again, and started rowing furiously. The boat headed for the horizon.

'Ashan!'

He said nothing. The boat rocked aggressively as he paddled.

'Ashan, why?'

He said nothing. Adorjan watched as the boat was led deeper into the shallower fog and onto deeper waters. They soon were passing the mouth of the shore and approaching the open waters beyond it.

Adorjan felt himself tightly grip the net on the boat's

aft. He felt his hands shaking. He braced for what awaited beyond the last morsel of fog lingering in the sky.

The fog broke, and light erupted, blinding him. It shone atop all the waters up to the horizon and beyond. His eyes burned, and his skin was flushed with heat. He and Ashan cried out in surprise and pain, hiding their eyes in their hands.

Adorjan saw blue all around him when he managed to open them again. They rode under a perfect sky and atop beautiful, calm waters. It was the spectacle of a new and vibrant morning. Adorjan and Ashan looked from whence they came, dumbfounded. There was only a fog atop the sea, with no islands or land in sight.

EIGHT

There was something deeply disconcerting and awe-inspiring about the vast open waters, despite the comfort of a clear morning sun reflecting upon them. Adorjan had never been in so empty a place, out of sight of his home and with nought but water and sky as far as the eye could see. It was a sensation that forced upon him a sense of insignificance and humility. The world had never felt as large as it did then. He and Ashan looked about the place in stunned silence. Their boat matched the slow and calm sway of the sea.

Ashan stood frozen, paddle in hand, brow furrowed and mouth agape. He and Adorjan looked back towards the fog they had come through. There were no cliffs, no mouth of a cove, no rough waters or dark clouds—there was only a lonely fog sitting on unblemished water. *My eyes don't deceive me,* Adorjan confirmed. *These waters are supernatural. We were wrong to come out tonight. Is this what you saw, Quy?*

Adorjan and Ashan waited quietly together. They waited with silent anticipation of a new change. Adorjan felt sick with stress, helpless at the mercy of whatever these nonsensical waters would subject him to. He looked out again over the vast cloud of fog stretching out on the sea, back to where their island should have been. The gravity of what had just befallen Adorjan slowly started to dawn on him, until it hit him hard—he had been subjected to something completely impossible. He had seen proof that something unnatural had descended on their island with his own eyes. Adorjan felt a pure form of terror for the first time, and he snapped.

'We shouldn't have come.' Adorjan felt words involuntarily leave his lips. 'We never should have come out here. Quy must have been lost in this place just like us, and we may never find our way back either. You have killed us by bringing us out here.'

'Quy's boat made it back to shore,' Ashan said, seemingly unmoved. 'It didn't steer itself. If Quy had ever come here, his boat made it back somehow.'

'Is this enough for you?' Adorjan was now shouting. His voice echoed in his ears. 'What now, Ashan? Will you still mock our tattoos and belittle our beliefs after this? Is there some natural cause for this, too? This is more than superstition—this is reality. Something has come for us.'

Ashan showed no sign of hearing Adorjan and appeared lost in thought. He dipped his paddle back into the water and slowly rowed. The boat drifted towards the fog, which resided where their island should have been, following the natural flow of the gentle tide. The sound of his paddle amplified the silence that surrounded them.

Adorjan watched with incredulity and confusion, but did not stop him. He looked on anxiously as their boat neared the fog. Impulse brought Adorjan's hand to the water, and his fingers stroked it as the boat drifted along. The feel of the water was slightly calming and grounding, being a sensation Adorjan knew well. The sea's touch was colder than ever, its chill running through his blood. Adorjan could see nothing in it but seemingly endless darkness. Even the sea itself seemed unnatural in this place.

The morning sunlight slowly faded away as the fog once more surrounded them. A new change in the water and sky came about suddenly. Adorjan was blinded by a stark shift from daylight to darkness. Sunlight was replaced with dull moonlight in a ruptured night sky. The boat was hit by a wave, and the sound of crashing waters filled the air. Sea water soaked Adorjan's skin and the boat's deck. They sailed now in heavy wind and rain. They sailed through the mouth of the island's cove, with their home shore almost in sight.

Adorjan met Ashan's eyes again. They betrayed pure bafflement and wonder. They both looked again to whence they had come. There, they saw nothing but a horizon they had seen a thousand times before, shrouded by fog.

Adorjan collapsed to his knees and held his aching head in his hands. He felt the effects of the herbs in him again—effects that were usually calming were now oppressing him with anxiety and exhaustion. The absurdity of what had just transpired felt impossible to digest, and he couldn't even bring himself to try. He wished for nothing more than the relief of solid ground and respite.

'Adorjan!' He raised his head at the urgency in Ashan's voice. Ashan was looking up. Adorjan followed his eyes and saw another absurdity. Something was falling from the sky—something smaller than he but larger than any flying creature. Adorjan only saw it clearly as it touched the sea, but it was enough to recognise the young girl.

Her name leapt from Adorjan's lips. 'Umbra!'

A little girl saw hazy beams of light blending with a dark sky. She saw the rippling light of a setting sun colliding with the sea and the glow of a rising moon stroking the clouds. She stood submerged in water. Her skin felt pleasantly freezing. Somewhere beneath her feet were the winds and clouds, just out of her reach.

The sea in which the little girl stood was devoid of life, devoid of movement, and heavy with peace. It was not quite silence touching her ears, as nested within it was a deep and relentless pounding, like a soft and everlasting heartbeat. The rhythmic nature of the beat felt as if it came from her chest. It sent ripples through the water around her.

Sunlight and moonlight kissed the sea, coursed through its body, and gradually died. It became so dark in their absence that she knew not whether her eyes were closed or blinded. The light left words in its wake—words too dark to see and too distant to hear. She instead felt them seeping into her skin along with the chilling tides. They stroked her mind with jarring delicacy and trepidation. She felt them calling to her from beyond the water, from where dim moonlight began to rise again.

The tides around the little girl changed. The water ripples further and further from her in waves. What had been silent waters became a cluster of echoes like those born of thunder. What had been dark waters now had light seeping into them again until not even a shadow remained where she stood.

A harsh wind hit her wet skin. Air forced itself through her lips, settling in her core. It clung to her like a disease and burned her. It lifted her from her feet and took her towards the clouds above her. The seas became distant below her feet. Up as high as the clouds, she couldn't breathe.

The clouds dissipated as the light from the sea followed her. Before her was a colossal full moon. The light it radiated was too bright for her, and she closed her eyes. The words calling her from the sea found a new clarity and gripped her mind firmly —

Nisi eam..

Adorjan clumsily made for the side of the boat. Umbra's body was already sinking before he caught sight of her again. Sense abandoned him, and instinct firmly took hold. He heard Ashan call out his name too late as he leapt from the boat and into the sea. He could barely feel the cold water on his skin, even as his body was submerged. He could see nothing but darkness, no matter how frantically he looked. He reached his hands out around him and felt nothing but water.

He tried to scream Umbra's name. A hollow, awful sound left his mouth, as did much of the air in his lungs. His body started to ache with his breath already spent. Instinct commanded him to reach up and haul himself out again. But as he raised his hands, he could not tell whether he was reaching up toward the surface or down toward the depths.

Adorjan realised, with the growing pain in his core and the tightening of the water's restraint, that he was drowning. Panic flowed into him. He reached out again to no avail. The cold now touched his bones. His consciousness started to fade, and water flowed into his core. His body went limp, and the pain in his head began to subside.

A thunderous sound and the sensation of wind woke Adorjan up. He gasped, and air hurried into his lungs so fast that they burned. He had enough strength to open his eyes and see himself being hauled back toward the boat. He felt Ashan's strong arm around him as they floated on the water together.

'Grab her!'

Adorjan heard Ashan's words, but could not process them at first. Then he saw Umbra lying on Ashan's shoulder.

'Now!'

Adorjan did so and laid Umbra on his own shoulders. It took all his strength to stay afloat until Ashan climbed back aboard and took Umbra with him. Then it took all his strength to climb back into the boat himself.

He slumped onto the boat's deck, heaving. Umbra was out beside him. Her skin was as pale as the fog, and her eyes were closed. He saw her chest rise and fall, but her breathing looked short and laboured. She looked terrible. Adorjan reached out and laid his hand on her. She was cold to the touch.

'Lay on her,' Ashan called out. 'Keep her warm.'

Adorjan did so. He lay on her with his face to the deck. He could not contain himself and began to weep. He put his face in his hands as if to hide his shame. Ashan took his paddle in hand and rowed hurriedly toward the shore.

The furious waves on the way home were not loud enough to hide Adorjan's weeping from his ears.

The words touched the little girl's blood and forced her eyes open again. Against the backdrop of a warm moon stood a silhouette upon new clouds—a little girl with long, locked hair flowing around her face in the harsh and bitter winds. Where her eyes and face should have been, there was only blackness. She was like a shadow.

Nisi eam.

Her voice was a whisper that filled every morsel of the air. She reached out her jet-black arm and offered her hand.

The little girl's vision blurred as she gasped for the heavy air suddenly filling her lungs. She reached out through desperation and instinct towards the shadow's hand, which drew ever closer. She managed to stroke her fingers. They were cold and hard as stone.

The little girl felt a new sensation on her feet. She looked down to see the sea rising, overcoming the clouds and reaching out to her. She felt rage coming from the waters as they gave birth to a colossal wave with a peak higher than she could see. She heard a blood-curdling scream as the water overcame her and the shadow, forcing both of them into its embrace.

Water flowed into the little girl's body once more and inspired something close to ecstasy within her. The shadow was before her once more, sinking into the water. Umbra saw fear in her empty face. The shadow reached out once more with a trembling hand. Umbra gripped her hand and held her tightly.

Light touched the water's depths. It shone onto the shadow's face and eradicated the blackness on her skin. Her eyes were still possessed by darkness, and her skin was pale like the moon itself, but it was unmistakable — the face the little girl saw was her own.

Umbra.

Something changed within her at the sight of herself. Her arm relaxed, and her mind was at peace. She looked upon herself with strange numbness.

She let go.

Nisi eam.

The face of the girl before her shifted from terror to contentment. The sea's depths drew her deeper and deeper until even the light fled from her. The shadow was left alone in the depths, with nothing but the words resonating in the air to keep her company.

Umbra.

Umbra's eyes finally opened at Varyis' touch. She was lying on her back and stared up at a straw roof. She was wrapped in a thick sheet and shivered within it.

'Umbra,' Varyis said.

He touched Umbra's hand with a delicacy that was unlike him. Umbra stared dead into his eyes, and Varyis looked into hers through the blurry vision of his tears. Dull red blended with the whites of her eyes, and they were trapped in dark circles. Above her eye was a cut in her brow that was swelling and turning purple. Varyis' stomach churned at the sight of it. He felt sick at the memory of his anger getting the better of him and of the bowl flying from his fingers.

He gripped Umbra's hand tightly. All manner of

emotions in the form of memories flowed into him in this moment of holding a loved one by the hand through their pain once more. There was no response to his touch. It was as though she were not present.

'How do you feel?' Varyis managed to force from his lips.

Umbra slowly and tiredly blinked but said nothing. She looked around the hut, as though it were alien to her eyes. Varyis tried to reach out further, but his hand would not obey. It hung over the cup, and there it remained, shaking violently, feeling less and less like his own. He looked up, but his daughter would not meet his eyes. She instead took the cup herself and sipped from it.

Varyis felt blood rise to his temples and his teeth gritting. His body stopped shaking.

'They told me you fell from the sky,' he said with some anger. 'What were you doing?'

Umbra met his eyes again, her face still devoid of much expression. 'From the sky?' she echoed. 'I thought I fell in the sea.'

'I know that already,' Varyis spat out, raising his voice. 'What were you doing in the sky?'

Umbra blinked slowly. 'I was climbing...and I fell. From the rocks. Not the sky.'

Varyis felt something in him snap. He practically shouted, 'You were climbing? In the dead of night, in the pouring rain, you went climbing on rocks? Are you dense? Is this how you spend your nights away, rather than working or cooking? You're not to go out after sundown again. You will come home after your work in the fields and stay there until morning. What foolishness took over you? To risk getting badly hurt, or worse—what were you trying to do?'

Umbra hardly reacted to Varyis' harsh tone. She still stared at the roof and quietly said, 'I didn't want to be home, Father.'

Those simple words, spoken in such a calm and soft voice, touched Varyis' heart and dissipated his anger. It had been so long since his heart had been so deeply and harshly struck that he could not comprehend the sensation he now felt. Guilt? Sadness? It was most likely an unnatural union of both and more.

He felt Umbra's hand slip out of his as his feeble strength left his body. He stared at his daughter's face, who looked right back at him. They sat together silently for a long time, looking at each other like strangers.

The exchange was broken by a voice.

'Varyis.' He looked up. Vada looked down at him with concern plastered on her stern face. 'We should let Umbra sleep a while longer,' she softly said.

Vada helped Varyis to his feet without waiting for a response. Varyis leaned on Vada as he walked on his trembling legs. He looked back upon his daughter once more. Her unyielding stare was devoid of any emotion, as though she had no face at all. Varyis realised something with excruciating clarity as he left his daughter to her respite—*I do not understand this girl.*

NINE

Adorjan could no longer bear the isolation and self-imposed despair. He'd stared at the familiar hole in his thatched roof for hours. Sunlight had slowly given way to moonlight, and he had barely moved or eaten since morning. Sobriety had never felt so painful.

He spun his old bamboo pipe between his fingers, over and over. Sounds of waves and the gentle pattering of rainfall rang over and over in his brain. He still felt the chill of the seawater on his skin and shivered from it. He was so lost in the recent memory that when the bamboo pipe clattered on the floor, he gasped for breath as though he were drowning again.

Adorjan finally stood up and stormed out of his hut, with only a vague purpose in mind—he yearned for some respite, and his shame-riddled brain offered none of it at home. He waded through the fog and made for the coast. The evening shore was typically quiet. The waves had quietened greatly, and there was no sign of the storm that had plagued it not a full day ago.

The sea brought no calm to his stormy mind. Along with the soft pattering of the waves was the sound of his screams resonating in his brain. The cold water touching his feet brought him immeasurable shame and guilt, as the memory continued resonating in his mind's eye. Returning to the coast only clouded his mind further.

Never again—those were the old words echoing in Adorjan's mind. *Never again. I'll never be so useless again. I'll never be pathetic again.* These promises repeated in his brain for a time, perhaps even leaking out onto his tongue, as he stood at the shore, blinded to the tides.

He must have spent longer than he realised. There was a familiar boat approaching when his eyes next opened, the sight of it another cause for shame. *Ashan.* Something like anger rose in Adorjan's stomach as Ashan's boat drew closer. Soon, he could see Ashan himself, setting his anchor down into the water.

'What were you doing?' Adorjan yelled out to him. If Ashan heard him, he didn't show it. He finished setting his anchor and dove into the water. The anger set further still into Adorjan. He waited a moment for Ashan to appear on the shore, and yelled again—'What were you doing on the water, Ashan?'

Ashan looked back at Adorjan, silently and intensely.

Adorjan felt anger build up that he could not contain. 'We almost died, man. *Umbra* almost died. If that doesn't keep you away from the sea, what will?'

'Are you seeing trees again?' he said, pointing at Adorjan's hand. Adorjan only then realised he was tightly gripping his old wooden pipe. He did not remember picking it up when it fell in his hut, and must have done so through instinct. His stomach sank at the thought. 'Maybe I'm just a figment of your imagination, too.'

'I'm sober,' Adorjan spat out.

'If you say so,' Ashan said with no hint of a smile.

'Answer me. What were you doing at sea again?'

Ashan's eyes narrowed. His brow twitched. 'And what is it about the sea that scares you so much?'

Adorjan groaned, incredulous. 'After all we just went through, you have to ask such a stupid question?'

'*All* we went through. Which *part* scared you?'

'All of it!'

Ashan shook his head. 'Then you're a fool—an idiot and a coward.'

Something bubbled over in Adorjan at those words. He grabbed Ashan by his collar, enraged. He thought he was a hair's breadth away from striking him. He didn't realise he had already done so until his hand started aching. Blood started leaking from Ashan's nose. Adorjan may have struck again had Ashan reacted in any way that wasn't so indifferent. Adorjan saw vitriol in the eyes glaring back at him.

'For once,' Adorjan slowly said. 'Just once, be serious.'

'*Serious*,' Ashan echoed. Blood flowed across his lips. 'How's Umbra doing? Has she woken up yet? Did she seem okay after all she just went through? It must have been traumatic, after all.'

Adorjan froze, taken aback. Something like guilt tugged at his heart, for a reason he couldn't comprehend.

'Don't bother answering that, I know you can't,' Ashan continued. 'Because you haven't been to see her, have you? I'm betting you haven't seen anyone since we got back. You just holed yourself up in that room as usual, putting that smoke in your body. Or maybe you *are* sober. Who cares?

'And who cares about what happened to us out there? You obsess over what you don't understand, what you can't understand, and ignore what's right in front of your face. All that should scare you is that Umbra almost died, and would have had I not been there to drag her out of the water. Just like *you* would have died if I didn't drag your sorry self up too.'

Adorjan's hands loosened from Ashan's collar. 'That *does* scare me. It's all I've been thinking about.'

Ashan struck his arm away. 'Stop lying to yourself. A man who is afraid for another's life isn't *angry* like you are. You're angry at yourself. You're bitter because you were a liability out there, rather than her saviour. You jumped in that water against your better judgement, not for Umbra's sake, but for your pride. You're turning to anger so that you don't have to face the fact that you're *ashamed*. So, don't bother trying to berate me. Get your *own* ship patched up before telling me *mine* is sinking.'

Ashan shoved something into Adorjan's hands. He had been so enraged he didn't realise Ashan carried anything. He looked down at a net partly full of fish in his hands. Ashan left Adorjan staring at the net, full of anguish and shame. Blood seeped from a fresh cut on his knuckle onto the sand.

Umbra sat across from an ageing, deteriorating man sitting on his floor bed, who was savouring every minuscule bite of boiled fish and seaweed from his bowl. He stared intently at nothing in particular, seemingly mesmerised by another small new hole in the roof of their hut, which still leaked a soft stream of rainwater into an old wooden bucket on the floor. So intently he seemed in a vacant thought that he had not met Umbra's eyes since she returned from her daily labour. She had soon returned the favour and barely looked at her father since.

Her hands ached from her work in the paddies, which had been more exhausting than usual. Her blood still felt cold in her veins, and the aftermath of the cold seawater chilled her bones still. Her bowl remained half full, with her appetite having abandoned her. She knew not the source of unease that constantly plagued her from within her hut's walls and kept her reckless. Nothing about this place felt safe or like her own home. It was claustrophobic and hot, like drowning in boiling water. It was as though this were the only place in the world while she was trapped in these walls, and the world neared total collapse. She longed for nothing more than to run away from it and back beside her lonely friend.

Umbra looked to the outdoors. It still rained heavily, and the wind had become aroused with the night air. She could hear it from where she sat, and it was oh so enticing. It drew her to her feet. It moved her away from the suffocating fire. It muffled the ageing man's voice until it embraced her under the safety of the night sky. She was suddenly hit with the orchestra of the storm—a crescendo of thunder and the crashing of angry waves.

Every step in the sand of the shore felt like a step

towards a haven. She knew not how many days had passed since she fell into the waves, but they were far too many days spent away. She begged in her heart that the whale still waited for her. Its silent words played in her mind still—how it pleaded for her to stay, begged her not to be left alone. *Stay. Stay.* Her promise plagued her as her first broken one—*I'll be back tomorrow.* She hurried as fast as she could.

The rocks were slimy and lashed by waves. Freezing water thrashed her skin as she climbed, her hands raw and bleeding from the sharp edges. She looked beyond the cliffs. The mist and rain were not so heavy that she could not see the shore. She saw the silhouette of the whale lying still upon it. She saw something beyond it there, as dark as the night itself and colossal—unfathomable to her.

A colossal creature loomed peacefully beside the whale, with the two green slits at its peak, which were surely eyes. It was so dark, it seemed made of shadows. The being's eyes locked onto Umbra. Her blood warmed at the sight of them, and an alien sensation ran through her. She was afraid. Truly afraid. She stared at a very embodiment of the unknown in its eye, and it terrified her. Yet her arms did not let up, and her feet drew her ever closer. Closer still. Her feet touched sand, and her hands were relieved. She approached the whale and the creature beyond it— slowly but without fear. Something akin to relief swept over Umbra. *The whale was not alone for so long.*

She drew closer still, and a peculiar realisation came to her—the being that appeared colossal from a distance was far less so when up closer, imposing though it still was. The being stared at her intently and emanated an ambience that was overwhelming yet embracing. Its being was contagious and all-encompassing. From the creature, Umbra sensed…exhaustion. Exhaustion and pain of the heart.

It broke its stare and looked down once more at the whale, which exhaled softly beneath it. Umbra laid her hand upon its cold skin, as if through instinct. It was wet for the rain, and it breathed as though it hurt to do so. Umbra remembered seeing this creature from the rocks, lording above the whale with the backdrop of a similar night sky. She remembered the stream of water that poured onto the whale. She looked upon the whale with pity and sorrow. The pain of the dark creature's heart bled onto her own.

Umbra realised her hands still held the unfinished bowl of fish and rice. She emptied the bowl onto the sand and ran for the coast. She filled it with seawater. She made back for the whale and poured the water upon its skin.

A slit opened in the whale's skin, where one great eye glinted, fixed on Umbra. It was huge and shone like moonlight. It was beautiful, yet the sight of it filled Umbra with sadness. It held a look of fear and anguish. Umbra once more heard the whale's voice in her blood—it told her to *stay*. Then she heard a new voice with her ears as the whale moaned with a new cry. It was so imposing that Umbra had to hold her ears, yet so feeble it inspired pity.

Umbra ran for the coast again, with desperation in her spirit. She filled her bowl once more. She turned. The shadow loomed before her, blinding her to the whale. She looked up and met its bright eyes, straining her neck. They locked eyes only for a moment before the creature shifted past her and seemed to be consumed by the water.

Umbra waited for what felt like a long while, and the

creature did not resurface. The waves, however, seemed to calm somewhat, and the rain eased. The storm was passing, faster than the clouds ought to have been able to disappear. She made back for the whale and poured her bowl on it again, once more meeting its eye. The water from her bowl was quickly overwhelmed by the rainwater on the whale's skin. She looked over the whale's body, sunken into the sand—immense and motionless. She looked down at the tiny bowl in her hands. She dropped it onto the sand, suddenly feeling insignificant.

She looked again into the whale's eye, where rainwater pooled like tears. She laid a hand on its skin, as it softly moaned again. She was resolute as ever that the whale would not spend its last moments alone.

Umbra said, 'I can at least stay with you for tonight.'

TEN

The rain finally seemed to let up. The once-rampaging rain and wind were now reduced to a gentle breeze and light stream of water. Cadeo gently tapped the beams of his t'rung again with his old pair of wooden sticks from inside his hut. He absentmindedly played a lesser-known tune, slow and devoid of rhythm. The tone would continuously and gradually fall from high to low, wandering unpredictably. It was a melody that made Cadeo's hands and eyelids heavy with tiredness, perhaps due to its sleepy cadence or the detriment of his age. The sticks had never felt so heavy.

Cadeo did not know why he had the urge to play this song on this night, nor why he played any song at all. It was a song he conceptualised many decades ago for no particular purpose that he could remember. So long had it been that he was unsure if he played anything resembling how it would have sounded back then. He believed, though, that his heart wouldn't have felt as heavy when he made it as it did now. He would not be hitting the t'rung with the same vehemence he now did, even if the sound back then would have been louder by way of his youthful fingers. *When was the last time I felt anger like this?*

Gratus sat beside Cadeo. He felt her eyes on him, quietly watching with an air of politeness. Cadeo kept playing, letting instinct replace memory and allowing the song to change as his hands saw fit. They hit the t'rung softer now, making the song barely audible to Cadeo's ears. He played for a long time while the rain outside subsided and the wind slowed to a near halt. His arms ached terribly, but still he played until the sticks fell from his fingers and clattered on the ground. Cadeo's lungs ached as he realised he had been holding his breath. He breathed deeply and lay down with his shaking hands.

'This is a surprise,' said a strong and beautiful voice. Cadeo finally met Gratus' gaze, who wore a warm and curious soft expression. As he so often was, Cadeo found himself lost in her eyes. They were as deep and dark, yet shone as brightly as they had their whole life together, even as the skin around them wrinkled and dried. 'I had forgotten that the t'rung could play any other song but the one to guide the fishermen home.'

Cadeo could not bring himself to smile at the jest. 'Well…there is no one to bring home on this day.'

Gratus held out her hands, which held a bowl of rice soup. Cadeo looked at it with some sadness and wondered how much longer such meals would be readily available.

He gratefully accepted. Gratus laid her hand upon his. It was warm and soothing.

'It has troubled you so much?'

'It was reckless, Gratus.' The words left Cadeo's lips quickly and easily. 'We have already lost one fisherman recently. What if we had lost them both, too? We would have had less able hands, and this drought would have been all the worse for it. Curiosity dulled their senses, and they could have doomed us for it.'

'And yet, had they not gone to sea, we would have instead lost Umbra,' Gratus said.

Cadeo grunted. 'That girl is even worse. To be in the sea during a storm, she has no sense to begin with. Varyis needs to get a tighter hold over that one.' Gratus' hand left Cadeo's, and the warmth went with it. Cadeo immediately felt ashamed. 'I did not mean that.'

'Of course you did,' Gratus said. 'You are just not accustomed to anger, and I am not accustomed to seeing you like this. What truly troubles you so much, Cadeo?'

Cadeo sighed. No matter how many years passed, Gratus' eyes saw through all the hardened skin and bones that covered his heart, and brought it to his face to see in its truest, ugly state. She was, of course, correct. The feeling of frustration and impatience had perhaps become a daily occurrence in his old age. But *anger* had been alien to him, so much so that he couldn't recognise it himself anymore. He struggled to form the words to respond because, in truth, he did not know where this anger came from himself.

As though reading his heart once more, Gratus said, 'Do you still believe yourself leader of this place?'

Cadeo rubbed his tattooed arms, the words seeping

deeply into him. 'I am obviously not. Not in their eyes,' he said. 'Else none of this would have happened. A leader must guide his people from danger and prosperity, but in that, I am failing at every count.'

Gratus now stood. The brown tips of her locked hair swayed around her knees.

'*That* is not where you are failing, old man,' she said. The sternness of her voice made Cadeo raise his head. Her eyes carried an intensity completely unlike her. 'Who of this island has ever called themselves a leader?'

'Arinya did. Do you not recall how she used to call herself our shepherd? And no one in this town would have argued against her being a leader, even during the famine.'

'And you have told me many a time that she was who made you strive to be a shepherd yourself. What does being a shepherd have to do with being a leader? A shepherd protects, nurtures and guides all under his care. A shepherd does not wait to be acknowledged before doing his duty. And a shepherd does not blame those under his care for losing their way—he makes haste to guide them back. *That* is why you are angry, Cadeo. Because you feel so far away from who you want to be.'

Cadeo sat dumbly, mouth agape and staring into Gratus' eyes. Such strength, such conviction, such unbridled certainty in her words. She was angry too, and as her words sank deeper into him still, he knew she had a right to it. *Ever unmovable and ever present,* Cadeo thought of her. He reached up to take her hand once more. She did not pull it away. *I have taken this for granted for far too many years.*

'You are not so far from a shepherd as you think,' she softly said.

'I am,' Cadeo said, without hesitation. 'I am very far. You are right, always. When was the last time I took action to protect?'

'When you last played that on the shore,' Gratus said, pointing at the t'rung.

Cadeo faced the ground once more. 'Whatever unseen force is out there does the protecting for me. I am but a conduit for it when I play. And even that force seems to have forsaken us in these times. It brought a boat back to us, but left Quy for the sea.'

'No force plays that instrument and gives our people a cause for hope but you.' Gratus gripped his hand back firmly. 'And what of those you helped to raise as your own? Look no further than Ruhan to see how becoming you can be as a shepherd. In him, you raised a loving and diligent man who is a pride for his people. Were fate kinder to us, Amado would surely have been the same.'

Cadeo could not hold himself at those last words. Something in his heart dissipated, something that clung to it and fed from it like a parasite. He felt a lightness in his spirit at its absence. A tear trickled down his cheek. 'Thank you,' he managed in the softest of voices.

Though Gratus' face stayed stern, her eyes smiled in the subtle way only Cadeo could see. He took his sticks into his hands and played his t'rung once more, through instinct rather than memory. Gratus sat by his side, her head on his shoulder, as he played through much of the night. His hands slowly returned to playing the song of his youth, with a touch more vigour than before. His eyes began to close at some stage, even as he played. The t'rung made a beautiful tone when it was permitted to. Cadeo became a mere conduit for its will to be heard, and felt joy at the prospect while it lasted.

Only when his hands grew tired once more and the music naturally slowed to a halt did he realise Gratus had fallen asleep on his shoulder, and he had a new listener in his home.

Ashan stood cross-armed at the hut's entrance, looking down on Cadeo with his characteristically unreadable expression. He gave Cadeo a slow nod. *That was pleasant*, was what Cadeo saw in the gesture. Cadeo nodded back. Ashan's eyes switched to Gratus, whose eyes were peacefully closed. He gave Cadeo another look, which said *another time*, and turned from whence he came.

'I'm not asleep,' Gratus said, slowly raising her head. 'Do you need something, Ashan?'

Ashan turned back to them and politely bowed his head. 'A private word with Cadeo. But it can wait until later.'

Cadeo gave Gratus a quick look, and she gave him a soft nod.

'It is okay,' he said to Ashan. 'We can talk now, and it need not be private.'

Ashan looked puzzled, but walked in to sit before them on the ground. 'It may not be a matter *she'd* want to or should hear about.'

'About the famine,' Cadeo asked.

'In part.'

'She has most of the same memories of the last drought that I do, and she knows as much as I do—about what is happening now. Firstly, though, you went to sea again?'

'If I didn't, who else would?' Ashan said. Cadeo had to scoff a bit. Ashan's abrasiveness was an insurmountable hurdle to understanding the man at times, and was a painful but much-needed breath of fresh air at others. This time felt more like the latter. 'You told me before that people saw strange sights,' Ashan continued. 'Things like shadows?'

'Colossal shadows,' Cadeo confirmed. He knew better than to press further in vain, but the line of questioning piqued his concern. *You saw something out there yourself, Ashan. Something that would scare even you.*

'Do you remember how they were described?'

'A little. I remember talk of dark people who were as tall as the hills and reached even the clouds.'

'But the sightings were rarely consistent,' Gratus said. 'Some were tall as the clouds, some were like our own shadows. Some arrived in a storm, some when there was no rain. Some were completely dark, while some had eyes that glowed green. Arinya believed it was psychological— one man sees something strange, others follow in panic. The sightings weren't consistent, so that explanation became easy enough to accept.'

'Easier, but not impossible,' Ashan stated more than he asked. 'Did these people have any commonalities?'

'Commonalities?'

'Were they all young, or old? Workers, or homebodies? Were they otherwise sick, or on any medication?'

Cadeo and Gratus looked at each other, both sharing the surprise that this had never been questioned before. 'Not that I can think of,' Gratus said. 'Ashan, why do you ask all this?'

'You cannot *both* be so blind,' Ashan said, not kindly. 'Fear has already spread through the people. They are all on edge, and it will only be so long before they lose their senses if this goes on much longer. We've no fish to eat, we only have so much rice left, and the harvest is many weeks away.'

Gratus smiled. 'No, Ashan,' she firmly said. 'That's no reason to be so specific. You are asking about *shadows*. You, or someone else, have seen something.'

Ashan said nothing.

'Are you now doubting your own eyes, Ashan? Are you starting to believe there may be things your eyes can't make sense of?'

Ashan said nothing and scowled. It was unlike him to be lost for words, and the sight fascinated Cadeo. His adoration for his wife grew ever larger. 'Didn't you always reject superstition, Ashan?' Gratus said, with a hint of mocking in her voice. 'Haven't you always mocked the art on our skin for that reason?'

'I reject abstract ideas, not what is right before my face.'

'And what is in front of your face now?' Cadeo could not help but interject.

Ashan did not answer. He took a long breath and said — 'One more question. You both maintain that you do not know how the last famine ended?'

Cadeo was taken off guard. His breath hitched, and a tightness gripped his chest. Of all the questions Ashan could have asked, this hit the hardest. It was like an echo from a song he had long tried and failed to forget. It was all Cadeo could do not to let the anguish show on his face.

He and Gratus looked at each other, then he firmly said, 'Of course.'

'Fine.' Ashan bowed his head, then left as quickly as he had entered. He left the flap of the hut open, exposing Cadeo and Gratus to the elements.

Cadeo and Gratus sat in mutual silence for a long while

after Ashan left, holding each other's hands tightly. The silence pressed down on them. Cadeo sensed Gratus felt the same shaken spirit, with the most torturous of memories being unearthed.

He was the first to break the silence. 'Polite as ever,' he grunted and sealed the flap of the hut.

'Also discerning,' Gratus said, laying down. 'Discerning, inquisitive and relentless. Maybe he has the best chance of making sense of all this. Even if it is because he seems to be the only one trying.'

'*Sense,*' Cadeo echoed. He lay down beside his wife and embraced her. 'Making sense of the nonsensical is not always virtuous. Sometimes it is just a waste of time. And the boy is still cutting his hair, see? He has neither sense nor maturity.'

Cadeo felt Gratus grin on his shoulder. 'You know,' she said. 'You know who may have had his temperament? They would almost be the same age.'

Cadeo scowled. 'Absolutely not.'

Gratus smiled harder still. 'Amado would probably have grown in much the same way—reliant on his own eyes rather than that which his eyes could not see.'

Cadeo smiled a little himself. Though the pain of Amado's name on his ears would never fade, it was pleasant to talk about him openly. He took Gratus' candour as an invitation to do so.

'*We* would have raised him into a good, faithful man,' he said. 'One like Ruhan. He and Amado would have grown up as friends and shared a similar outlook on life. Ashan had no one to learn a sense of spirituality from. Lestari and Adhiarja lived only ever with practicality in mind and tried to raise him in their image, never looking at life beyond flesh and blood.'

'Yet, Ashan is not like his parents were,' Gratus said. 'Would they ever have marched up to our home and so brazenly probed into our past like he just did? They wouldn't ask questions and instead accept everything exactly as it is. They surely tried to raise Ashan to be the same way, but he could not be more different to them. He is courageous, ever questioning why everything is as it is, and rarely accepting the answers he is given. The man Ashan has become is more a product of his environment than his parents' influence. Ruhan was always more agreeable as a child than Amado was. Amado would have been a product of that same environment. Perhaps even more so than Ashan, with two fossils like us trying to fill his head with superstitions and traditions.'

'Until those superstitions proved to be a reality,' Cadeo said. 'Then his mind would have been changed, just as Ashan's has now.'

'Don't get ahead of yourself now, old man. All Ashan did was ask more questions.'

Cadeo could not deny the truth in her words, as usual. *Amado would have grown into the finest of men with you to guide him as you do me, Gratus.*

Cadeo struggled to find sleep that night. Speaking of that painful time stirred a storm of thoughts he couldn't quiet. But that one question stuck in his mind, like a thorn wedged deep into the flesh. *How did the last famine end?* His answer had been honest, he knew. He did not *know*. Yet something pulled at his stomach and gave him deserved doubt.

Sleep eluded Cadeo. Some unseen thorn still twisted in the dark recesses of his mind—a guilt that felt ancient and buried, but still alive beneath the surface.

ELEVEN

Adorjan rose from another restless slumber to face a brand new day. The effect of the herbs still lingered in his brain from the night before, and his home still had the distinct smell of fragrant smoke trapped in it. His pipe had fallen from his fingers, scattering ash along the floor—evidence of an artificially induced sleep.

It was to be another day of expected labour and responsibilities. Another day of smiling through gritted teeth under the pretence that all was well in this place, that all was well in Adorjan's head. It was a day he could not willingly face—not right now and maybe not for a while. Several reasons and excuses had flowed through Adorjan's head last night as to why he felt even more restless than usual, why his own company put him at such unease. The answer was ultimately obvious, and accepting this was what drove him to the pipe once more—Adorjan was still riddled with guilt.

Ashan had the right of it, Adorjan was greatly pained to admit. Adorjan was not uneasy out of concern for Umbra, nor was he shaken by how close to death she had come. He was *angry* at being confronted by his own inadequacies. He was bitter that he had been a liability to Umbra and Ashan. All this stemmed from his dependency on an unnatural high, which he once more retreated to when faced with the truth of his self. Ashan had stopped short of calling Adorjan pathetic, but Adorjan now did so himself. *I'm… pathetic.*

Adorjan couldn't face others with such heavy shame and self-loathing, yet he couldn't bear to face it alone either. The latter was particularly true. He managed to drag himself from his floor bed, swaying on his feet with his head spinning. He could think of only one person he could bear to see right now, and whom he knew would feel better for seeing. *She'll again berate me when she sees me like this*, he knew. *But I deserve at least that much.*

He had a half-finished bowl of now slimy rice and grasshoppers for breakfast. He felt a little more sober with something in his stomach and strong enough to walk. It was early in the morning, as Adorjan could tell before he even stepped outdoors. It was not easy to feel or see the sun for the fog, but the early morning air had a certain purity, an intangible *feeling* that Adorjan had long grown accustomed to. His mind, always on his duties and the paddies that demanded his care, never allowed him to sleep for long enough to miss the morning air.

Adorjan found that he was becoming familiar with the fog, and it held less of the portentousness than when it first arrived. He could make out the horizon in the mornings despite it. He could still hear the soft trickle of the morning tides. He still felt the coarse sand seeping between his toes with each step. The morning was how it always was, and time moved on as it always did.

He knocked on his aunt Vada's hut. There was no answer or light from within. He made for the grassy hills to climb to the only other place she would be at such an hour—Burial Hill. The walk was not a long one, yet the climb uphill was tiring, even for Adorjan's young legs. It was also a climb that brought sorrow with it—his feet usually only touched this grass to mourn both new and old deaths. Adorjan hoped he was correct and that his aunt was at the top, lest he had invited more darkness into his heart for nothing.

Indeed, there Vada was at the peak, kneeling among the idols and busy at work. Adorjan knew his aunt would often visit this place, though he had never known why, nor had he thought to ask, assuming it was to pay respects to the dead and to be lost in memories like everyone else.

'I'm tending to the flowers,' Vada said without turning her back, as though reading her nephew's mind. 'I'll be out of your way in a moment.'

'Do you always tend to the flowers up here, Auntie?' Adorjan asked.

'Oh, Dory,' she said. 'Whenever I can. They have a habit of attracting weeds, and they're far from water, so someone has to do it. Though they're doing better than usual with all this rain, I suppose.'

The flowers were a vibrant tone of pink and red,

forming a harsh contrast against the serene backdrop of the idols and the sea. They were small, and the idols towered above them, but there were many.

'What's their purpose?' he asked.

'Purpose?'

'Are they for your medicines? What do they treat?'

'Nothing at all. They're just here to look pretty. They make this place a little less grim, don't you think?'

'Maybe a little,' Adorjan said, though he wasn't so sure himself. *Nothing is pretty enough to make death any less grim.* 'Isn't that a waste of energy, Auntie? Climbing all this way just to care for flowers with no purpose? We don't have much to eat right now. You ought to save your strength.'

'Someone woke up chipper this morning,' Vada laughed. She finally turned to see him and fell quiet. Adorjan was suddenly conscious of what a state he must have looked in. The herbs still clung to his brain, and he could feel it in his eyes. He felt the wind brush against remnants of tears on his face that he hadn't realised had fallen. It was an effort to stand with any dignity, and he felt himself hunching over.

Vada had a face that always seemed to smile and exude joy, even as she frowned now, at the sight of Adorjan. He managed to meet her eyes and waited for her to say something, anything. She didn't talk for a long while, and her look became intense and unreadable. Adorjan felt more and more vulnerable as they locked eyes, as though he were naked before her in every possible sense. He was the first to break their stare, looking to the ground and searching for words to say, but found nothing. He didn't know what to ask for or how to put what troubled him into words.

Vada softly spoke first.

'It's not a waste of energy, coming here,' she said. 'I do it because these flowers are pathetic. Yes, they're pretty and worth keeping alive for that alone, but they're a pain in the rear. They grow in a terrible place, far from water and constantly exposed to sunlight, which always makes them thirsty. Well, they're well fed for now, but now they have no sunlight because of all this fog. So, if these flowers have sunlight, they won't have water unless I bring it. If it rains and there's fog like this, they have water but won't have much sunlight, no matter what I do. And on the rare days that they have both, they still get overgrown by weeds unless I help them. They're pathetic.

'All this could be solved if only they had a brain and some feet. Then they could move down the hill and closer to the shore, where they'd have plenty of water and no weeds to worry about. Or I suppose they could decide to do nothing at all and keep having some fool like me come up here day after day to keep them alive instead. But, had they the will to move for themselves, they might have grown three times bigger by now, and maybe been three times prettier. Sometimes, inaction is the easiest choice, but the most painful over time.'

Adorjan nodded quietly and in contemplation. As ever with her abstract words, the meaning behind them was simple to comprehend and easy to digest—*you're miserable because you're inactive.* Even less than the chastisement he had expected, these were the last words he would have wanted to hear, and they made him feel no better, but they gifted him with a feeling far beyond temporary relief or affirmation.

'Didn't *you* plant these flowers here?' Adorjan said.

Vada smiled again. 'Don't judge me. Now I have something that can't live without me.'

Adorjan laughed, or rather scoffed.

'Anyway,' Vada continued. 'I've done all I need to for them this morning. As promised, I'll leave you in peace.'

Vada descended the hill before Adorjan could protest, and was soon out of sight. Burial Hill was almost silent without her. The flowers at Adorjan's feet flowed gracefully with the wind and were beautiful in their vibrant tones, even without the sun to shine on them.

Adorjan hadn't fully appreciated until today how beautiful the rice fields usually were, when all was right with the world and nature took its course uninterrupted. Something was alluring about the uniformity of this place built upon generations of hard workers, of its humble appearance yet complex needs. Even the feeling of his feet sinking slowly into wet mud and the plant stalks between his fingers as the sun beat down on his body was inexplicably therapeutic.

But the fields today were bleak and grey, devoid of beauty or elegance, even with the rice in the paddy standing uniformly. This was just a stretch of wet land in this fog, representing another long stretch of labour to come for the simple purpose of survival. It was labour for the benefit of his future self—sowing what couldn't be reaped for weeks, surviving meanwhile on the last harvest. It was, for the first time, a vicious and brutal cycle in Adorjan's eyes, bordering on *futile*.

Yet, his hands toiled as they always did, without question or hesitation. This was devoid of usual chatter and liveliness, despite Thi, Lihn, and Kien having returned to the field. Everyone worked efficiently and silently. The plants grew healthily, yet there was none of the enthusiasm and excitement one would expect. Perhaps, Adorjan considered, the hunger had taken a deep hold of his people, too. Perhaps harvest was no longer something to be celebrated, but simply a time of relief.

Umbra worked in the fields again, too, for the first time in many a day. Adorjan left her be as they worked, much to his shame. The sight of her still stirred nervousness in his heart and stomach. *I can't continue for another day like this*, he resolved. And so he approached her during their break. He asked her to work beside him before they finished for the day. She muttered something sounding like *okay*, and that was where their talk finished. That was the first time he had looked her in the eye since that day at sea—a realisation that did his mood no good.

As the sun started to set, Adorjan finished planting all but a few hollow bamboo poles in the soil, in preparation to drain the water from the field in the coming weeks, on the day before the harvest. It was the work Adorjan found the most exhausting, but also the most fulfilling. It was a fine way to mark the soon-to-come end to a season of labour.

Umbra came to Adorjan before she left, as promised. Adorjan surprised himself with how nervous he was, standing before a skinny little girl, glaring up at him expectantly. *Not another day*, he reminded himself.

Adorjan spoke frankly, lacking the energy or self-awareness to don his usual smile and warmth.

'Can you help me set the last bits of bamboo?' he asked.

'Me?' Umbra said, confused.

'It shouldn't be just me all the time. It would be a nice change of pace for you, too.' It seemed like a lousy excuse once Adorjan said it out loud, but Umbra didn't protest. She worked with Adorjan for perhaps another hour, diligently and efficiently as ever. Though she was brooding, she was typically inquisitive. She was always curious about the *why* of her work, and a girl who took pride in her labour even at her age. By the end of the hour, Adorjan was convinced she would know more about these fields than he did by their next harvest. She had a way of working with the soil and grain that was beyond normal, as though she had an *understanding* of the earth that ought to be reserved for someone ten times her senior. Adorjan could see why she had always been so insistent on working the fields and preferred tending to them over learning any other skill. *The fields have been calling to her, not the other way around.*

He sounded the horn, and Umbra joined him for his rounds through the paddy. He complimented his people's work and thanked them for their labour. Indeed, they had little zeal left, and it seemed an effort for most to muster thanks in return. Most left the fields before Adorjan could reach them. Thi and Lihn were the only ones he was able to thank.

'You're welcome,' Lihn had curtly said with a glance at Umbra. 'Excuse me. I'll be going home to eat…something.'

She took her leave, and Thi was on her heels after her usual smile and nod in returning thanks. Adorjan decided not to take their abrasiveness to heart, as he was tempted to do the very same, wanting nothing more than his bed and his herbs. It did not seem to bother Umbra either, thankfully.

Adorjan finally broached what he had intended to since he awoke, before Umbra left for the day herself. He asked her to stay a while longer, so that they could talk.

'You're going to ask me what happened that night at the sea,' Umbra said. 'I've been asked many times now, and I don't know what happened. I don't remember.'

'So I've heard,' Adorjan said. 'We may never know what happened there. But why were you climbing the rocks in the first place? Surely you can remember that.'

Umbra said nothing, looking at Adorjan, confused. He wondered if his tone was perhaps too harsh, but he persevered.

'And not just that. I've spoken to your father. You've been going home late at night, sometimes not until after your father has gone to sleep. Are you still climbing rocks? After what happened to you, are you still taking such risks? What have you been up to, Umbra?'

Umbra did not miss a beat and said, 'I still come to work, and I still keep my father fed. I only stay away at night to be alone. So why do you need to know what I choose to do at night?'

Adorjan found no words to respond with. Umbra was always straight-talking and otherwise unassuming, yet never so abrasive and self-assured. And above all, Umbra was not wrong. Adorjan saw now his naivety, to think he could approach Umbra so directly and demand anything from her while he saw her as a *mere* child. Adorjan had heard from Varyis that Umbra had changed since the incident, as though the ordeal had aged her and made her eyes perceive the world around differently. Adorjan now understood what Varyis had been trying but struggling to say. Umbra truly had changed.

Umbra allowed the question to go unanswered and left Adorjan to stand dumbly behind her, watching her go. She stopped before she stepped out of the paddy and looked down at one rice plant. She knelt and pulled it out of the ground. Adorjan could see a tone of yellow on it, the subtle colour change that indicated an early disease.

Before she was out of earshot, Umbra turned back around and bowed.

She said, 'Thank you for saving me that night.' And with that, she was gone.

Adorjan went from confusion and shame to concern at Umbra's last words. He was convinced now that she had changed, and likely not for the better. She spoke not with the words of a child he had watched grow, but with those of a stranger.

He stayed only a little while longer before leaving the field himself, with renewed intent and purpose. He looked over the rice with diligent detail once more. The rest of the plants looked healthy and green. The disease had not spread, and removing that one plant would help ensure a healthy harvest for the others.

He had a lingering thought as he made his way home — an observation that gave him pause for reasons he did not understand.

Umbra has never bowed before.

TWELVE

Umbra left the fields behind, exhausted in every way. Her arms hung painfully at her sides from the strain of work. Her legs and feet barely kept her upright, causing her to sway with every step. Still, she walked purposefully, forcing herself to summon whatever remaining strength she had left to make her way home.

She longed for bed, longed for respite—she could hardly remember the last time she slept. She spent most of the night staring into the dark after she returned home from the beach, with sleep still eluding her. Something would gnaw at her each time she closed her eyes, as though her brain fought against respite. She didn't intend to chase sleep again tonight and wouldn't return home until the sun started to rise. Perhaps sleep would find her on the shore, for now more than ever, she found the sound of waves and rain on sand to be the most soothing of all. She had grown fond of the whale's hum, too and wished to hear its voice every waking second.

But Umbra had also grown deeply afraid of what else awaited her at the beach. The image of that colossal dark entity possessed her mind's eye and shook her to her core. The memory of that *thing* now felt like an abstract dream for its absurdity, yet she did not doubt that it had been real. Perhaps she was drawn to that beach again now as much for that entity as for the whale, by fascination more than she was repelled by fear. Umbra followed that fascination again once her work was done.

Umbra passed by her home but didn't need to enter. She was tempted by the smell of rice from within, as it reminded her of her hunger. But she picked up the bucket she had left behind her hut that morning and made straight for the beach once more. She thought about her father on the way and how he seemed to be cooking more often these days. All her life, she had accepted that her father's condition would only worsen, and he would only become more dependent on her as the days went by. She wondered if his self-sufficiency was a sign of healing, but decided instead that she was being naive. More likely, he just had more strength left that she realised, and her daily absence meant he was forced to care for himself in a way he used to have the luxury to ignore.

Varyis' hand shook viciously. His whole body was weaker and further beyond his control than on most days, as even the slightest movements and the most menial of tasks took significantly more effort than, perhaps, ever. Moving outside to relieve himself had taken far more of the afternoon than it should have. Speaking with Vada during his check-up left him short of breath. Dousing the fire under the pot of cooked rice and vegetables took all he had left in him for the day.

Her diagnosis was not surprising to him—his body was deteriorating, and her treatments were doing nothing to slow his decline. The herbs would instead ease the pain.

'I'll keep helping you however I can,' she had said. 'But I'm sorry to say that it's up to your body what happens here on out.'

Varyis had grunted a thanks. He felt no better or worse for her words, as it was nothing he had not expected to hear. He would live on while slowly falling apart and doing what he could each day to make the process bearable. His body would continue to deteriorate for the rest of his days, and he had had years to come to terms with that already.

He crawled his way back to his floor-bed, and even this was agonising for the sores his many days and weeks spent lying on the floor-bed had sprouted all over his body. He coughed and spluttered uncontrollably, and it hurt to breathe. He felt himself deteriorate further each time he lay there. He found himself wondering how many days he had left trapped in his four walls, how long it would be until his body gave in. He took his recent self-sufficiency as a sign that he had a while to go yet. He was unsure whether that was a hope or a lamentation.

He waited for the rice to cool. He left Umbra's portion in the pot, knowing better now than to wait for her. He only knew she came home at all these days for the empty and clean pot she left behind in the mornings. But Varyis could not help himself and still stared at the outdoors while his food cooled. Only recently did he realise the joy he used to feel when she came home, when she cooked for them and when he had company again for the nights. *No, not joy,* he reflected. *That is relief. I took the girl for granted too much to be joyful. I hardly know the girl. I'm still yet to even see her laugh or cry.*

Such thoughts were the sole reason he was grateful for these lonely nights now, for they forced upon him reflection and introspection. *I have had no reason to question myself, no reason to reflect and no cause to change, until now.*

The worst of it was the words Umbra said from her treatment bed, which still echoed in his head. *I didn't want to be home, Father.* She had said it with such certainty, so calmly and with no meekness. Varyis had been angry for a while, as was his way and so often his first instinct. Yet with the benefit of reflection, he could not find it in himself to stay angry. He instead became sad with the burden of realisation. It was the most natural thing for a little girl not to long for a broken home, for there was nothing less welcoming than an angry and bitter father. *Of course, she wouldn't want to be home with me. I don't even want to be home myself.*

Varyis spent each night lamenting the man he was, lamenting that it had taken such heartbreaking words to see his own reflection, trying to convince himself he need not be this way until death came for him, yet doubting his ability to change.

Yet, for now, Varyis had no choice but to change in the smallest of ways. He gave up on waiting again. He ate the fruits of his labour, left alone to do so once more. He watched the outdoors still as he did so. It was a calm and quiet evening.

The fog made for a bleak backdrop at the beach. It was unsettled, flowing along the shore and out to sea with the steady winds. Umbra watched the beach and the whale on the sand from the rocks. It lay still as a corpse, but she could hear its hum and feel its voice through her body.

She watched a long while, with fear coursing through her blood. She looked through the haze for an unnatural shadow beyond it. She looked far up into the skies for deep-green floating eyes and the trickle of flowing water. There was nothing to see, no matter how long she seemed to wait. Yet something stirred inside her—nameless and unshakeable. Beyond the fear was a feeling that had no name, yet one that felt more real to her than even the cold evening air on her flesh. She had to ignore her every instinct to move forward and for her feet to touch the sand.

She moved tepidly toward the whale, with the feeling within her only growing ever stronger. She looked about her all the while, feeling more oppressed by the mist and the darkness of the evening than usual on this day.

The whale's eye opened as she drew closer, and it watched her sleepily and dazed. A light had seemed to have faded from its beautiful eye, and it blended easily with the mist before it. So different it was and so devoid of intent that it enamoured Umbra once more. It was like looking at an eclipse, at a moon with no light. The sight of it drew her closer with no more hesitation, and she rested her hand upon the whale's hide.

The whale hummed once more at its touch, feebly.

Umbra had grown accustomed to the whale's voice, as she had never so intently listened to a sound. So much so that the voice now was like its own entity. She now could sense the pain in it, the fear and even the relief to have company.

'I'll stay with you tonight, too,' Umbra said. 'And every night from now on. I'll sleep here beside you.' The whale's hide was dry and hard. It felt like the whale ought to be in pain from this alone. 'Wait a second.'

Umbra carried her bucket to the shore and filled it. It was rather small, only able to carry fish for a few days before the famine. To soak the whale would take many trips and a lot of energy. *Maybe I won't sleep tonight either.* Umbra was reminded once more of her hunger as she struggled to fill the bucket, but she didn't mind. The sensation wasn't new to her, and there was always food to come in the mornings. But she also felt faint and dizzy. No doubt the consequence of the day's labour was now in full force. She didn't mind that either.

Umbra turned and was frozen in place, met by the sight she had dreaded. Two slits of dull light floated in the sky in the form of eyes glaring down on her. Something resided beside the whale, with barely a tangible form and almost perfectly cloaked by the guise of night. The being was not nearly as colossal as before, but its formlessness was like that of a nightmare. It was as though Umbra stared at a hazy memory, or the manifestation of a lacking imagination.

Yet, Umbra stood firm. A wave of unnameable emotions and sensations ran through her blood, yet none of them were *fear* anymore. She slowly drew closer to it. The being that existed in her recent memory, empowered by her youthful imagination, bore no resemblance to the being that now looked down upon her. The emotions in her blood became clearer as she drew closer, until she could distinguish one with clarity when she was within touching distance—*sadness*, bordering on mourning. The feeling came with no logic or reason, yet was as real to her as the wind on her flesh.

The being's intangible *body* flowed along the ground as though it flowed on calm waters. It kept flowing past Umbra and slowly submerged itself into the waters. She watched still as it emerged again moments later, larger than before. It moved past her again and loomed over the whale. Water poured from its *face* and onto the whale's body. The whale stirred under the water's weight. Some of the cold water splashed onto Umbra's face.

It's helping. It's keeping him alive, just like me. Joy welled up in her at this realisation. Perhaps she had known all along, and had merely abandoned fear before she understood why. But this absurd and incredible sight before her made her certain—*this creature is a friend, too.*

The last of the water left the creature, and it became shrunken once more. Umbra understood, now with a clearer mind and heart, that it was tired. She picked up her bucket and filled it once more with renewed vigour. The bucket was too heavy for her to carry when filled, so she instead dragged it in the sand. Half the water had splashed out before she could pour it on the whale's hide. Then she ran back to the water and filled it again. Then again. Then again.

The creature watched as Umbra spent all the energy she still had, then rose once more and worked along with her. The night passed unnoticed by Umbra. When the moon reached its highest peak, a new sound flowed into the air. The whale hummed once more, a hum unlike any Umbra had heard before. It was not the same hum she had grown accustomed to that comforted her like a blanket. This one was lowly and weak, and seeped out of the whale's body. It felt like a scream condensed into a whisper.

Its eye fell open, its vibrancy all but gone, and it looked at Umbra. It moaned at the sight of her, even weaker. Fear found its way to Umbra once more, and it was swiftly overtaken by panic as realisation hit her. The whale was *dying*. The whale was conscious that it was dying. The whale knew that it could do nothing about it. Umbra was watching the beginnings of a loss before her eyes.

All the while, unknown to Umbra, the strange dark creature grew once more, lording over Umbra and the whale. It called out to the sky in a silent voice. The sky quickly heeded its call.

Unknown to Umbra, a great downpour was presently being born.

Rogue winds were born from a night of calm and tranquillity, fuelled by anger, pain and fright. Clouds formed by way of sadness and grew heavy with rain. Such were the makings of a terrible storm never before witnessed on the island, brought about so swiftly that its birth would go unnoticed by most. Birds and insects did not have the instinct to flee until they were already caught in the heart of it. Each wave of the sea grew beyond its natural scale and lashed out at the sand with a new fury. Each raindrop was like an arrow piercing the flesh of the land. The spectacle would be clear to see—for even the unnatural fog plaguing the land fled before the storm's rage.

All the while the storm raged and spread freely, a crack of vivid green light lurked in the sky and shone upon the body of the strange creature watching from the horizon.

THIRTEEN

Umbra watched on from the cave at the foot of Burial Hill when the rain first started to batter the whale's body. It was like a gift from the sky, a final effort to save her friend's life. Yet it appeared to be in vain as the whale remained still, and its moan became weaker still. The downpour created a terrible sound on the beach, like a thousand fists pounding the ground. The whale's corpse was pelted by the rain. Umbra could not see the dark creature anymore as the whale hid her from the sea, but she could *feel* it in every drop of water and every howl of wind. She and it shared the same faint hope—that the water would be enough to rouse the whale back to health, that this storm could create a miracle that her hands and bucket could not. But even as the whale's flesh was drenched, Umbra knew deep down that the storm was futile.

Umbra's instinct took over her. She ran out into the sand and stumbled over it until she was with the whale again. She laid her hand upon its cold flesh. She embraced as much of the whale as she could in her arms, feeling its body rise and fall with the last of its vigour.

'I'm here,' were the only words she could find to say. 'I'm here. I'm here.' She closed her eyes and whispered these words to her friend, over and over, all the while not breaking her embrace.

One more moan flowed from the whale. It was the quietest of all, but Umbra felt it trickle through her arms and into her bones. She felt the pain nestled within the voice and felt the pain herself. Too soon, her voice was the only sound to her ears. The whale's body lay with perfect stillness, and it fell silent as its beautiful eyes finally closed.

Umbra felt the whale's life extinguished through her fingers. She held nothing more than flesh and blood in her arms.

She sank to her knees, her hand on the whale's hide. The only sound was her breath, ragged in the silence. She witnessed the end of a life, and the moment was not lost on her. Never had she come face to face with morality to such a degree as to witness a final breath. She couldn't grasp what she'd seen—only that it mattered.

Then, the tragedy of this event began to dawn on her in some small way. The end of life was final. She would never hear the whale's hum again, never see its beautiful eye open, never spend another long night bathing its body. More than witnessing the end of a life, Umbra had witnessed the loss of a friend. *I'm alone again.* She wondered if she could have done more, if things could have been different. *What if I didn't fall into the sea? What if I saw the whale more often? What if I had poured water on the whale earlier? What if I didn't try to keep the whale to myself and I told the others? What if I didn't stay away from the beach for so long, and I wasn't scared of that creature?*

She put her hands upon the creature once more. Its flesh was cold.

'I'm sorry,' she said. 'I'm so sorry.'

Umbra let something out of her spirit, something she did not know she had been holding. Her sorrow gradually compounded her guilt, and she felt a foreign release in her. Her eyes welled up with tears, and they flowed down her face like a waterfall. She sighed and groaned, unable and unwilling to stop the tears from falling. Her spirit let go completely, and Umbra released a terrible scream to the heavens. She felt herself *break* on the beach that night, alone.

All the while, the strange dark creature grew once more, far more colossal to lord over the beach and cliffs. It grew and flowed away from the shore until its intangible body blended perfectly with the skies, and it lorded over even the island itself.

Umbra's scream was drowned out by the scream of a rousing wind and a growing tide.

Cadeo had been standing atop Burial Hill when the winds began to change, and a strange light emanated from the sky. He had been particularly restless that evening and had no appetite for supper. It was not unusual for Cadeo to be out for a while longer after his evening walks, and he knew

Gratus would not worry. The loving woman that she was, Cadeo knew she would keep his rice warm and his tea freshly brewed when his appetite finally returned.

Still, he found that recent sunsets invoked in him an urge for music. He would have the impulse to play his t'rung not far from his hut, trying and failing to produce new melodies he could repeat and perfect. Each session instead would become one of improvisation. Poor improvisation at that, but he could feel his fingers becoming more accustomed to the unfamiliarity of each melody and his brain letting go a little of the need for control each time he played.

This evening, however, had been different, and Cadeo was plagued with sadness and anxiety. His impulses led him to the top of this hill. With some hours of meditation and reflection, he came to understand the source of his anxieties. *I am wasting time with personal leisure,* was his conclusion. *As my people face a potential tragedy with which I am all too familiar, I waste time easing my own heart.*

Yet Cadeo was conflicted, for he knew instinctively that this musical habit held some purpose and value that he was only beginning to reap the benefits from. It had been too many years since Cadeo created anything, too long since his hands had been busy with productivity alone. This, though, he believed to be the core of his anxiety. *Am I making something meaningful in my music, or just running from my helplessness and duty?*

His introspection was brought to a harsh end when he felt the locked hair on his back flow with fury and water falling upon his face. He opened his eyes to a sobering sight that would be implanted in his memory for the rest of his days, like a vivid and abstract painting. What had been another foggy sunset before he closed his eyes mere hours earlier had become night with dark, heavy clouds. The sea had grown as furious as the wind, and the sandy shore had drowned some of the sand, reaching as far as the stilts of the huts along the beach.

But the strangest of all was the green light tearing the very sky in half. Cadeo could not describe the tone of green beyond calling it *incomprehensible*. It was vivid, brighter than the healthiest foliage in the height of spring. Cadeo may even have thought it beautiful, had it not been accompanied by chaos and nature's fury.

He was hit with renewed and indisputable realisation. *Nothing about this famine is natural. We face something beyond our comprehension and reach. Heaven itself may be holding our fate.* A natural tone of lightning cackled from the clouds, and rain struck the land with all its strength.

Cadeo trembled. He watched the scene before him with almost unblinking eyes, his mind a haze. *What can I do?* He sank to his knees, crushing the pink and red flowers beneath him, which too had been roused by the wind. He watched the strange green light gradually fade. He watched, along with the idols on the ground, until that light was gone and left an ever-furious storm behind. *What can anyone do?*

A new gust found the top of Burial Hill, strong enough to take Cadeo off his knees. He was thrown away from the edge and back from whence he climbed, rolling down the hills into rocks and soaked mud. He cried out in pain, but could not even hear his voice for the sudden onset of thunder and rainfall. His hip ached terribly, and his arm became numb. He found his way back to his feet with great difficulty, fighting not to be blown down again. The pain was enough to force some sense and urgency back into him.

He worked his way back down from the hills. He moved as fast as he could through the pain, which was no faster than the pace of his evening walks. He groaned and yelled many a time at the cold on his skin and the hard rain striking at his face. It practically blinded him, and he made most of the journey with his eyes closed. He knew well enough the makeup of this hill, the feel of the ground he walked on, and the greenery stroking his legs as he went, that it was not so difficult to find his way.

It was all he could do to stay on his feet by the time he made it back to the bottom. The wind was no calmer. Its fury had brought about another unnerving scene. The shore and the beach were all but gone, drowned out by the sea. Cadeo stood up to his knees in seawater and all manner of sea debris. Only their stilts kept the huts upright —they rose from the water like spires. Cadeo found himself once more stunned and lost in a moment of disbelief. Everything before him was natural, a possible reality without the interference of heaven or any other power beyond nature. Yet the suddenness of the change, the drastic shift from the home he knew all his life to the place he now beheld, was like a dream from the deepest of waking sleeps.

Adorjan was in his hut when the rain began to fall. It was a restless night in which he hadn't even tried to find sleep, enjoying the relief the herbs and smoke once again brought him. He had fought for a time to resist them, to keep his sobriety and to remember the self-hatred he had felt when the smoke was still in his lungs while at sea. But his internal fight ended when he realised that it had no purpose—it was only him in this hut, and there was no one depending on him here, no one to save. Adorjan was beholden only to himself on this night, and so he decided to indulge once again.

The herbs bestowed upon him the vision and sounds of the sea, along with a strong sense of peace and ease. Adorjan felt as though he were drowning, and that the water was sweet in his lungs. The waves would lift him from his floor-bed and set him down again with each stroke, as if to rock him into a deep sleep.

But he was pulled from his waking slumber by the feeling of real water touching his face. He looked up through the hole in his roof and was startled to see a clear night sky. He had grown so accustomed to haze that seeing stars between clouds was like a glimpse into the past, before such hard times and when food was plentiful by comparison. More rain fell on his face. The drops became plentiful until they flowed through his roof like a river through a natural valley. Adorjan rose and swayed on his feet, gazing up at the roof in awe. Never had he known the rain to fall so heavily, even in his waking dreams. He stood in a blend of reality and dreaming, as the herbs still gave him visions of the sea, even as the water filled his hut and cooled his feet.

That blend was soon shattered as his roof caved under the weight of the rain and wind, filling Adorjan's room with straw. The rain struck his skin painfully, and the wind blew through to his bones. His temporary serenity and sense of awe were swiftly replaced with bafflement and denial. His room was being torn apart from within, his floor-bed carried away by the waters outside, and his utensils becoming debris. This was a storm of abnormal fury.

He moved before he realised it. *That's right, the people,* he vacantly thought. *I must check on everyone in this storm.* Near subconscious duty took him outside to an incredible and disturbing sight.

The mist was indeed gone, and Adorjan could see as far as the horizon for the first time in weeks. He could see fractions of the night sky through the rain clouds, where the moon appeared to melt through them and drip onto the sea. There were small but vivid cracks of a bizarre green light parting the clouds, in a tone that looked unearthly and wholly unnatural. But what held his sight above all was horrific. Filling a sizeable portion of the sky was a *man*. He had a colossal face that was so dark that it was stark even against the night sky, lit in part by the vivid green glow from his eyes. It was the being from the sea— the same, but much absurdly massive. Its empty face turned toward the island—toward Adorjan. The totality of the sight before him was like a twisted form of art, pulled from beyond his deepest imaginings and terrors.

A bolt of lightning flashed in Adorjan's eyes, close to the island, and blinded him for a moment. Then the *man* vanished along with the bolt. But the sight of it was firmly imprinted into Adorjan's mind, and his heart thumped without restraint. He fell to his knees, short of breath and shaking.

'*It's just the herbs again,*' he repeated to himself over and over. '*It's the herbs.*' He cursed himself again for falling into this state once more, where he could trust neither his eyes nor his mind to keep a hold on reality. He forced himself to look at the sky, but the *man* was certainly gone, as was the vivid green light in the sky. All that remains before him is a furious mess of rain and lightning.

Then Adorjan began to hear the sounds hitting his ears. Amid the thunder and wind was the sound of destruction, the sound of wood being split and torn apart. His home was barely recognisable when he turned and saw it. Its structure was gone, and what stood before him now was nothing but a pile of wood and straw. That he was blessed with such a beautiful sea view also meant he was exposed to the elements more than most.

Adorjan suddenly felt a deep dread and raced down the hill as fast as his feet would carry him, hit with the realisation that his house wasn't the only one so exposed to the sea. Aunt Vada's house was in the hills and naturally protected by the cliff faces, giving Adorjan hope that her home was in a better state than his.

He momentarily stopped in his tracks when he reached the bottom of the hill. Rather than the supple sand of the familiar coast, his feet and shins met cold water. The coast was all but gone, swallowed by an oversized sea. The huts stood on their stilts like risen spires from the water.

Cadeo stood before Adorjan, watching the bizarre scene. Adorjan waded through the water and shook him by the shoulders. Cadeo faced him with a vacant glaze over his eyes.

'Oh, Adorjan,' he said, his voice belonging to a man who felt every bit of his age.

'Cadeo, why are you out here? Go home and get out of this storm.'

'Home.' Cadeo's eyes sparked to life as he echoed the words, then reflected terror in realisation.

Cadeo took off and waded through the water as fast as his old legs would carry him. Adorjan ran along the coast and up the next hill towards his aunt's house. The rain seemed to pour ever harder the further he went. He looked out over the sea on the way, but there was only the darkness of the night looking back at him.

Streams of water and debris flowed down Vada's hill and took Adorjan off his feet many a time on the way up. He was exhausted when he was only halfway up and was forced to crawl the rest of the way on his hands. He crawled blindly through the rain and mud, striking his face, making his way through memory alone.

Vada's hut was still standing in the face of the hills, unharmed. Adorjan had built it with his own hands and had been insistent on it being nestled into a crevice and surrounded by stones and trees. Whether or not he had foreseen how protected the huts would be from the elements, Adorjan was now grateful and in awe of the man, for the hut had barely been touched by the wind nor been struck by even a single stray stone.

His aunt Vada stood some distance from her hut, more exposed to the storm than her home was. Adorjan found the strength to get to his feet and hobbled over to her. He screamed her name, but could not even hear his voice over the wind.

His hand was finally on her shoulder, and he pulled her into an embrace.

'Auntie,' he screamed again. 'Get back inside!'

Adorjan tried to pull her, but she would not move. He then saw her face, lit by the increasing lightning bolts. She looked over the sea and wore an expression Adorjan had never seen on her, or perhaps on any other person. It blended terror and incredulity into one unnameable and abstract expression. Adorjan followed her gaze and no doubt wore a similar face when he saw what she did.

The colossal *man* was before them, standing so tall that the clouds were like a crown upon his head. He was moving. He brought his hands up to his eyes and held his face in them. He slowly turned his body and drifted further into the horizon until they could barely see his silhouette. The storm began to settle as he moved away— the wind waned and the lightning abated.

Adorjan held his aunt's hand. He could not form a rational thought in his mind or bring any coherent words to his lips. He instinctively deciphered the feeling coursing in his heart as hopelessness in the face of a new reality.

All the island people who saw that sight in the storm shared in the loss of rational thought and coherence. All joined together toward a new life of irrationality.

FOURTEEN

Cadeo moved with single-mindedness, spurred on by terror—and by shame that Gratus wasn't his first thought when the storm came. Shame that he spent so long standing in a daze after seeing the state of his island and was only moved into action by the words of another. Cadeo would never know all that had come to pass in that time he spent standing there, nor even how long he stood for. Yet, he knew instinctively that he could not go on calling himself a shepherd after this night, no matter what awaited his people on the other side of this storm. His age had been a valid and convenient excuse for his shortcomings as a self-proclaimed shepherd since this famine had started, but his shame on this night went far beyond the weakness of age and spoke to his shortcomings as a mature man. The storm gave him a profound learning and humbling experience that he would not soon forget.

The rising seawater slowed him down on his way home so much that his hut never seemed to get closer. He was surely within sight of it, but his failing eyes could not see so far in a nighttime storm like this. Cadeo's father had built the hut he now lived in higher on the hills than most others. He had always been conscious of the changing tides at night and often told Cadeo's mother how the others on the island lacked foresight when they built their huts, that wooden stilts wouldn't be enough to protect them when nature turned angry enough. On perhaps the only day since his hut was built, Cadeo was grateful for his father's decision, whether it was a result of foresight or the paranoia his mother seemed to believe it was.

It also meant there was always one final climb after Cadeo's walks to tire him out. His father also had the foresight to dig a small valley with steps made of dirt to make the climb easier, likely planning for his twilight years.

Cadeo reached the hill where his home was. There was nothing there. Where his hut ought to have been perched, there was now nothing. His hut was gone, as were the trees that had grown alongside it, as were the valley and the steps. Where there was a carefully crafted home was now a river of wet mud and debris still flowing from the peak with reckless abandon. The lush greenery, the pale sand at the hill's base, and the ancient trees lording over where Cadeo's home used to be—nature had claimed it all, and only emptiness remained.

At the base now were the remains of what used to be his home, now a mess of wood and straw, drowning in a pool of mud.

Cadeo forgot about the storm, about the island being overcome by the sea and the peril of his people. He rushed to the wreckage and tore at the debris with bare, bleeding hands. He screamed at the top of his lungs. Gratus' name poured from his lips, but it would have sounded like a wild wolf's howl to anyone's ears. He pulled at the debris and mud with all his strength, so intensely that his hands bled. The panels were too heavy for him to lift, and he tried to dig around them. A wild stream of water flowed down what used to be his father's valley and made his work all the more difficult.

So intently and desperately did Cadeo struggle against the wreckage that he did not realise he had a helping hand beside him, until they spoke up.

'You're sure she was here?' Ashan asked, hauling wooden slabs and digging through the debris with his hands.

Cadeo barely heard him and did not respond, but it was enough to quiet his screaming. He began to pray under his breath as he kept digging, and his hands continued to bleed.

'Please, god of the wind and god of the sea, whoever you may be. Do not take her from me —'

Cadeo reached for a slab — then froze. It was slick with red that the rain could not wash away. There was a mass of it under the slabs, in the same tone of red that poured from his hands. Under the night's shadow, the blood seemed to take over his hand and drown it in darkness. Cadeo groaned. He plunged his hand into bloodied rubble. In it was the wet and mangled flesh of a body. He barely suppressed the urge to vomit. His mind was empty of all thought except disbelief and a yearning to prove his eyes wrong. He pulled at the slabs with all the strength he had left. It refused to move even slightly. He kept on pulling, even as the wood burrowed into his hands and broke his skin. He bled more.

'Stop, Cadeo,' he barely heard as Ashan laid his hand on his shoulder. 'Let go.'

'Ashan!' Cadeo screamed out. 'Help me! Get her out!'

He was pulled away with Ashan's strength, so harshly that he fell onto the sand.

'Don't torture yourself like this, old man,' Ashan said.

'Ashan, damn you!' Cadeo kicked out at Ashan's legs, who didn't flinch. 'Get her out! Don't leave her like this!'

Ashan gripped Cadeo's shoulders and pinned him down on his knees.

'I'm sorry, but…Gratus is gone, old man. You don't want to see her like this.'

Cadeo tried to smack Ashan's arms away, but he was too strong. 'Why do you stop me?!'

'You think she'd want you to see her now? For you to remember her like this?'

Cadeo fell silent, weakly clawing at Ashan until he had no strength left. His body, mind and spirit gave up. He slumped over in the sand. Blood covered his face as he brought his hands to it and wailed. He wept so hard that his eyes hurt. He screamed so loudly that his lungs burned. He held onto Ashan so tightly that his hands turned purple. He utterly broke down.

Cadeo never noticed how the storm abated, how the rain let up, and the clouds passed by as quickly as they had come. He never saw the dawn.

FIFTEEN

Ashan took a moment to admire the most beautiful morning in weeks. The morning after the turbulent storm was striking in its calmness. He hadn't realised how much he'd taken the sky for granted—its shifting colours, its vastness—until the fog tore it away. It had made the world feel small, knowable and too intimate. He never felt alone in it, even while at sea or anchored off the shore. This clear morning brought a feeling of solitude and peace again, as Ashan could once more marvel at how small he was in a massive world.

It felt alien to walk on the island again, to have solid ground under his feet again. If only rice and vegetables grew on the sea, he would not need to set foot on solid ground again. Since the fish had died out, he had to come back to the island more often than he would like, but he always returned to his boat as soon as he was able. Today, he walked as though he were exploring a new land. Huts old enough to be called *ancient* were damaged or destroyed. Much of the sandy shore had been eradicated by the tide. Foliage on the hills had been crushed by mudslides or uprooted by wind. Everything had changed in just one night.

Cadeo's hut had been damaged the worst of all, and it had been the only one to collapse. The others had roofs or walls missing, or holes in them caused by debris, but they were still standing. Ruhan had already started patching homes with yarn or old wooden beams. He presently worked on Nghi's by the shore, so engrossed that he didn't notice Ashan pass. *Ru will have his hands full with all these repairs*, Ashan thought with some sympathy. *I don't envy him. It's far too much for one pair of hands.*

He later passed Thi and Lihn. They were brooding and didn't even seem to notice him. They stared at the ground, lost in conversation.

'If the paddies are still in any shape at all, that will be a miracle,' Thi muttered. 'That storm may have condemned us to starve.'

'It's not like you to be so pessimistic,' Lihn said.

Ashan walked on. It was, for the most part, the atmosphere he had expected — people quick to rebuild but found wanting in their ability to comfort themselves. He expected that they would once again lean upon superstitions and fantastical ideas to find reason in their hardship, particularly after they learned of Gratus' death. *Her death may not have been the only one in such a storm. I'll find out before long.*

He had had a lot of time to himself to think on his boat, to ponder Cadeo's words about the famine. He concluded that it didn't much matter *why* these things were happening, only what could be done about them. He had grown accustomed to perils at sea, to trusting his instincts and eyes, and to flee or fight as needed. Most had never experienced any significant adversity. They were now encountering a hardship they could do little about, and they would soon learn how they could cope with a sudden realisation of their vulnerability. Tougher times were now here.

Ashan soon reached the cave nestled in the hills, where Nota lived. He had not intended to go, but he seemed to have done so while walking absentmindedly. There was light coming from inside. The cave was, of course, undamaged by the storm.

A pot of water boiled on a fire inside. Nota sat on the ground and painted the large flax linen spread along the walls. An ever-growing number of wooden figures littered the floor, all abstract and disturbing to Ashan's eyes. Some vaguely resembled contorted human bodies. Some looked like celestial bodies with faces or other distinct features. Some resembled nothing at all, yet even those somehow stirred strange feelings in Ashan when he saw them. One was phallic and not at all abstract. He had outright asked Nota about that one when he first saw it. She'd just replied —'Every part of the body deserves to be immortalised through art. Even yours.' Ashan had not raised the topic since.

'As you can see, I'm perfectly fine.' Nota presently said while she painted. 'But thanks for coming all the way up here to check. You're too sweet.'

Ashan quietly groaned. *She's in this type of mood, then. I should have stayed on the boat.* He had thought the tragedies of the night before would dampen Nota's typically flippant nature, evidently mistakenly. He sat down beside her and watched her hands at work. She painted with a dark green ink that smelled of ivy berries.

'Is that a rice plant?' he asked. The painting was detailed and vivid. It was simple by Nota's standards, but it stood out amid the others on the canvas for its realism. Her skill was undeniable, as ever.

'Mm-hmm. A tattoo for Cadeo,' she said.

'Cadeo? He came here already?'

'I saw him walk by the cave this morning.'

'Then, how could you know that he needs a tattoo?'

She looked at Ashan, deadpan. 'I know what grieving looks like. And it's not hard to imagine what happened in a storm like that. He'll come by when he's almost done, so I may as well have a tattoo ready. I thought a rice plant would be a suitable way to remember Gratus, since she worked at the paddies for so long. That, and there's hardly any space left on his body, so it would need to be something long and thin. What do you think?'

'I think I'm sorry I asked.'

'That reminds me—bring one of Gratus' hands when you come by again, would you? Doesn't matter which one...actually, make sure it's her left hand. I'll prepare it for the tattooing before Cadeo comes.'

Ashan took a long breath. 'We're done talking.'

'Hmm. Have I offended you already?'

Ashan said nothing.

Nota snorted. 'You can think these superstitions are stupid all you want. But who are you to rob him of his wish to mourn as he sees fit?'

'Yeah, I've heard this a thousand times before. I do no such thing. He and everyone else can mourn in whatever sick, twisted way they want to. It's still sick and twisted.'

Nota smiled. 'But they still find it healing, regardless of how sick you think it is.'

'Delusion isn't healing. Treating ink on their skin as a ward against some obscure danger that they can't even articulate isn't healing either.'

'Hmm. *Delusion* is a strong word. That sounds like projection. Are you just a little superstitious after all, and just in denial? Or, is it *because* they don't exist that--'

'This looks a lot like Gratus,' Ashan said, picking up one of Nota's wooden figures from the floor. It had Gratus' mild expression, distinctly long and thick hair, and tattoos crafted perfectly.

Nota smiled again. 'That's because it *is* Gratus.'

'She died only yesterday. You made this in one night?'

Nota's smile faded.

Ashan set the idol down and looked at Nota intently. 'Did you have this ready before she died? Does that mean you've made one for all of us in preparation for our death? Tell me you're not that death-obsessed.'

Nota picked her brush back up and painted again. '... I'll get her hand later myself, if you're gonna be like that.'

Ashan gladly stood to take his leave.

'Is Cadeo, you know...okay?' Nota's voice was softer as she asked. 'Do you think he should be alone?'

'I don't know. I don't imagine so,' Ashan said. 'But I don't know where he would have gone now. I was with him when he found Gratus last night. I thought it better to leave him alone after that.'

'You shouldn't have. To lose a home and a loved one in a day is cruel and difficult to bear alone.'

Ashan looked back at Nota. She carried on painting the rice plant with her back to him. It dawned on him that he had been insensitive to her in his dismissal of Cadeo's grief. Nota too had lost her family and her home on the same day, and knew more than anyone how Cadeo would be feeling. She had once told Ashan that she had moved into the cave for her artistry, to be closer to nature and easily inspired. But Ashan had come to believe that that was an excuse she told herself, and that she could not bring herself to live in her parents' hut after they died. She had given up her home to Adorjan, and Ashan doubted she had returned to it since.

Ashan had forgotten all this while speaking so frankly about Cadeo's loss. He couldn't leave Nota like this.

'It's nice,' is what Ashan settled for.

'Hmm?'

'The rice plant. It suits Gratus well.'

Ashan left the cave before Nota could respond.

Adorjan had not seen another soul yet this morning except his aunt Vada, who had practically hauled him up and forced him out of the hut. He had woken up that morning from several nightmares with green thunder and giant shadows, in an inconsolable mood. He was painfully sober and terrified. He obsessed over what he saw in the storm, over the dark and unfathomably massive *creature*. It was so firmly imprinted in his mind that he was unsure if he was sleeping or awake at times in the night.

Vada looked in only slightly higher spirits than he,

though it was clear on her face that she had not slept much either, and she had shed tears in the night. She had convinced him to get up and eat breakfast—a small portion of boiled rice, seeds and seaweed. Adorjan had forced it down his throat at her demand, but was sure it was delicious in hindsight. Vada then convinced him to get outside and spend time comforting their people, despite his protestations.

'I'm afraid, Auntie,' he had admitted. 'I don't have the heart to face the others right now.'

'Everyone else will be thinking the same thing,' Vada had said. 'Someone has to do it first, Dory. That, and it's better to see the island now than stay here and imagine what you may see later.'

'Then, why don't *you* go?' Adorjan had asked.

'I will, after you do. That will give me the courage to go too.'

That had been enough to bring Adorjan outdoors. He couldn't say he felt much better for it, but he had more clarity of mind now that he could see the storm's effects for himself. He couldn't deny the relief he felt to see only a calm sea and clear sky when he left the hut, and no fog or creatures in sight.

There was such a thick atmosphere of despair and sadness that it was almost tangible. Most huts had been damaged, and debris was scattered about the hills. The sea had not receded much, and the surviving huts by the coast were now on stilts atop water. The beach at the foot of Vada's hill was gone. It was a sobering view, like Adorjan had woken from reality into a dream.

The destruction reminded Adorjan of his own experience in the storm, how the rain invaded his home and the wind tore it apart. He held onto a faint hope that he had hallucinated, that the herbs were inspired by the storm to show him such a sight, but he already knew it was a hope in vain. Indeed, what remained there was a mess of wood and straw, with barely enough shelter to hide from a single raindrop.

Adorjan looked at his broken home, resigned. He mourned very little for it. Its absence only brought deflation, for he had failed to care for such a gift responsibly. *How am I to look Nota in the eye and tell her this has happened?*

He put his hands to work and dug through the wreckage. He searched and worked for a long while before he found it—his pipe wrapped up in his floor bed. It was dirty and scratched, but otherwise in remarkable condition. The herbs inside it were soaked and ruined. A sudden, fleeting anger came over Adorjan at the sight of it. *Of all things to survive this storm.* He almost threw it out to sea, but could not bring himself to. Though it was an object he resented, it had earned value as memorabilia, if nothing else. He instead tucked it into his trousers and moved on with one more glance at his hut. *It can at least be used for firewood to warm our breakfast,* he bitterly thought.

Breakfast. The thought brought another realisation to Adorjan along with a fresh wave of dread. He made his familiar daily trek through the hills with urgency. The walk was more tiring than usual due to the damp soil. It boded ill for what awaited him at the top.

What he saw was even worse than he feared, and it almost brought him to tears. He stood before what used to be the paddies of rice that would soon have been ready for harvesting after a season of tender care. But there were no green plants to be seen, nor could one tell that they once grew in a body of water. The paddies were ruined, smothered by a mudslide along with everything else on the trail down from the hilltop.

Adorjan was at a loss. He set his hands into the mud and touched the spoiled rice beneath it. He felt the results of their months of labour, that which his people rested their very survival on, dying in his fingers. He closed his eyes and thought only of the sensation in his hands. The feel of healthy soil and nurtured rice was familiar enough to him that he did not need to touch it for long to know there was no life left there. The storm had killed their harvest.

Adorjan looked at the clear sky from where the storm had raged mere hours earlier. The night was hazy in his mind, but he remembered parts clearly—the dread of rushing to his aunt's place, the relief of finding her and her home unharmed. And that *creature* he saw in the storm. Adorjan missed the days when he doubted his own eyes and believed that creature to be born of his imagination. He missed the ambiguity that came with the herbs and his addiction. But he believed now that it did not matter that he could not trust his eyes while his mind was not his own, because he could not deny what he felt and saw now that he was sober. Nor could he deny what his aunt Vada had seen for herself.

Along with the monster that plagued his memory, Adorjan was terrified by his powerlessness before whatever had come for his people.

Varyis shook violently on his back, feeling weaker than the

day before, as he did each day. His body felt less and less like his own with each passing day as he became a helpless slave to deterioration. He felt miserable.

He was woken up that afternoon by a breeze through a new hole in his roof, which gave him a new view of the sky. Vada had spoken once about the lingering fog that had stubbornly stuck to the island and how, in her words, the world felt small while the fog lingered. Varyis had grunted unsympathetically, with a response akin to *try having your world be four walls and a bed.* Now, seeing the sky for the first time in many weeks, it was as though the fog had never happened, and Vada may as well have been recounting a fairy tale.

Varyis' eyes went to the floor by the cooking pot when he was awake enough to recover some coherence. Umbra was nowhere in sight, and there were no signs she had returned yet, even to sleep.

Damn this petulant child of mine, Varyis bitterly thought, not for the first time recently. He had started with frustration and anger at Umbra's constant inconsideration to leave him unfed and to worry so soon after her ordeal at sea. That anger gradually turned to a dose of shame last evening. He remembered Umbra's words again—*I did not want to be home, Father.* He realised that those had been the last words he and his daughter shared, and he had not done much to resolve that, though nor had he been given much opportunity to do so. He had resolved to understand Umbra's words and to ask the question he should have asked at the bedside—*why not?*

But that moment of introspection was broken by yesterday's storm, which had appeared from nowhere to the sound of a wild wind and heavy rain. Panels were torn from Varyis' roof, and the rain soaked everything inside. He lay down on his back all the while, helpless and panicking. He could think only of Umbra having no roof over her head and only hoped she had found shelter in someone else's home.

By the end of the storm, Varyis was freezing, and his home was just about still standing. The roof was all but gone, made up now of only a few wooden panels and with all the straw blown off.

He spent every waking moment since the storm hoping to see Umbra coming home. It hadn't happened. He was determined to stay awake until he saw her, yet now he woke to the sight of a clear sky and still no Umbra.

He presently hauled himself toward his cooking pot and basket of rice. There was very little left, perhaps enough for a few more days at most. He found some firewood that had been protected from the rain and was still dry enough to ignite, and began to cook enough for two portions. As the rice was brought to a boil, Varyis wondered—*would the rice fields be able to withstand a storm like that?*

Someone finally entered the hut when the rice was almost ready. But Varyis was distraught to see it was Ashan.

'I know it's been a while,' Ashan said. 'But I thought you'd be a little happier to see me.'

Varyis realised then that he must have been scowling and probably looked a mess. He didn't bother to put on any pretences, least of all for a friend.

'I'm disappointed that you're a man.' Ashan furrowed his brow, and Varyis elaborated before he could retort. 'I meant *Umbra.* I'm waiting for Umbra to come back.'

'Back from where?'

'The storm.'

Those two words were met with a beat of silence as Ashan grasped their meaning.

'I haven't seen her, I'm sorry,' Ashan eventually said. 'But I'll look for her.'

Varyis nodded with a grunt of gratitude.

'I'll have to search on foot until I find my boat.'

'Hmph. A storm like that could have carried it anywhere. I wouldn't count on finding it again.'

'Oh, I guess you wouldn't have seen outside. Part of the beach was submerged last night. If anything, the boat's probably on a beach somewhere. But I doubt it's still in one piece.'

Varyis grunted again, with some unease. A twinge or worry cropped up in him again with news of the severity of the storm. He could only hope that Umbra was not near a shore when the tide rose.

'Well,' Ashan started, breaking the silence again. 'I'll get to searching. I'll let you know if I find her.'

'No need to let me know if you don't,' Varyis said. Ashan nodded. 'Have some rice, since you'll be searching on foot.'

'You have enough for two portions? Don't waste it on me,' Ashan said harshly. 'Umbra will be hungry when she's home, I'm sure.'

Varyis grunted again, acknowledging the reprimand. He paused before he said. 'Thank you. For saving her that night.'

'You don't need to thank me.'

'I will anyway. Listen..since that night…something has changed her. She's different—she feels far away.'

Ashan listened intently. 'Different how?'

Varyis too a moment to find the words. 'She's not an emotional girl. I've never even…seen her cry before, but she sometimes seemed close. Now, I'm not sure if she's even capable of it. It's like…she's lost something.' Varyis tried to grunt but coughed instead. His body burned, like it was being torn apart from the inside. Whenever he thought he was becoming accustomed to the pain, it worsened.

He spoke again when he caught his breath. 'It's pathetic, isn't it? A parent being so far from understanding their child--' Varyis violently coughed again and struggled to stop himself.

Ashan gave him a cup of water. Varyis drank and sighed. 'Just be gentle if you see her.'

Ashan nodded. 'I'll be back if I find her. And I'll need to fix this roof too.'

'That can wait. I'm sure others need your help more than I.'

'Varyis, you're by far the most in need.'

'Hmph. I doubt that. I still have these four walls. Can that be said for everyone? Was anyone hurt last night?'

'…there's a lot of damage. We'll soon find out how much.'

'Then find that out first before you make any promises to me.'

Ashan stood to take his leave. He said, 'You need to stop being ashamed of asking for help, Varyis. At least not from me.'

Ashan left him alone again to dwell in his worry and frustrations. The rice was ready. It smelled tasteless.

SIXTEEN

Little had changed. The paddies were still mired in mud and debris—except for one patch Adorjan had toiled over all day. One rice plant had resurfaced from the mud, but it was mangled and crushed. He unearthed one plant. Then another. And another. Each one the same—crushed, hollow, their grains spilt onto the earth. Even the bugs and their predators had abandoned the paddies.

Adorjan fell onto his back in the mud. He thought the earth itself had given up. The soil felt wet but dead—soft to the touch, but lifeless beneath. Realisation hit him hard as the dead rice plants stroked his back. *We've only the reserves of rice left. Soon, only vegetables and seeds. Not enough. Not until spring. Not to rebuild for the next harvest. And what if another storm comes around?*

Adorjan gasped like a man drowning. His heart pounded against his ribs. Sweat broke across his skin. He slammed his fist into the earth—again and again—until blood seeped through the mud. And he struck at it still, even as pain rose through his arm and to his shoulder. He rose to his feet and struck harder still. A groan escaped him. Then a shout. Then a scream so deep that his stomach burned. He then slumped down on the earth. His throat hurt, yet he felt better for it.

He smiled as he realised that he had never before screamed, nor had he ever been angry. It was a nasty feeling, but the relief of the aftermath was blissful. It was a relief that rivalled even that which the herbs offered him.

Soon, a woman appeared standing above him, her face cloaked in shadow with the sun on her back. He knew it was Nota for the wooden charms hanging off her long hair.

'It was hard to ignore the screaming,' she said, answering Adorjan's unspoken question. She spoke calmly, her face drenched in shadow. 'The rice is dead already. Screaming and lashing out won't change that.'

Adorjan held his bleeding fist in his hand, only now feeling it ache. He looked down at the dead paddy. Some sense of calmness came over him with the truth of her words.

'Isn't it funny?' he asked. 'So much rain, yet we will still starve.'

Nota sat beside him. Her old clothes were covered with colourful stains and dirt, yet she smelled of herbs and flowers. She looked relaxed now that Adorjan could see her face, and not at all in grief.

'How..?' Adorjan started. 'How can we hope to survive when the sea, the skies and the very land are against us?

What are we to do?'

Adorjan could feel Nota sigh beside him.

'Why are you asking *me*? Who could ever answer something like that? The sky and the wind and the land will do whatever they want. I have no answers for it. I'm just an artist.'

'Just an artist? Then what is all *this*?' Adorjan held his arms out, both covered in vibrant pink lotus flower tattoos, all designed and painted by Nota's. '*You* design these wards and put them on our bodies. *You* protect us from the elements and anything that means to harm us. Where is this protection now?'

'*You* call them protection and wards. *I* call them tattoos. Are you trying to guilt an artist for doing their job well? Then I'll ask you this, farmer. Look around you. Look at these paddies and plants that have now died under your care. Are you to blame for all this?'

He felt some shame from her words, but he didn't back down. 'This was not under my care—it was beyond my control. Beyond anyone's control.'

Nota glared at him. 'Because nature is not controlled or tamed by any one man, is it?'

That gave Adorjan pause. He softened and felt himself calm again at the realisation that Nota blamed only nature. *She doesn't know about the creature. She didn't see the creature during the storm.* He found that he could not tell her at that moment, for he saw her calmness in a different light—saw that it was fuelled not by strength but by ignorance. He did not want to steal that ignorance from her. He was jealous of her for it.

'I'm sorry,' was what he said instead.

'If you're sorry, don't say stupid things like that again.

And don't ask me for any more art if you're so quick to discard it.'

Nota had a unique way of speaking, even when outraged. Her words would be harsh, yet easy on the ears and even a source of comfort to those willing to listen. Adorjan embraced the feeling of shame her words gave him.

'Even though the paddies are dead, they are quite beautiful,' she said, looking out over the rice again. 'You did your job well, farmer.'

Adorjan almost smiled as he raised his head to look over the dead fruits of his labour.

Instead wore a face of shock for the colossal figure darkening the afternoon sky before him. It was far in the distance, beyond the hills that lorded over the paddies, but it stood far taller than even them. Its glowing green eyes were vibrant even in the midst of the bright sky and were piercing. They watched Adorjan as the creature moved closer and climbed over the hills.

Adorjan grabbed Nota's hand, and he stumbled away from the paddies. He ran as hard as he could, dragging her behind him.

'Where are we going?' he heard Nota ask. He didn't answer and had no answer. His feet guided them to wherever they stepped, with no guiding or rational thought in his head but to flee.

They fled to Nota's home, to her cave in the hillside close to the paddies. Adorjan fell to his knees inside, gasping for breath. Something resembling his senses began to return to him now that he was in the cave's walls, surrounded by Nota's ward paintings and wooden figures. *Why do I even run? Nowhere is safe.*

'It would have been polite to ask before taking me home,' Nota said with a laugh. 'What was that about?'

Adorjan looked at her incredulously. His face must have been a sore sight, for even Nota's demeanour changed at the sight of it. *You didn't see it. Only I saw it. Was that the herbs again? But last night was not the herbs. I've not smoked, but I still can't trust my eyes?*

He put his face in his hands and wept. Tears flowed easily, and a groan came easily to his lips. He felt something break in his mind—something that used to force shame or dignity upon him when tears threatened to fall. He let go of whatever that thing was that held him and let his anguish seep out of him, from his eyes and his mouth. He cried and groaned for ages, yet there was always more anguish to release. Even when his energy left him and he fell silent again, the anguish clung closely to his heart. He knelt on the floor of the cave with his face to the ground, exhausted.

'Are you done?' Nota finally said, with no hint of humour or softness in her voice.

'I'm losing my mind, Nota.'

She knelt before him and raised his chin with her fingers, forcing him to look her dead in the eyes.

'So what?' she said. 'Those tears better not have been only for you, and you'd better have cried for the whole island. Or do you think you're the only one who is losing their mind? Fish died at sea, we couldn't see the sky for months, and now everyone is about to find out that we're doomed to starve. *Who* were you crying for?'

'Me,' Adorjan said, with little hesitation. 'I cried for *myself*. The others can cry for themselves, if they feel like I do.'

Nota let go of Adorjan's chin, which fell to his chest. 'Get out. Cry somewhere else.'

Adorjan gladly stood to do so. Angry at Nota's abrasiveness, he wanted to be anywhere but with her. But another form of anger took hold of him first, before he could leave the cave—anger at her impassivity. Anger that she could so easily dismiss his dejection, having felt none of it herself. Bitter words came to Adorjan's tongue, and he did nothing to fight against them.

'Your family hut—it's gone. It got destroyed in the storm.' He turned to look at her back. He spoke, trying to match her dismissive and harsh tone, with only a hint of sympathy. 'I'm sorry.'

Nota fell silent for a moment. It was a brief moment, but long enough for Adorjan to savour her dejection, the shift from her usual aloofness into a moment of hurt. Adorjan could not see her face, but he knew the words had touched her heart.

She picked up her brush and started painting a half-finished piece on her wall. 'That's a stupid thing to be sorry for,' she said. 'That pile of wood and straw wasn't my home. That storm took nothing I hadn't already let go of. I live *here* now, and this cave won't ever be destroyed by mere wind and rain.'

'But you have memories in that hut. You're not sad that those memories are gone?'

Nota looked away from her art for a moment. 'Memories are in my head, not in that hut. That's where *you* lived. You should be more worried about your own home and doing what you can to survive. You still have *your* family to take you in, don't you? Just as you had *me* give you that pile of wood and straw when you needed it.

Maybe now you should consider building your own home.'

Adorjan was left feeling no better for indulging in his bitterness. He felt a self-loathing deeper than any before. He was ashamed that he allowed himself to be so vulnerable with someone else, especially someone he knew to be lacking in empathy.

He learned that day that his sadness was not to be consoled or soothed in this place he called home.

'By the way,' Nota said before Adorjan took his leave. 'Ashan came by earlier to ask if I had seen Umbra. She's been missing since the storm. I thought you'd want to know.' Nota gave Adorjan a look of disgust and dismissal.

Umbra. Missing. Guilt hit him before concern. He hadn't even thought of her once since the storm. He immediately understood Nota's meaning. *You have more to worry about than just yourself,* was what he heard, and she was probably right. Umbra once again showed Adorjan what he was lacking with her helplessness—a sense of responsibility and a capability to justify it.

Adorjan left the cave with dry eyes and a vow that no one would ever see him shed tears again.

SEVENTEEN

It was the day of Gratus' burial. In Cadeo's absence, there was a consensus that Ruhan was the closest to Gratus and best suited to choose her final resting place. He chose to burn her on what remained of the shore near Cadeo's broken home. He stacked the firewood there himself and carried her body there. It had been almost completely crushed, and Gratus was barely recognisable. Ruhan had gone to some length to ensure no one would see Gratus in that state until her body was already set ablaze.

It had been many years since Ashan had been present for a burning, and he chose to keep his distance this time, too. He watched on from on the hill where Cadeo and Gratus' home once was, far away enough that he could not hear their prayers, but close enough to see them weep. Thi and Lihn cried the most. They could not look at Gratus until she was almost reduced to ashes.

It was unsettling to watch, even for Ashan. And it was striking that Cadeo was absent for any burning, least of all Gratus. No one had seen him since the storm. There had been open murmurs that Cadeo may have already been dead himself, that perhaps he had thrown himself into the sea in his grief or died in the hills from a broken heart. The islanders had decided to proceed without him. Ashan could only imagine how he would feel when he found out he missed this burning, were he still alive.

Cadeo looked over the sea from the heights of Burial Hill.

He had witnessed much change in the sky over the last few days from this lonely spot. He had felt the wind settle after the storm and seen it carry the fog away with it. He had seen the sun rise and set in all its exposed glory. And now, some days after the storm, he felt the wind begin to stir again. What had been a warm afternoon breeze turned into a heavy wind. The flowers around Cadeo's feet swayed along with the change as though they clung to the ground with all their strength.

He barely noticed. He looked out to the sea but only saw what his mind's eye had stubbornly shown him since the storm—nothing. Nothing but the memory of Gratus' body beneath the rubble. Nothing but the memory of his children, Amado and Adra, sinking into the sea until the depths swallowed them. Nothing but constant reminders of his newfound loneliness and unending failure as a shepherd. To have even failed to care for and protect his own family, he would never have the right to refer to himself as a shepherd again.

Cadeo stood alongside the burial figures of his people, some of whom had died during his lifetime and some long before. There were some whom even Cadeo didn't know the names of, since their names had long since been lost to time, and the rotting wood was all that was left of them, the only proof they had ever lived at all. Gratus' idol would soon be made and erected. As would his own. As would everyone whom Cadeo had ever known, even a child like Umbra. Then, not long after, all their names would be lost to time as well.

Cadeo wondered why the figures were set to watch over the sea at all. Perhaps now that the sea was empty and dead, it felt more like a foe than an ally. Perhaps if this new famine ever ended, he would look upon the sea favourably again, and the figures' eternal watch would make sense again.

For the first time, the cycle of life and death looked utterly pointless. The fleeting joys while he lived no longer seemed to justify his life or balance the pain that life had brought him. There was no meaning to be found in the end of such a life, as any number of years of life would feel like far too few. He saw no purpose anymore—his heart still burned with love, but there was no one left to love.

Cadeo wished more than anything to join Gratus, to feel the warmth of her flesh again, to hold her in an eternal embrace wherever she now was. It was all he had longed for in the days he spent on this hill. He had already come close to doing so many times.

If only he could will himself to take that one step off the edge of Burial Hill.

Ruhan looked at Ashan partway through the burning. Ashan didn't need to be close to him to know he was glaring with judgement and some resentment. *You ought to be burning her with me*, was what Ashan imagined he would say. No matter how often the topic of superstition and customs arose between them, Ruhan never softened to Ashan's repulsion, and he never gave up in trying to guilt him for it. Though he was sickened by how he embraced every custom this island had, Ashan at least respected Ruhan's persistence. But on this day, he took Ruhan's glare as a suggestion to leave the people to their customs in peace.

He happened upon his boat after he spent most of the day wandering the island. He had decided to venture as far from his people as he could, and even climbed across a cliff face to reach a beach he knew to be remote, under the arch of Burial Hill. He had sailed past it many times but never had cause to set foot on it. He would sometimes see Umbra sitting there. She was always alone and would stare at the sky or over the sea. He was concerned for a time about Umbra's apparent desire for isolation, until he realised his hypocrisy. He instead respected Umbra for seeking out peace of her own accord. He now realised that Umbra would have sought that peace out during recent storms and fog, regardless of how perilous the climb to the beach would have been. That was probably why he had found her at sea that day, because she had tried to make the climb and fallen. He decided to keep that information to himself, lest he steal away any more of her peace if her hiding spot were to be discovered.

It was also what brought him to her favourite beach in

the hopes of finding her here, but she was nowhere to be seen. He instead found his boat on the sand. The beach was smaller than before as the shore had risen and devoured a part of it. The boat had surely been carried there by a strong tide. The storm had had its way with it and damaged the hull. The stern had been shattered, and the rudder had been warped. One side had been torn away in part, where the oar would rest. It may not have been beyond repair, but Ashan may as well have built a new boat from scratch with that amount of effort. He was without a boat and therefore without a home.

He was more annoyed than sad at this realisation. He was only glad that he had the good sense to keep Quy's boat ashore. Everyone else seemed to have forgotten about it, so he was free to make it his own.

Ashan happened across something far more interesting and surprising on the beach—a whale. It had probably washed up on the shore in the storm as well, since it was freshly dead. It was a small one, perhaps an infant, which meant it had a thin hide and tender meat. That meant it would be both easy to slice and eat.

Ashan found a spear in his broken boat and stabbed the whale. The spear pierced its flesh with just a few thrusts. He would need Adorjan to help cut the whale up and share it before it started to decompose, but he allowed himself a sigh of satisfaction and relief. *The island will eat for a few more days.*

Adorjan had not been at Gratus' burning. Ashan found him beside the rice paddies shortly before sunset. They were in a poor state, as Ashan had imagined. It had been some years since he had seen them for himself, but he always knew how much Adorjan cared for them and how he had taught others to do the same. He always had an affinity for this place, even as a child. It was one of the few traits Ashan understood in him, as he had a similar affinity for the sea, even since before he was old enough to sail. This sight of fields overrun by mudslides must have been devastating for him, and Ashan expected that it would further damage his already fragile mental state.

Adorjan slept by the paddies, next to a small patch that looked like he had been trying to restore. His efforts were futile, judging by the state of the rice plants he had unearthed, but Ashan respected that he was trying rather than sitting idly by as he had come to expect of him. He decided to let Adorjan have his rest and would instead have him help with the whale in the morning. Ashan would do what he could himself until then.

He borrowed Nota's largest and sharpest caving tools on the way back to the beach. The sea was calm when he got back, and the climb across the rocks was an easy one. The beach appeared darker than usual, even for the evening, as Ashan struggled to see the whale until it was right before his face. Nota's stone knife pierced its flesh after some effort. Ashan prepared for a long night of labour.

The knife sank deeper into the whale's body, and it began to bleed, the blood flowing out from its grey skin like a small stream before it washed away in the seawater.

A strange, unpleasant sensation came over Ashan before he could fully slice off the first chunk of flesh. He felt cold and began to shiver. The air became thick, and it was hard to breathe. The whale gradually disappeared from his sight, slowly hidden by a thickening white cowl in the air.

The clear sky the island had been blessed with for mere days had been temporary, as had the return of natural order. The fog swiftly returned and covered the entire sea and land. All Ashan could see was a tide rolling up against the shore and blood-soaked sand. He heard what sounded like thunder out at sea and experienced the closest thing to *panic* that he ever had. He experienced the fear that came with the awe of nature. Another storm was brewing on the horizon.

The tide rose, unnaturally fast. He soon stood in knee-high water, and there was no longer a coast before him.

Something was in the water, something small.

Ashan took it into his hands. It was a dead fish. A long-dead, rotten, grey fish with the texture of slime. Its mouth hung limply, and its eyes glared distantly. It was like an unworldly being, unrecognisable even to the eyes of a seasoned fisherman.

Something else rubbed against Ashan's skin in the water, against both his legs. Ashan looked down and stumbled backwards with surprise.

More dead fish. Many of them were trapped in a calm tide. He looked out to where the shore had been and saw only dead, rotten fish floating on the surface around the whale. The water felt unnaturally cold.

It feels...lifeless. The water, the sand and the air—the beach itself feels like it has died.

The water seemed to come to life and flee from his feet. It recoiled swiftly until the sand beneath it was exposed again, leaving the dead fish in its wake. Ashan looked to where the water had fled. His head ached again with incredulity and bafflement.

Something approached from the horizon with a great

fury. A sole wave of water rushed toward the island. Even at such a distance, he could see that the wave of water was immense as it warped the sea with its approach.

Ashan was moved by the pure instinct to survive. His feet took him to the base of Burial Hill looming far above the beach, and he laid his hands on it to climb.

A terrible and piercing *sound* stopped him. It was like an echo not heard only with his ears but with every morsel of his body. It ran through his bones and froze him from the inside, as though both ice and fire had been poured into his blood. He couldn't call it a scream as it was not a sound or sensation he could so easily name.

He clutched his ears in vain. His head felt set to burst.

The sound of rushing waters gradually grew louder and could be heard even over the scream in Ashan's head.

He clung so hard to the rocks that his fingers bled, and the pain was sharper than that in his head. Ashan breathed in as deeply as he could. His heartbeat slowed a touch.

One hand, he commanded himself. It took all his strength to take his bleeding hand from the rocks and to reach higher. *One foot,* he commanded himself. He found a new footing through strenuous effort. He climbed through the pain.

Ashan continued to will himself into movement through the pain, all the while resisting looking out to where the wave swiftly approached and grew all the louder.

But soon, Ashan felt a spray of water on his body as the colossal wave found the shore. It reached as high as Ashan with a great force. He clung to the rocks with all his remaining strength and but couldn't hold on against the force of the rushing water pulling him.

The sound never seemed to die. Ashan could not feel himself being thrown about at the sea's whim. He felt only agony as the world went black.

Cadeo saw another change in the sky, one far stranger than the many he had seen from Burial Hill. There was a green light that shone brighter than any afternoon sun.

Something stirred in his heart at the sight of it, something that he could not comprehend at first. He felt both afraid and angry with no apparent cause. It stirred up long-buried feelings and emotions that he instinctively tried to suppress, but he could not stop them rising to the surface along with scattered memories that accompanied them.

Those memories had become hazy over time, but he now saw them clearly. Along with the sightings of colossal shadows in the last famine, the green light in the sky was seen often. Cadeo himself had only seen it once before on the night he took Amado and Adra out to sea for the last time. That light had always been seen at the same time as something absurd—a sudden downpour, a drop in temperature, an unexplained change in the sea tide.

On this day, fog presently returned to the island and the sea when the light shone again. Cadeo watched the haze materialise from nothing.

Fear found Cadeo's heart easily again.

He screamed out with all his might and being. Only heard his scream, as the rousing wind, angry sea and thunder drowned out his voice. He screamed in anger. He screamed in terror. He screamed in bafflement at how he still had a yearning to live in the face of doom. He screamed for as long as he could.

Even his scream was without purpose, for nothing made sense to him anymore.

Ashan's eyes shot open. He gasped amid deafening silence. The world looked grey and blurry until his vision began to clear up through slow blinks. He was on his back in wet sand, looking up at lingering fog. It was already nighttime.

He pushed himself to his knees. He was freezing, and wet sand clung to his itchy skin. The pain in his head had receded, and the scream-like sound had been silenced. So abrupt an end it was that Ashan wondered for a moment— *am I dead?*

But a pressure remained in his head like a breaking dam. He stroked under his nose where he felt a trickle. Blood was on his fingers.

He was on a beach—Umbra's favourite beach. The tide had receded, and the sand was no longer submerged. The sea looked calm beyond the haze.

The beach was lonely. The whale was gone. There was no sign it had ever been there at all.

The sky was the natural colour of nighttime.

EIGHTEEN

Umbra had watched the fog return from her hiding spot by the rice paddies. She had fled the dead whale hours ago, seeking comfort in the only other place she felt at ease — but the paddies, too, were ruined.

What remained of the water was tainted by debris, as dull as the grey sky. The rice plants were broken and smothered under mud. They looked more like dead fields than paddies soon to be ripe for harvest.

She'd laid her hands on the soil. It felt cold, as though all its life had faded. The rice would never grow again, and the paddies would have to be rebuilt. There would be no harvest, and Umbra would have many days spent in hunger ahead of her. She wondered how they would survive until the rice could grow again and the fish would return.

Even here, the whale haunted her. If she had brought water sooner, perhaps it would still be alive. Her presence in its last moments felt hollow and meaningless. All her work—caring for the whale, nurturing the rice—had been futile. *I don't know what to do anymore.*

Her downcast heart took her away from her hiding spot by the rice paddies. She snuck to Vada's hut. She peeked her head inside, and Vada was nowhere to be seen. So, she searched through the boxes in her place. One looked as though it had once been full of rice and was now almost empty. Another had an unpleasant fish scent but was empty. Others had sacks of herbs that she didn't know, but they all combined to make a strange but pleasant aroma. Then she found Vada's box full of tools. She found what she had come to the hut to find—a small stone knife.

Vada often carried knives like this with her, but Umbra was not sure what she used them for. She guessed it was for gathering herbs. The stone blade was sharp and well-kept. Umbra promised herself that she would only use it for a moment and return it.

She went back outside, where she had a view of the sea before her. It seemed a fitting place to her, and one that was comfortable, giving her the conviction to do what she needed to. She took a long breath, then unravelled her long, locked hair. It hung down as far as her hips. She didn't think of her hair often, but she was already lamenting its absence. She had been excited at the idea of her hair becoming long enough to touch the ground, at it being a youthful black at the tips and a mature white at the roots.

She hesitated—the symbol of her life and wisdom, soon

to vanish. The weight of it felt like punishment enough.

She held some of the locks on the side of her head.

She cut one lock. It took effort, even with the sharp blade.

It was so light in her hands, almost weightless.

Another lock fell. Each cut hurt more than the last..

Then she cut another.

Each one hurt more to lose than the last.

'Umbra,' she heard as she took hold of another lock. Vada approached her hut with a bundle of herbs in one hand and another knife in the other. 'What brings you--' Vada went silent when her eyes fell on the cluster of hair in Umbra's hands. Her face changed, and she looked as distraught as Umbra felt.

'Child,' she said, slowly and deliberately. 'What's happened?'

Umbra said nothing. She looked down at her hand again as though broken out of a daze. The sadness in her heart rose anew and harder, as the permanence of her actions now dawned on her.

Vada set the herbs and knife down at her feet.

'Whatever happened, you mustn't...this will not do,' she said. Her voice was calm, but Umbra felt her hands tremble as she stroked her hair. 'Whatever's happened, whatever you may have done, it will pass. You'll forget it one day. Don't lose this part of yourself over a moment that will soon pass.'

Vada held out her hand expectantly, looking at the knife Umbra still held. She bit her lip and looked down at the ground. She dropped the hair she was holding. She fled to the hills again. Vada's voice calling after her gradually faded as Umbra lost herself in the fog.

She was soon back at her hiding place by the paddies. She sat there for hours, still holding the stone knife. She marvelled at it for a while in the shadows of neighbouring trees, unsure what else to do. She had lost the conviction to cut off any more of her hair. She regretted the locks she had already cut off.

She heard a scream near the paddies while she sat there —a deep and guttural scream. She fled to hide by a tree. Adorjan and Nota were there by the paddies together, and Umbra realised the scream must have come from one of them. She decided to stay hidden—she wanted nothing more than to be alone, and she didn't want to be seen here. She was relieved to see them eventually run from the fields together, and she was left alone again.

Umbra spent another night there, sleeplessly. She was utterly exhausted and hungry, tired of being outdoors. She decided to wander the island, avoiding anyone she could see. She walked near Burial Hill and saw Cadeo at its peak, so she swiftly took her leave. She saw destruction throughout the island, with some huts badly damaged, and some even missing roofs. Much of the plant life had been damaged by mud. It made for a devastating walk, seeing that her home was barely recognisable.

She eventually made her way to her hut, which she was relieved to find was still standing, and only the roof was damaged. She stood outside it for a long while, both hesitant and scared to enter. She thought about her father for the first time in days—about how angry he would surely be. Had she anywhere else to go now, she may well have never entered this hut again.

But Umbra was driven inside by some concern for her father, and shame that she had not thought much of him over the last few days. She needed to know that he was okay after the storm, and perhaps he had not eaten since she last fed him. She felt that he would have a right to be angry, having left him to fend for himself for so long.

Umbra breathed a long breath and finally entered her home again.

Varyis was full of conflicting emotions as he held a lock of coarse, thick hair in his hands—anger, confusion, and relief. He was coughing, and the pain in his chest was almost unbearable. His body and mind were particularly fragile this day. He was constantly dizzy, forcing him to drift in and out of sleep.

Vada had visited his hut not long ago with freshly picked herbs and had brewed some medicinal tea for him.

She told him that she had seen Umbra. That she was alive and well. That she had gone to her hut and stolen her knife. That she had run away when confronted.

Varyis was at first deeply grateful to Vada to know she was safe and well. Then, he was infuriated that she had not come home despite being well for all that time.

Vada knew Varyis well and had noticed the change in his temperament and the anger he could not hide.

She had put a lock of hair in his hand with no explanation. He knew it to be Umbra's. It smelled softly of salt and fire smoke. It was a stark tone of black with a faint sheen, just like her mother's. He looked up at Vada, confused.

'Go easy on her. She needs it.' That was all Vada had said. They were Vada's last words before she departed.

Varyis still presently looked at Umbra's hair in his

hand, full of longing for her to come home, to see her himself.

Then Varyis finally got what he longed for.

Umbra came home soon after. She stood by the entrance of the hut and stared silently at Varyis on his floor-bed. Her skin and clothes were covered in dirt. She was ashen, and she shivered. Her hair was dishevelled with dirt and leaves clinging to it. It fell messily around her waist.

Varyis forced himself to sit upright and look his daughter in the eyes. He struggled against his shaking body and fought through the pain. It took him a long while.

Umbra watched him with a static gaze. Her eyes were vacant, as though she saw nothing at all.

They stayed this way for a long time, in a strange stand-off that neither was willing to break. Umbra's shallow, laboured breath echoed through the hut.

Varyis couldn't speak, unable to find words to convey his vexation, anger and profound relief.

So he didn't speak. He dragged himself across the floor to the cooking pot and poured out a small portion of what remained of their rice in a bowl. It was now cold and had a stale scent. His hands shook as he held it out and offered it to Umbra. She still didn't move. She looked down on her father with the same cold gaze.

Varyis couldn't hold out the bowl for long. He set it down before his strength gave out.

They shared silence once more.

'Do you even care anymore?' he said.

He looked upon his daughter.

He finally saw it.

Tears.

Umbra was *crying*.

Varyis trembled. He came to a sobering and painful realisation as Umbra began to sob out loud—

I don't know what to do.

It was Umbra who moved first. Varyis only saw that she had held Vada's knife in her hand when it fell from her fingers and pierced the ground.

'I'm sorry,' she said with a feeble voice.

She ran and embraced her father. She nestled her face in his chest and sobbed harder.

'I'm sorry. I'm sorry.'

She held Varyis' arms so hard that they ached and began to shake again.

Varyis still found no words to say.

The best he could do was to embrace his daughter as she cried without restraint.

Umbra put the first spoonful of rice in her mouth. It tasted foul. She fought against spitting it back out. She instead took another mouthful.

Her stomach churned at its unpleasant texture. But she was grateful, regaining a little strength after eating her first meal in days. She remembered the paddies—ruined, dead, desolate—with each mouthful. It moved her to keep on eating until her bowl was empty.

It was a pleasant feeling to eat a meal made by her father's hands.

Umbra felt warm in her home.

Varyis watched his daughter eat the last spoonful of rice from her bowl. It was clear to see how foul it must have tasted and how much she struggled to swallow it all.

Yet, for the first time in years, Varyis felt full of contentment.

Umbra lay down to rest on Varyis' lap. The smell of salt and smoke flowed from her.

Varyis finally allowed himself to smile.

NINETEEN

Cadeo leaned on trees and rocks as he climbed the hills, each step threatening to fold his legs beneath him. He felt every bit of his age as he dragged himself through the fog to Nota's cave. It smelled of herbs and cooked rice. She sat against the far wall, painting a vibrant but small mural. To Cadeo, it looked like a mess of colours and disjointed shapes with no cohesion.

She didn't seem surprised to see him, but something akin to sympathy passed over her face. Cadeo was conscious of the sorry, shameful state he was in. He hadn't bathed in days, his hair was unkempt, and he only had the strength to keep standing by leaning on the cave walls.

Nota beckoned him to sit. He did so, stumbling to the middle of the cave and easing down onto her floor bed.

She gave him a bowl of warm rice soup flavoured with an assortment of herbs without him asking. Cadeo hadn't the presence of mind to thank her aloud or otherwise acknowledge the gesture for the sacrifice it was. *There is not even enough food for you right now,* he thought. *How foolish to waste a precious bowl on an old man.*

But he accepted it with a feeble nod and ate heartily. Nota waited patiently and silently for Cadeo to finish before she presented two bowls filled with colourful ink— one green and the other light brown. They smelled of ivy berries.

She held out to Cadeo a couple of sharp bone shards. He took them gently into his hands. They were incredibly light and a perfect tone of white. He felt, as he always did, that they were an abomination—a premature reminder of the end of life that ever lurked. He felt a new wave of sorrow at their touch. They were light yet burdensome, as though they were carved from both grief and comfort.

He wiped away a single tear from his already red eyes.

'It's Gratus' hand,' she said. 'I thought it would be fitting, since you were always holding it in yours. Now she'll always be holding you, in a way.'

Cadeo was touched. It was an incredible display of empathy and understanding he had not come to expect, not from Nota of all people. He only replied with a quiet *thank you* under his breath.

She didn't seem bothered by his apparent indifference. She took back the shards of Gratus' hand and dipped the sharp edge in the dark green ink to soak.

Cadeo just nodded his head without turning around and held out his arm. The art mattered less than ever, and he wanted nothing less than to sit for another. He was here only because Gratus would have wanted him to be, and she would not have accepted him abandoning such a custom.

Nota took his arm and silently got to work.

The procedure was painful, as it always was. The tattoos along Cadeo's back had been the most painful and taken the longest. They were seaweed and flowers that were to protect him while he was a fisherman. The pain this time paled in comparison to those and to all others. Though he could feel Gratus' bone in his flesh, it was as though his skin were hardened and more numb. Cadeo took it as another sign of ageing, that he couldn't feel pain the same way as before, and that the softness of youthful skin was all but gone.

The two of them sat in silence as Nota worked. Cadeo spent the time looking vacantly outside, where a shattered pattern of sunlight reached the ground through the fog and shone on half-dead foliage. Birds and insects sang as the day carried on as always. The island teemed with life amid the destruction and death.

'Is there a point to this?' Cadeo eventually said. He didn't know whether he spoke to Nota or himself. He spoke only for the sake of speaking. 'Gratus had tattoos all over her body. Amado and Adra were too young to have their first. Yet all were killed by nature...Gratus by the land and my children by the sea. Why should these tattoos protect only me?'

She stopped her work as Cadeo spoke.

'Has my life been built upon false faith in the wards of tattoos and music? Why would *any* of those who have been set on Burial Hill have died, were our faith rewarded? But if my faith is in falsehoods...what have I been living for?'

183

Nota said nothing, carrying on with her work. Cadeo pondered his question in the silence between them, but came no closer to an answer in the hours that followed.

'It's finished.'

Her voice woke Cadeo back to the present. 'Hmm?'

'Your tattoo. It's finished.'

Cadeo looked upon the work of Nota's hand, stunned.

'It's apt to remember Gratus by, don't you think?' she asked.

It was unmistakably a rice plant, yet it was not a natural one. The green and brown shades merged in a spiral-like form, as though they embraced and fought one another all at once. The result was a piece of art that would remind Cadeo of the concept of conflict itself, a tattoo that would put him at odds with nature, with its cruel relentlessness. It was remarkable.

He was in awe of the piece and its designer, but he couldn't bring himself to be grateful. For he did not yet know if he could call it a ward as he always did, or if he would come to resent it.

'What you said sounds like mourning to me,' Nota said after a while. 'If you weren't asking those kinds of questions— of yourself, of your family, of what you call *faith*—you wouldn't be in mourning. I won't answer those questions for you. No one should. This is *your* mourning, and I won't rob you of finding your own way to heal.' She placed the bones in Cadeo's hand. They were vibrantly coloured and shining like beautiful seashells. 'What *I* do has nothing to do with faith. There's nothing inherently magical about carving ink in your flesh with your loved one's bones. My only job is to colour on your skin that will have meaning to you. And to make you look pretty.

Whatever you put your faith in is up to you.'

Cadeo lowered his head, accepting the words not with gratefulness but with understanding. He nodded once more. *This burden is mine alone,* he determined. *As it is meant to be.*

The two fell silent together again until the ink dried and his tattoo was set.

Umbra opened her eyes from her father's lap, woken up in the night by a hollow, deep sound. She listened. She heard it, yet not with her ears. The sound rippled and echoed within her in the form of a voice with intangible words, yet she understood all of them. It was a sound that roused her instincts, her emotions, her conscience—all that was intangible in her.

Umbra was standing outside before she intended her body to move, drawn by the sound almost as though against her will. She was met by a thin fog on the shore before her. Most of the sand was still submerged by the sea, and the water softly flowed under her hut. The sound came again. It was closer than before, yet no louder. She began to follow it. The water she walked in reached her knees. She walked along what remained of the shore. The soft waves became silent in her ears as the sound drowned them out again.

She walked for a long while, as far as the cliff face that led to her favourite beach. The sound came from beyond it, where her friend's life had ended. She watched the cliff face and Burial Hill looming above her. She hesitated. She tried to will herself on, but her body wouldn't move. She began to shake. The rocks before her looked insurmountable, the beach unreachable.

The sound came again in the tone of a beckon, of a plea. It was closer still, as though it came from beside her. Still, Umbra didn't move. She didn't want to proceed, yet didn't want to retreat. She was not afraid of what awaited her on the beach—only saddened by the whale that would not be waiting for her. She lacked the heart to face that empty shore.

Then, a large figure appeared beyond the white veil. It drifted toward her from beyond the cliffs and from the beach where it had beckoned her. Its dark body was a dark contrast to the white sky, like a black hole in the clouds. It drew close to her, staring at her with glowing green eyes. The sound had stopped.

Umbra was not surprised to see it, nor was she as fearful of it as she once was. She no longer saw an entity to run from. What she felt now was peace, as though she looked upon an accepted part of her life — something closer to her than her own people. For it spoke with a beckoning voice she wanted to heed.

It was smaller than before, now a little taller than a man. It reached her and was close enough to touch. There was no sound anymore, and the two looked upon each other. So close up, the creature didn't look to have a body at all. It looked like it was made of the mist, or the dark shadow of it. Like it couldn't be touched by flesh or the elements, yet the fog swirled around it like it would for a living thing.

It opened a hole where its mouth ought to be. Something came pouring out of it and onto the sand. A pile of stones. They were colourful and glistened in the muted moonlight. Umbra picked one up. It was a vibrant red tone, like a dying rose. It was smooth to touch. It was striking and unique.

'What is this?' Umbra asked.

The creature looked down on her and made a sound like a groan.

Umbra looked up at it. Its words were clear to hear, yet she could not grasp their meaning. She had never heard the words it used, nor had she heard any words uttered in such a way. Her mind struggled to comprehend, to the point that it was painful.

She set the stone down before the creature. She looked up at it questioningly.

The creature looked down at it. Then looked back at her. All silently.

It soon drifted towards the shore and submerged in the sea. Then it was gone.

Umbra picked up another one of the stones. It was a blue deeper than dawn and a strange shape with many sharp edges. It was coarse to touch and felt like hundreds of small stones were huddled together in an embrace. They were beautiful, almost unworldly in their vibrancy.

She couldn't fathom what their purpose could be. She wondered if this was what rocks looked like from the bottom of the sea, but wondered why the creature would bring them to her. They meant nothing to her.

She heard the water splash. The creature was before her, its mouth open once more. It knelt in the sand to set something silver and thrashing at her feet—a fish.

It was as long as Umbra's arm and had immaculately shiny scales. A mackerel. She dropped the stones to lay her hand on it. She had almost forgotten what the touch of scales felt like. She picked it up into her arms and embraced it, as though to prove it real to herself. It felt even larger in her arms. It was enough for a couple more days' worth of meals for her and her father.

Umbra felt a tear running down her face with this realisation, but rather than sadness, she felt a profound relief. She allowed more tears to fall as a mark of elation.

She hadn't noticed the creature returning to the sea again. Then the water parted for the creature once more.

It arose from the sea, now much larger. It stood above Umbra, as large and tall as the whale was. It looked full, like a filled sack.

It opened its mouth once more.

Umbra had to back away from the creature for the sheer amount of fish that fell out of it. A school of them hit the sand as a pile and were sprawled out. There were dozens of fish of all kinds—some were barely as large as her hand, others were even bigger than her mackerel. Enough fish thrashed around to feed all her people for a week.

Umbra's elation turned into shock and bafflement. She looked up at the creature, utterly lost for words. The creature groaned—

Its words were still incomprehensible to Umbra, yet they were soothing. It was like listening to a lullaby, arousing a feeling like that which The Wandering Fisherman did. They inspired a daydream of being welcomed home from a long voyage. Contentment.

The creature returned to the sea once more.

It was even larger when it surfaced again and rivalled even the size of the whale.

Its mouth fell open again.

TWENTY

Quy's boat was exactly where Ashan had left it—on a lonely patch of green beside the west shore. It had been untouched by either the storm or any hands, left exposed to the elements to decay. Moss had settled on it, and the wood was slimy with dew. Parts of the hull had been rotten since long before the boat had been abandoned— more evidence of Quy's negligence. Ashan was constantly coating his own boat with fish oil, back when they were in abundance, to prevent exactly this. He was certain Quy had never done so himself, as he sporadically saw Ruhan doing so for him.

Ashan imagined that it only had a few more journeys left in it before it either sank or spent the rest of its days washed ashore. The recklessness and negligence of his friend never ceased to amaze. He resented that he had to put his trust in such a vessel.

He dragged it to the water and rowed purposefully. It was eerie how calm the waters were and how gentle the wind was on his face. The raging tides and torrential rain were now like distant memories.

Dead fish and famines, shadows of giant men, storms and tidal waves. Something insane is happening to this place.

Ashan beckoned for the *supernatural* to come for him once more.

Quy's boat passed the edge of the bay and approached deep waters. The boat felt much like his own to steer, and he quickly felt at home again. Some seawater crept into the hull after the boat passed over each wave, but it stayed afloat.

Ashan rowed the same way he had when they found Umbra at sea, the same way Quy had sailed when he disappeared. Adorjan had seen the shadow in the distance soon after they passed the bay. Ashan watched intently as he sailed. He saw nothing out of the ordinary, just fog and calm waves all around him.

The fog became thicker the further he went, until he could only see his island as a dark silhouette. He wasn't worried about finding his way back to shore, as he knew these waters as though they were a part of his flesh. To sail came naturally to him, even more than walking. He saw waves and storms as companions along his voyages.

The island was almost out of sight. He began to feel the unease that came with such solitude, and he was nervous. He could not imagine what was about to befall him, nor did he fully understand his purpose for being here. It dawned on him that following in Quy's steps meant he had resigned himself to die. He didn't hesitate to sail on.

I'd rather die knowing the truth than live in fear like the others.

He soon experienced the extraordinary again.

The fog ended. Day turned into night. A colossal sound erupted into his ears. Quy's vessel was almost capsized by the force of the waves. Lightning flashed and thunder roared. Ashan was thrown off his feet. He grabbed the boat's tiller instinctively. The boat was thrown from one wave to another. It was all he could avoid falling overboard. He lost orientation, unable to see the moon or stars for the stormy clouds. Darkness tossed him from side to side. Lightning tore open the sky again, each flash coming faster. They were all that lit his way.

This place did not feel normal, not a normal storm or sea. Ashan felt some inexplicable malice there, as though nature itself had gone insane with anger. Beyond the ferocious storm and the stirred waves, something about this place made him afraid.

More lightning revealed something in the sea, for a brief moment.

A man *stood* in the water. A creature. It was colossal, dark as the sea depths. Then he was gone with the lightning.

Ashan fell off his feet. He was too stunned to scream.

The lightning flashed again. The creature was there, even larger. *A black body and a head coming out of the water,* Ashan heard in Adorjan's voice. *As high as the clouds...this is it.*

Light shone on the shadow once more, and it was larger still. Rather, it was *closer.* A pair of green lights lit from his face, like twin stars.

He came closer to the boat. Lightning flashed again, but the creature was clear to see now without it.

Ashan gripped the tiller so hard that he felt splinters in his hand. He heard his heartbeat even amid the crashing water and thunder.

He looked up at the creature's green eyes, which glared right back at him.

He drew closer, flowing over the water like a formless shadow.

Its glare made Ashan feel cold. They emanated the same malice as the storm.

He was right beside the boat.

Some clouds overhead parted and made way for a new green light, as vivid as the creature's eyes.

He sank deeper into the water. Ashan could only see his head and shoulders. It never broke its glare.

Many feelings and instincts ran through Ashan's mind —amazement, fear, awe, disbelief. One thought and feeling reigned above all others. Anger.

Is it you? Are you the reason my people starve and die?

It leaned in toward the boat, as though in response to Ashan's thoughts. It loomed closer still until its huge, void-like face was all Ashan could see. A pair of colossal hands, also drenched in shadow, rose from the water.

It brought them up to its face and clasped its head.

A sound burst from it, louder than thunder and deeper than the darkest eclipse. It was akin to a groan, yet carried the shape of a word that Ashan could not comprehend.

He saw before him the silhouette of a man in pain. Or a man losing his mind.

Sense and reasoning abandoned him as the creature stood in the raging surf, rain and lightning striking from clouds torn by green light. It was like a scene from a dream no fleshly man could ever conjure.

Ashan spoke to him.

'Who are you?' he screamed as loudly as he could. '*What* are you?'

The creature took his hands from his face. He looked down on Ashan's vessel again. Another sound seeped into Ashan's ears—softer than before, yet almost deafening. It made the sound over and over. They had the shape of more words, and were as incomprehensible as the last.

Ashan opened his mouth to scream out again, but was halted by a terrible and piercing sound, not heard with his ears but with his blood. It sent an ice-like chill through his veins. It was the same sound he'd heard on the beach when he found the dead whale.

He covered his ears in agony. But it was in vain.

The sea grew angrier.

He was thrown overboard and into the water.

He was tossed from one wave to the other, barely able to move for the sound echoing in his blood.

The sound was relentless and overbearing, robbing his instincts and coherence. It was all he could hear, even as the water crashed around him.

He saw the two green eyes of the creature above the water, its head dimly lit by the light in the sky.

Ashan reached out to the fading surface. Perhaps it was out of desperation, or perhaps the anger he felt for that being was beyond his comprehension or strength.

Regardless, it was for nothing.

That he felt no more pain was the sole mercy, as he fell into an unnatural sleep. The relentless sound faded.

The silence that ensued coaxed him to sleep like an unnatural and terrifying lullaby.

Ashan opened his eyes and stared up at a thin sheet of mist, squinting for the dim midday sun, breathing in a refreshing sea breeze.

He lay in the middle of Quy's dilapidated boat and floated on calm water. His island home was before him, and drew ever closer without wind or oars to guide it. Quy's boat brought him home, as if of its own accord or by the will of the sea.

Ashan questioned whether he was dreaming or if he had passed into a next life.

There was something slimy on his skin. He looked in the hull of the boat around him and was brought back into the present by what he saw.

Fish. The boat was full of them, of many breeds and sizes—so many that the boat struggled to stay afloat. All of them were either freshly dead or still thrashing around.

Ashan held one in his hands, scarcely believing his eyes. *Why,* was all he could think, his mind still lost in a fog. *How? How am I alive?*

Quy's boat found the shore before long. It set itself down, with the coast as a natural anchor.

There were more fish on the beach. Many more. Ashan's eyes ran up along the shore, and he saw no end to them, as far as the fog allowed him to see. He could barely see the sand for the fish atop it. Most were freshly dead, some were slowly dying.

He climbed out of the boat and walked among the fish with bated breath. He touched some, picked some up, and held some as they died.

He saw another silhouette in the fog as he walked. It was the shape of a little girl with long, unkempt hair, standing beside the shore.

'Umbra,' Ashan called out, baffled. 'Umbra.'

She did not respond.

He walked toward her tepidly. He called again, and she still did not respond.

She stood facing the sea, looking at a large mackerel she held in her hands. Her eyes were practically unblinking and bloodshot, and she stared vacantly in a daze.

Ashan reached out and put a hand on her shoulder.

Her face shot up. Her wide, bloodshot eyes met his. She glared back at him, vacantly. The look on her face was empty, devoid of expression. Ashan took a step back from her, instinctively.

'Ashan,' she finally whispered.

'Umbra,' he said. The sound of her voice was jarring to her ears after all he had *heard* at sea. It was enough to centre him, to feel alive again. 'What happened here?'

Umbra looked down at the fish in her arms, then back at him.

Her face changed. She smiled. It was an expression so unlike her that it was disturbing. Ashan grew tenser still.

'Ashan! Look!' she cried out. 'Look.' She held the fish out for him to see. 'Fish. There's fish everywhere. We can eat again. Everyone can eat again. I...I'm going to tell Father.'

She ran off without waiting for a response. Ashan watched her go until she disappeared beyond the fog.

He was left alone with the dead and dying fish. She was right—enough food for the island to eat for days surrounded him.

But he felt anything but happy for it. He had never felt so uneasy, so disillusioned.

Nothing here made sense. Nothing could be explained with anything close to reason or logic. Ashan was lost. He was terrified.

He looked out to the sea from where he came. There he saw nothing at all.

TWENTY ONE

Cadeo woke sometime near midday back in Nghi's home, on one of the many floor-beds Nghi had made. He was disoriented after a night of strange and hazy dreams. Wooden idols and paintings came to life and spoke in strange tongues, in a place made of clouds. He had been more of an observer in his dream than a subject.

He felt better after he regained some coherence. It dawned on him that it was the first time he'd slept since Gratus had died, despite seeing several sunsets from atop Burial Hill in that time. The rest and a modest meal in his stomach boosted his spirits, even if slightly.

His arm ached more than the day before, and his freshly tattooed skin felt tender to touch. He looked at the art with a fresh set of eyes. It truly was beautiful and impressively detailed. It was now the most vibrant tattoo on his body and stood out compared to the others that had dulled over time.

Nota had been right—a rice plant was an apt choice. It would remind Cadeo of the years Gratus worked at the paddies, from her years as a young, vigorous, and abrasive woman, to when she grew slow, old, and mild-mannered. This would be his favourite tattoo.

Cadeo's entire body was now fully covered. There was barely a patch of skin left for even the smallest piece, save on his neck and his face, which he preferred to leave untouched. This would likely be his last tattoo. *It means my life is almost done and ready to be left behind,* he reflected.

He thought again of Gratus, Amado and Adra waiting for him in the next life. No part of him looked upon the approaching end with anything but longing. *You all won't be alone for long.*

His t'rung stood outside Nghi's home. He marvelled that it had survived the storm, and he was grateful that his tendency to leave it on Burial Hill had spared it from the worst of the storm. Nghi had told Cadeo that he had found it almost completely undamaged at the base of the hill when he helped Ru take care of Gratus' body. Cadeo did not have the desire to play it again, but he had yet another cause to be grateful to Nghi. It would be kept at his home until that time to play it came again.

Cadeo set out for his habitual daily walk. He thought about his people as he went, about how they were faring since the storm and whether their huts fared better than his. He was ashamed to realise that that was the first time he had thought of any of them in days. He thought they were within their rights to be angry at him for abandoning them in such a time of need, but he was duty-bound to accept whatever they expressed. He made a full-hearted promise while he was still alone—*I will never abandon any of you again. I will be a shepherd once more.*

As Cadeo approached the shore, he saw that there was something else at the coast. There lay fish in the sand—many of them. They looked freshly dead. He picked one up in his hands, scarcely believing his eyes until he felt the scales in his fingers.

His bafflement was broken by the sound of his people's voices further down the beach. They carried disdain and anger. He followed them and saw a group huddled together in the fog.

'—without knowing why.'

'What else do you need to know?!'

Cadeo recognised the voices immediately—Ruhan and Adorjan, respectively. Most of the islanders were gathered there too—Vada, Ashan, Nghi, Lihn, Thi and Kien.

He felt touched at the sight of them. They each looked so different from even the last time he saw them, each looking tired and famished. He saw how diminished the island now was with Gratus and Quy gone.

His people barely acknowledged his presence, invested as they were in the argument before them and the piles of fresh fish at their feet.

'We're not touching these things until we know what brought them to us,' Ruhan was shouting. 'Until we can be sure it is not another omen.'

'*Omen*,' Adorjan echoed. He held an empty sack in his hands. 'We have had omens for months now, and been cursed to die. You would demand our people starve when food is right before them?'

'Should I be right, this food could bring us even more hardship. Look around you. This isn't natural. This cannot mean anything but disaster for us.'

'Then I will try on all our behalf. If I'm still alive tomorrow, we will know this fish is no omen.'

'One day is not enough. And one person is enough to bring evil on us all!'

'Evil,' Kien echoed in her rarely heard voice. She spoke softly from under her straw hat and the bark cloth hanging from it. '…Evil.' She nodded.

Adorjan groaned. 'We haven't the luxury to fear evil in even our food. You've seen the paddies by now—the rice is dead, the paddies destroyed. It will be weeks until we can restore them, and many more months until harvest. Once we've eaten our rice reserves, we will have nothing left to eat. Nothing but seaweed and herbs. We are sure to die. Here we have a chance to survive. We may even have enough to sustain us while we mend the paddies and plant again.

'Who's to say this fish is not a gift from the sea? Would you risk throwing it away because of fear?'

Ru shook his head. 'Or a *test*. We've had no fish for months, and it must be for a reason. Can you stand there and tell us with any confidence that this is not either an omen or a test from the seas?'

'What choice do we have?' Adorjan shouted again. No one replied.

He turned to Ashan in the silence that followed. 'Say something here?'

Ashan stood a distance from the others and was quietly observing until now. It was a rare sight to see him among his people, and that was not lost on Cadeo. Ashan looked as uncomfortable with it as he would have expected.

He shrugged. 'I have nothing to say. I'm taking a share

of fish to eat regardless.'

Ruhan erupted. 'Did you not hear me? I don't care what you believe, but what if you bring ruin to us all?'

'At least I'll have a full stomach.'

Ruhan was attacking Ashan before any could react, grabbing him by his clothes and shouting in his face. Adorjan and Nghi were on Ru quickly and pulling him away, as best they could, against Ruhan's strength. Ashan was unbothered and looked at Ruhan with an expression close to disgust.

Cadeo looked on at the scene unfolding, ever unnerved. It was perhaps on this very shore that the first instance of the disunity occurred so many years ago. He remembered the horrible feeling as he saw the people act in anger for the first time, and the unease that followed as any peace among them faded. As he looked now on the farmers and the fishermen, he saw the makings of disunity again. It was a most terrifying sight.

He mustered as much air into his lungs as they would hold and shouted at the top of his voice, 'Enough!'

Ruhan looked up, surprised and immediately softened when he saw Cadeo, only now noticing him, and he released Ashan. The three looked at Cadeo with some surprise. None had seen him for days now, and it was the first time any had heard him shout. They were unsurprisingly stunned.

'Each has their own choices to make and consequences to bear,' he said. 'Should your consciences trouble any of you so, then do not dismiss it. Leave the fish. But do not deprive the others of either the gift or curse they may be bringing upon themselves.'

Ruhan looked distraught. 'But Cadeo...' he started.

'But,' Cadeo continued. 'Any who choose to take the fish ought to work on restoring the paddies to repay the gift Adorjan claims this to be, under his guidance. Starting from tomorrow, with no exceptions.'

His people looked at each other. Though some looked distraught still, Cadeo could see them soften. Some of the tension left the air.

'We still have plenty of salt,' Nghi added. 'For any who take fish, I will bring some and help you preserve it.'

Adorjan was the first to move. He filled his sack with fish until it was close to bursting. He looked at Vada, who had been quiet until then.

'Auntie,' he said. 'Please--'

Vada took hold of the sack before Adorjan could say another word. 'So long as you come home and share them with me.'

'I will.'

Ruhan scoffed and walked away. 'This is a mistake,' he said as he went. 'We invite more omens to make our hardships even worse. We'll all regret this.'

Cadeo frowned as he watched him walk away. Part of him was proud that Ruhan had kept the faith and respect for nature that he helped instil in him, but Ruhan was always abrasive and at times judgemental for it. He hoped that his mind would change soon, and that he would take his share of fish too, for better or for worse. Cadeo would talk to him about it after he had calmed down.

The others left, one by one. Vada and Nghi took a share with them. Kien seemed to ponder for a moment before she left empty-handed, as did Lihn and Thi.

Ashan was the last to leave. He acknowledged Cadeo with a nod and approached him. Cadeo had not seen him since that storm. He had meant to thank him for being by his side when Gratus was found. But he felt nervous now that they were together, perhaps also ashamed. He began to realise how much that act meant to him and the kindness Ashan showed in being there with him. Despite their differences and how much disdain Cadeo knew he had for him, he was there. Cadeo wanted to tell him that he would never forget it.

But Ashan put his empty sack in Cadeo's hands before he could speak, then quietly took his leave.

Cadeo looked down at the sack, now alone on the shore. He stood there for a long time, contemplating Ashan's wordless message that he'd heard loud and clear —*make up your mind too.*

Cadeo pondered this over and over, but he could not deny that he came to the same conclusion regardless of how much he thought it through.

He filled his sack with fresh fish.

Vada had no doubts in taking the fish. She was glad that Adorjan didn't either, else she would have force-fed him his share if she had to. She walked home with the heavy sack of fish on her back. It felt wonderful to smile again. The last couple of nights had been spent fighting against her anxiety for Adorjan and the future. She constantly reminded herself that he just needed time and space to process the madness of the storm, as did she. But it was far more difficult to reconcile with what she had just seen.

She could not get that image of the colossal creature she saw that night out of her head. It followed her as far as her dreams and nightmares, followed her to Burial Hill as she tended for the flowers, followed her home—it deprived her of even a moment of peace.

All that kept her grounded was knowing that Adorjan would need her in the coming days, that she would need to be a strong shoulder for him. She thought that he was still the soft and delicate child she had held in her arms mere decades ago, in the pleasant days her sister still lived and loved him dearly. But now, she had a cause for rejoicing.

She had witnessed Adorjan becoming more of the man she wished him to become—one who stood firm with integrity, not swayed by opposition, who was willing and able to fight for his conviction. A man who *had* any conviction to speak of. She was curious what had befallen him during the last couple of days to have caused this aspect of him to rise to the surface, but she decided she would never ask him lest she deprive the man of keeping his journey of growth as his own. There was nothing for her to do but smile, for the first time since the storm.

Vada boiled water the moment she got to her hut and cooked one small fish for herself. She forgot to add herbs or salt in her eagerness to, yet it tasted incredible to her after so long without.

There was no sign of Adorjan before she finished her meal or in the hours after, but that was okay with her. There was plenty of fish for him regardless of when he returned, and she had his word that he would do so. She decided to use her time practically and made for the Burial Hill, spurred on by a satisfied stomach.

The flowers on the hill had been mostly untouched by the recent winds and rain, as were the idols beside them. They were slightly misshapen, but they were otherwise as healthy and vibrant as ever.

Vada spent a few hours on that hill caring for the flowers, watering them and cutting away weed sprouts. They were strong, but the fog needed to pass soon and make way for sunlight, lest they starved and withered. Keeping them alive was exhausting, and at times she was tempted to abandon them. But they provided her with some purpose in what would otherwise be a boring life. As did Varyis.

She thought about him too, as she did most days, with sympathy. There was nothing else to be done for him but to ease his pain while his body deteriorated. He only had so long left to live. He didn't seem surprised when she had told him, as he had surely felt it for himself and known it was coming for years. For all the pity she had for him, she was far more concerned for Umbra. She was a remarkable girl—resilient, smart, dutiful. But the day was coming soon when she would have neither a father nor a mother, and Vada didn't know how such a young girl would cope. *I'll be the closest to her one day,* she had accepted. *She'll need to lean on me, too. Still so many hardships ahead.*

Vada went home soon before sunset. Though it was already night, Adorjan had still not returned. She was instead greeted by a bizarre and putrid smell from inside.

It filled the hut and clung to its every surface. It was a familiar smell that took her a moment to recall with its intensity. It was the smell of food that had gone rotten.

It was the smell of a fish crate that had not been emptied in many days.

Vada looked at the wooden crate she had poured the fish into. Flies circled it and were frantically crawling inside.

The smell grew more intense the closer she got to the crate. She gagged and covered her mouth.

She opened the crate.

All the fish she had brought home were rotten. Their grey scales had turned brown, and their scales were reduced to ash.

Even with her nose and mouth covered, she was not prepared for the putrid stench that hit her. It was like being buried in the entrails of a long-dead sea creature.

She gagged again and ran outside to vomit. The smell followed her even there.

She groaned and gagged once more. Any of the ease she felt from the day had been shattered, replaced with anxiety and confusion.

Vada forced herself to go inside again, forced herself to confront the crate. She managed to throw the rotten fish out into the sea from her hill home and left the crate outside.

All the while, she thought about why. She thought about how such deterioration was possible in less than a day. No sensible thought came to mind. She instead resigned to filling the sack with fish from the shore again in the morning.

She tried to will herself to sleep. Most of the smell had gone from the hut by the time she lay down, but it was strong enough to keep her awake.

In the dead of that night, she was disturbed and startled by a voice outside her hut, whispering her name.

She thought for a moment of Adorjan, but realised he had no reason to call out, especially not in such a soft and timid way.

Someone called her again, a little louder. She got up

from her floor-bed. A visitor was standing in the front.

'Ruhan?' She could not see his face but recognised his uniquely thick hair and beard even in the dark. He stood by the crate, with one hand on her hut. He looked as though he were leaning on it.

'...can I come in?' he asked. He moved without waiting for an answer and stood awkwardly by Vada's cooking pot. She lit a piece of wood for them, and the light showed Ruhan clearly. He looked exhausted. His eyes were barely open, as though he were either in a daze or half asleep.

He sank to his knees before Vada could talk and set his forehead on the ground.

'I...' he began. 'Please, let me have fish.'

Vada gently lifted Ru's head. 'Don't bow, Ruhan.'

'Cadeo,' Ruhan said. 'He...he told me that I was too judgemental, that I treated you and the others harshly. I'm sorry. I know I don't have any right to stop you from doing what's right by you. You were right to take the fish. You, Adorjan, Ashan, the others—you were all right. Please, I know brought a heavy sack home. Let me have some.'

'But there's fish on the shore,' Vada said sympathetically. 'Why would you need ours?'

Ruhan looked Vada in the eye. He had a look of dejection, of a man at the end of his rope.

'I already tried,' he said. 'But the fish were rotten. Every one of them. They fell apart in my hands. And the *smell*...'

Vada backed away from him with renewed horror. '*Rotten*,' she echoed.

'What?'

'The fish. Mine turned rotten, too. All of them. I...don't understand.'

Utter defeat crept onto Ruhan's face as the meaning of

Vada's words sank into him. He was on the verge of tears while he looked at her. Vada wanted to reach out to him, to embrace him and reassure him. Yet she had neither the words nor the energy to do so, with their shared words sinking in for her too—*we've no more food to eat again. We're doomed to starve.*

The two looked at each other silently with shared and deepening despair.

Then Ru's face changed.

A new face was on him as he rose to his feet. It was a look that put Vada on edge.

'You lie,' he said, still looking Vada dead in the eye.

'Ruhan?'

'You lie.' He repeated. His eyes darted about the hut, from one crate to another, all of them boxes he had built for Vada himself. 'The fish...I can still smell fish. You must have--'

He opened a crate. It only had utensils. Then another with medicinal herbs.

'Ruhan,' Vada pleaded, fear starting to creep into her.

He did not reply. He kept searching, growing more aggressive. He tipped crates over and threw whatever his hands fell on. Falling wood and clattering utensils echoed in the hut, each sound making Vada flinch. Incoherent mumbling turned into frenzied shouting. He cursed, he accused, he screamed out sounds with no meaning.

Vada saw a madman before her. There was only a shadow of the boy she had witnessed grow into the most dependable and kindest of men. There was no pleading or reasoning with him.

Her instincts take hold of her.

She leapt onto him and struck at him with all her

strength.

He swung wildly and struck her on the chin, knocking her onto the floor-bed. The hut went darker in her eyes as she bled from her mouth. She realised her jaw was broken, as her scream was agonising.

Ruhan looked down on her.

'It's *you*,' she heard him say. He drew closer to her. 'And the others. I told you that fish was an omen. I told you they would bring evil on us. You ignored me. You've doomed us.'

His words were hard to comprehend as she fought to stay conscious, but the look on his face was clear. She had no name for it, never having the misfortune to witness it before that night. Only two words came to her mind — madness and malice.

The man who wore that face came descending on her, lashing out with something he held in his hands.

Vada screamed with all her being, with no one to hear her.

The scream was then silenced.

TWENTY TWO

There was a putrid smell in the dead of the night. Cadeo woke up confused and momentarily lost, not yet accustomed to the new surroundings of Nghi's hut.

He followed the smell to the sack of fish he had left hanging just outside. He had done so at Nghi's request, since he had shared Ruhan's fear of their sudden appearance. Nghi had said that letting the fish inside would invite evil into the home. Cadeo relented and agreed the fish would remain outdoors and be cooked on an open fire outside.

Now the sack reeked. Every fish inside had rotted. They looked and smelled as though they had aged weeks in a mere few hours.

Cadeo took the sack down to the coast and threw them into the sea, baffled. He wondered what could have befallen them, whether it had been a mistake to leave them outdoors, but he could think of no good reason for it.

On the coast, the smell clung to the air, lingering in the fog even after the fish were gone. He set eyes on what now lay in the sand and saw that it was not only his own fish that had gone rotten. They were all the same—decrepit, fly-ridden, turning brown.

He immediately remembered Ruhan's words and his vehement declaration that they were evil. Unable to deny what his eyes saw, Cadeo thought that Ruhan may have been right, may have proven to be wiser than him. *It was naive to think the sea would give us a gift while the land still torments us.*

He looked down on the fish, once more reminded of the unknown forces his people were up against.

Then he heard his name in the wind. It was uttered as a scream.

'Cadeo!' he heard again—bloodcurdling and desperate.

'Cadeo!' He made for the source of the voice a ways up the hills.

Nghi, Kien, Lihn and Thi were all drawn out of their huts by the scream. They followed him up the hill, where Ashan and Nota were together.

'What's happened?' Cadeo asked.

'We don't know either,' Ashan said.

Cadeo's name was called out again, closer. He now recognised the voice, even in its uncharacteristic panic. It was Ruhan's voice.

His people followed him to the source.

They first saw Adorjan, who had followed the voice before the others, now standing frozen.

Then everyone saw what he saw. Even in the dark of night, Ruhan looked wrong.

He whimpered at the sight of Cadeo, with his eyes full of tears. Blood soaked his clothes and covered his skin, with splatters on his face and in his hair.

He held out his hands before him, reaching out to Cadeo.

'Cadeo,' Ruhan said once more when he was right before him.

Cadeo laid his hands on his shoulders, unable to speak in his shock.

'I...' Ruhan said. His eyes were vacant, and his voice was little more than a whisper. 'I did something...bad.'

'What?' Cadeo managed to say. 'What's happened?'

Ruhan laid his hands on Cadeo, smearing blood on his clothes. He couldn't look him in the eye.

'Vada...'

Cadeo's eyes shot wide, and his blood froze. No more words were needed.

A tragedy had now befallen this island.

His eyes went to Adorjan, who was trembling as his eyes widened.

He bolted off into the fog. None tried to stop him.

'Vada,' Ruhan repeated.

He could not say anything more. He fell to his knees and sobbed uncontrollably.

Adorjan had never run so fast, yet the trek to his aunt's home felt never-ending. He was deprived of thoughts or reason on his way, utterly lost in panic and dread.

He finally saw her hut and slowed to a walk. Every step suddenly felt like his feet were made of stone. This place took on a new appearance in the fog. It was ominous and not of this island. It looked more like an abandoned shack, a mere building, than a loving home.

Adorjan dragged his feet to the entrance.

He forced himself inside.

There was the smell of blood.

He saw what used to be Auntie Vada.

She was a gut-wrenching sight, sprawled out and covered in red. Her face was swollen, distorted, caved in from broken bones. She was unrecognisable.

Adorjan approached her.

He laid his hand on her.

He embraced her.

He pleaded incoherently.

He embraced her again.

He screamed.

He cursed.

He fell silent.

He finally embraced her again.

Through it all, one clear yet illogical thought gripped him—he would not shed a single tear.

He succeeded. What ought to have been devastation and grief was overcome by rage.

Adorjan was outdoors again, with an unyielding purpose and a broken mind. He broke into a run. Time passed like a blur on his way.

He laid eyes on the fiend who had killed her. Her fresh blood was still all over him. He dared to weep.

Adorjan's hands were on Ruhan. They wrapped around his throat and squeezed it with all their strength.

Ruhan looked at him with fear. He didn't care. He squeezed harder.

Ashan was on Adorjan and pulling him away.

Adorjan screamed. He couldn't hear whatever Ashan and the others were saying to him. He screamed over the turmoil of his people. He screamed so hard that his lungs hurt. His hands still dug into Ruhan's flesh.

Then he was slammed onto the ground, hitting his head. He was pinned down, and his head ached. Everything went blurry.

He held onto his consciousness through rage alone.

The strength and will left his body. He lay helplessly.

He refused to cry.

Cadeo watched on as Ashan held Adorjan to the ground until he fell silent.

The others had long since backed away from Ruhan and Cadeo, seeing a monster before them. They stood at a distance and muttered in a panicked undertone. Ruhan stared at Adorjan, shocked and with bloodshot, dazed eyes. The change in the air was palpable and immediate.

Cadeo held his head in his hands as he felt it was bursting, smearing Vada's blood on his temple. He could not fail to see this disaster as the inception it would inevitably be—mass fear and doubt in one another would spread, giving birth to hysteria and disunity. That disunity amid starvation and the maddening fog would make life together a nightmare, a time of utter misery and terror, a time where death may become preferable to life.

Ashan's voice broke through Cadeo's lamentations.

'Rope,' he was saying. No one showed any signs of hearing him.

Ashan resigned and took off his top. He tore it into a long strip and bound Adorjan's hands behind his back.

Adorjan breathed heavily and groaned into the ground, but he did not resist.

Cadeo looked at the blood-soaked Ruhan. His heart bled as Ruhan looked back at him. He was back to being the boy, the man, he knew—the man who was dependable and abrasive, but kind and gentle. The man who, beyond his calm demeanour and intimidating vibe, was afraid. The man Cadeo had raised to keep traditions, superstitions and faith as his sanctuary. The fruits of Cadeo's labour stood before him, broken and covered in blood, as the man who would tear his people apart in the days to come. This was Cadeo's fault, too.

A shepherd protects, nurtures and guides all under his care, Cadeo heard again in Gratus' sweet, stern voice. *A shepherd does not wait to be acknowledged before doing his duty…does not blame those under his care for losing their way, he makes haste to guide them back…*

…you feel so far away from who you want to be.

Cadeo allowed the instincts of a shepherd to guide him. The burden of such a duty was heavy indeed.

'Nghi,' he said. 'Please get some rope.'

It started to rain. The islanders gathered around Ruhan, who was bound by Nghi's rope. They looked down on him quietly, in shock and disbelief, as he finished his confession. He spoke impassively with his tears spent while he admitted everything—how he had gone to her hut for the fish he had only hours ago rejected, how he had beaten Vada to a pulp with firewood when she had no fish to share, and how he kept on beating her even after she died for as long as his anger lasted.

He confessed it all and was met with silence heavy with incredulity.

All of it over a chance at a meal, which Vada did not even have for herself.

The disdain for Ruhan, for his actions and his madness, was palpable. None looked upon him with more disdain than Adorjan, who stood at some distance beside Ashan, with his hands bound. His heavy breathing was like an echoing scream compared to the silence of his people. None wanted to speak, and none knew what would come next.

None but Cadeo. He looked upon Ruhan alongside his people, not with anger or disgust, but with sadness. As he had watched Ashan bind his hands and feet, Cadeo had the time to solidify his conviction. Action had to be taken to prevent this disaster from birthing far worse. Yet, his wisdom and his feelings for Ruhan were at war with one another. They fought to reason on his behalf, to find some way to spare him the consequences of his madness, to show him mercy.

But the more Cadeo tried, the more he accepted that there was no reasoning against that which was right before his face. He could not deny his wisdom.

It was all Cadeo could do to resist screaming out in anger and sorrow. It was a difficult step forward to take.

'What now?' someone finally asked. All eyes turned to Lihn as she spoke. 'What are we to do? It is tempting to wait like this forever, but...'

Lihn unwittingly gave Cadeo a gentle nudge to break his internal strife. *You postpone the inevitable,* he told himself. *Do not endanger your people with inaction.*

He finally spoke.

'Ruhan must die.'

The words were even more agonising to spit out than he had imagined.

Cadeo felt everyone's eyes on him and looked into Ruhan's. They showed shock and fear in equal measure. It was a face Cadeo had prepared himself for.

He steadied himself. It was a moment of the utmost importance—demonstrating to his people what conviction looked like. Being closer to the man he had long wished to be for them.

'Ruhan must die for this,' Cadeo said, louder.

'Cadeo…' Lihn said, her voice quivering. 'H-how could you even—?'

'It is how it must be,' Cadeo plainly said. 'You all know of the famine from what your predecessors told you. I am all that is left of it now, the only one who lived it for myself. I tell you—I saw the madness that comes from starvation, how trust crumbles after a single act. Fear, doubt and suspicion take hold of us, and that will inevitably lead to more tragedy. Then, as those tragedies happen, they become…normal. Then it is only so long until we face complete collapse. Ruhan has done something unforgivable, and it will corrode us if we allow it to. We cannot allow this to lead to any more tragedies. Ruhan will serve as…a deterrent.'

'But *death*, Cadeo?' Nghi said.

'Ruhan killed, and must be killed in turn. I wish it were not so, but it is. We cannot treat murder as anything less than deserving of death.'

Cadeo's words sank into his people and were taking root. He saw and understood the conflict in them, yet the words were ringing as true to them, just as they had done for him. Their despair only gave Cadeo more conviction and more affirmation that his decision was a wise one. Now that they had been spoken to without any refute, his people would be united despite this tragedy. They would have each other to grieve with and eventually move on from the pain.

'You are truly willing to kill?' Lihn eventually said. 'Just as Ruhan did?'

'I'll do it.'

The words were spat with pure venom. Adorjan said them not with pleading, but as a demand. There was a yearning in his tone that bordered on glee. Cadeo understood and even empathised with his anger. He imagined if it had been Gratus whom Ruhan had killed, or Amado and Adra. He would have done anything to pay their killer back in kind. Cadeo did not have the heart or desire to deny Adorjan this chance.

He also doubted that he would have enough conviction to kill Ruhan himself. *I just pray that this will give you some measure of peace, Adorjan.*

'Not happening.' Ashan spoke before Cadeo could.

'Yes, it is,' Adorjan said through gritted teeth. 'I'll do it. No one else.'

'I won't let you.'

'It's not up to you!'

'Ashan,' Cadeo interjected, with a calmness but the same sureness of voice. 'I'm truly sorry. Ruhan is close to you, I know. He is close to me, too. But he must die for everyone's sake.'

'Not by Adorjan's hand,' Ashan said, unfazed by Adorjan's outburst.

'Don't you dare deny this of me,' Adorjan spat with

even more vitriol.

'Do you hear yourself? *Deny.* You wouldn't kill Ruhan righteously, but because you *want to.* I won't stand by while you kill out of revenge or spite. If he has to die, I won't let it be out of hatred.'

'Ashan,' Adorjan spat. 'My aunt Vada couldn't rest unless--'

'*I'll* do it, Adorjan. And I'm not asking your permission. Your hands are already tied.'

Adorjan stared dead into Ashan's eyes with contempt. He fell quiet with the truth in Ashan's last words being undeniable. Cadeo also saw the truth in them and felt some shame that he was so willing to allow Ruhan to die in the name of anger, that he was so quick to concede that he would do the same himself.

Ashan knelt before Ruhan, who looked to be in a quiet trance. 'You're to die for killing Vada,' Ashan said. He spoke softly. 'I'll kill you myself, and I'll do it without anger or hatred. And we'll allow you to choose the place. Where do you want your last moment to be?'

'Do not be so cruel as to force a man to choose his death,' Cadeo said firmly. He allowed himself to give some way to compassion one more time and laid a hand on Ruhan's shoulder. 'We do not do this because we want to, but because we must. I...my love for you has not changed and never will. This will always be your home, and we will always be your people. I...will play the song for you in your final moments to remind you of that, Ruhan.'

Ruhan looked up to the sky. He had no more pleading or fear in his face, only despondency. He looked up quietly for a long while, so long that Cadeo wondered if the words had reached him at all.

'The sea,' he then said. 'I love the sea…let me die in it.'

Cadeo walked beside Nghi, who carried the t'rung on his back.

Ruhan walked among the group. The descent from the hill to the shore was a silent one. The sea greeted them there with a beckoning tide. Nghi set down Cadeo's instrument in the sand. The time to play it again had come far sooner than he had thought, for the very worst of reasons. Never had the t'rung been called upon to sing for so devastating a cause.

Ashan guided Ruhan to the water.

'Do you have anything to say?' Ashan asked. His tone was soft. He sounded dejected and exhausted.

Ruhan turned around and faced his people. He stood tall, and his eyes were piercing once again.

'I'm sorry,' he said. 'Truly. That means nothing now, I'm sure, but…I have to say it regardless. You…you've always been good to me. You all gave me a life to cherish. I just…regret that it will end this way. Cadeo is right—you will survive this famine together, just as our predecessors did the last.

'And Adorjan. You hate me, as well you should. But don't hate Ash for this. He's saved you from becoming like me.'

Adorjan said nothing. Nor did anyone else.

Ruhan faced the sea after one final bow of his head.

'Sorry to have you do this,' Ruhan quietly said to Ashan.

Ashan's face softened at those words, seemingly against his will. 'Did you just apologise? This isn't like you at all.'

Ruhan grunted. He allowed himself a small smile despite it all. 'I won't forget that attitude of yours. I'm glad it will be you if it has to be anyone.'

'It was my choice,' Ashan said. '*I* had me do this. You didn't have me do anything. Don't be sorry to me, of all people.'

Ruhan looked Ashan in the eyes for the last time. 'Even now, when you're about to have my blood on your hands, you're trying to make me feel better. You're one of a kind, Ash. Don't ever change.'

Ashan laid a hand gently on Ruhan's shoulder. 'Farewell, Ru.'

'...Farewell, Ash.'

Ashan guided Ruhan into the foggy sea.

Cadeo played a melody.

It was the same song he had played thousands of times through his life to guide the fishermen home at sundown. For the first time, he played it for someone's departure, knowing he would never bring them home again. He wondered if he would ever be able to play this song again.

Ashan dunked Ruhan in the water, holding him there by his head.

Cadeo closed his eyes tightly. It was all he could do to fight back tears. *You must not cry now,* he reminded himself. *Your people look to you, now more than ever, for strength.*

He played on.

The melody swelled and drowned out the sounds Ruhan made in the water. Cadeo's music was all his people could hear as they quietly watched another tragedy in action.

They watched until the music ended. No more sounds

were coming from the water.

That night, with a heavy and crippled heart, Cadeo played the most beautiful music he had ever made.

TWENTY THREE

Adorjan had given his aunt's home a wide berth in the days leading up to her death. In hindsight, it was stupid of him. He always knew that a loving and warm home awaited him here and that Vada would be delighted to have him there with her. Yet, he had instead decided to sleep by the paddies, surviving by eating bugs and roaches. He worked tirelessly from sunrise until long after, yet made little progress. Spending the night outdoors somehow convinced him that he was working as hard as he could.

Finally, Adorjan made his way to the hut in the morrow after her death, after telling his people not to join him in preparing his aunt's body.

There, he hesitated to enter. Her home was still in disarray, her body lying on the floor bed. Flies had gathered around her. Her blood on the ground had turned dark and dry. Adorjan couldn't enter yet, enraged and devastated as he was at the sight of her.

He instead gathered his aunt's firewood into a stack outside. He'd never built the burning bed himself, but watched Ruhan build enough of them to copy it himself.

After it was done, he finally forced himself into the hut. Adorjan didn't and couldn't look at his aunt's body for long, nor at the blood-splattered and ruined hut. He didn't allow himself to imagine what Ruhan had done in this place, or what Vada's last moments were. He allowed himself only to be moved by duty, as one without thought or compassion.

He carried the body outside. It was light and frail even in his weak arms. He set it on the burning bed. Then, he set the wood on fire. The flames tore through Vada's body, and its smoke reached as high as the clouds. Only when her body was consumed and turned to ash did Adorjan allow himself to feel again.

Memories flooded so quickly that they overwhelmed him—new memories of Vada imparting her wisdom to him in the kindest of ways and old memories of how she would feed him and ease him to sleep when he first became an orphan. Back then, she often reminded him that the world had not fallen apart, even if it would feel like it for a while. She had been right, as Adorjan's parents were only a distant memory to him now. His Auntie had become his mother and father.

He watched his aunt become lost to the elements. The rage in his heart burned anew with the realisation there would be no more of those memories to be made. His rage became hatred.

I hate this life.

He'd spent so long now living hungry and afraid from day to day that he could hardly remember what life was like before it all. No, even before that creature and the fog came to the island, herbs were all that had kept him sane and all that broke up his monotony. Life had never been pleasant, nor truly felt worth living.

I hate this island.

He called this place home, not because he belonged here, but because he had nowhere else. Adorjan hated even the paddies now, for as much as they gave him purpose, they now tore it away. Now, they were gone and perhaps always would be.

I hate these people.

He looked down at his hands that were balled up and turning red. Those were the hands that should have killed Ruhan. Now he was burdened with hatred for the man that could never be eased, with revenge now forever out of reach. He hated all his people for allowing it to happen. He hated Ashan for taking that right away from him.

And more than anyone, he hated himself. He spent too long alone, dwelling on his helplessness and despair, and allowed tragedy to happen. He should have been home to stop Ruhan. He was now truly alone, and it was his fault. Watching his home turn into a living nightmare against which he seemed to have no recourse, he blamed himself most of all.

I hate it all.

Long after Vada's body was reduced to ash, the fire raged still.

Ashan set the wooden burning bed alight on the isolated

shore, hardly believing he was doing so. Ruhan's body lay on it, his face a picture of peace and contentment, until it was consumed in flames.

No one else, Ashan bitterly scoffed. *Not a single person willing to burn him, nor to help me build this. Not even to attend the burning.*

At first, he had decided this would simply be practical —else, Ruhan would have to be buried, and there would be no one willing to help with that either. Now, while he watched Ruhan burn, Ashan was glad he had done this. It was what Ruhan would have wanted. It was always he whom the others left to burn the bodies, and Ashan now felt for himself how much a burden it was. For Ruhan to have found purpose in such a thing…Ashan hated practices like this even more now.

He could still feel the moment life left Ruhan's body, could still hear his groans from under the water, quietening until they were gone. He could still hear Cadeo's song being played on the beach, that melancholic melody that always came when he returned to land.

He had no words for those who stood on the beach, who had watched the execution at a distance, after the deed was done. Spineless. Placid. Cowardly. So quick to wash their hands of the ordeal and become passive observers. So comfortable to watch the death of their own, so long as it wasn't by their own hand.

Ashan had no delusions—he was now a murderer. And his supposed kin had allowed him to take on that burden. Even Nota. He couldn't call her a friend now. He couldn't stomach the thought of sleeping in her cave again. He would go back to sleeping on a boat, far from her and the others.

Ashan had no cause to wait by the fire any longer. He left Ruhan's body to the flames.

He returned to Quy's boat further along the same shore. There, he was met with the same strange sight he had seen the day before.

After seeing that shore for himself, where every one of the fish had decayed long before their time, it was even stranger to see this again.

The fish in Quy's boat were still fresh and preserved as though they were newly dead. Not a single one had begun to rot.

Nota pretended to be hard at work fulfilling her duty. Cadeo had reminded the others that they would meet on Burial Hill shortly before sundown—an implied order for Nota to prepare the figures before then.

In truth, Ashan had been right. The figures had been completed years ago. *Partly completed*. Nota had developed a habit of crafting them while those they represented were still alive. They wouldn't be detailed until after they died, then she'd add their tattoos and wrinkles, and carve their hair.

Neither Vada's nor Ruhan's figure had any detail yet. Nota had never been called upon to prepare two figures at once before. Looking at Vada's figure now, she hadn't aged much since Nota had first made it. She only needed to shape her impressively long hair, and it would be finished. Nota knew very little about Vada and had never cared enough to. She was a truly plain, boring person. Still, she could not help admiring the calm and tranquillity that followed her everywhere. She sometimes wondered what her secret was to having such a peaceful spirit. She even felt calm now while looking at her figure's face.

It was not so for Ruhan. Nota felt uneasy looking at his face now. He had always looked rough and brooding, ever since they were children. He was often crass, dismissive and abrupt, even to those who were far older than he. His locks of hair were thick and never well-kept, and she doubted he'd ever trimmed his beard. But he was quite soft at heart and ever willing to aid when it was within his power to do so. That only made his brutality all the more shocking to Nota. He would be remembered now more as a murderer than a helper for his people, and she saw the tragedy in that. But that wasn't what unsettled her most.

Soon, his wooden figure would be set in the ground alongside those colourful flowers to overlook the sea, along with his ancestors and his kin's ancestors. His people would mourn him for a short time on Burial Hill before returning to their homes and scraping together whatever morsels they could for dinner. Ruhan's brutality would be a short legacy, and even that would fade with time.

Yet, none would remember Ashan holding him under the water. None would remember how every person in this place had killed Ruhan through their inaction, including her own. *Especially* her own. She had understood Cadeo had said Ruhan had to die, but she was conflicted. *It would mean we are to be killers too,* is what she had reasoned at the time.

But she had said nothing. Perhaps her words could have changed something, or been futile, but she had never even tried.

Nota felt uneasy seeing his face because it was a reminder, not of his brutality or of Vada's death, but of her people's haste to kill in turn.

He would be a reminder of her unwillingness to protest, of her lack of conviction, for the rest of her life.

Though Cadeo had said this had to be done in the name of unity, Nota never felt so far from everyone else.

Nevertheless, she presently took Ruhan's figure into her hands along with her crafting knife and worked on reflecting his likeness with painstaking detail.

Umbra finally set Vada's knife down. Her hand ached, covered with fresh calluses and small cuts. But what she had made was worth it. She picked it up in her hands and admired her work.

It was a figure of her whale friend. It was far smaller than she had expected from the block of wood she started with. It had fins that were far too thin. The body looked more like a sea rock than a whale's smooth hide, but Umbra was proud of it.

She thought she could now understand why Nota loved making figures of people after they died and why setting them down on Burial Hill was so important to everyone. Umbra's work over the last few days ensured that her friend would be immortalised and never forgotten. She felt she would become wiser with this reminder of her failure to her friend, ever present in her home. She was glad she had not cut her hair now and would thank Vada when she saw her again.

Umbra enthusiastically showed the figure to her father the moment he woke from an early evening rest. He took it from her hands and looked at it tiredly.

'What *is* this?' he asked, confused. He laid it gingerly

on the ground when his hands started to tremble.

'…a whale,' Umbra said with a pout. 'Can't you tell?'

'A whale? Whales have fins like a fish. Why doesn't it have any? Or a tail?'

'It *does*. Look,' Umbra said, pointing out the thin blocks of wood at its side and rear. 'Here and here.'

Varyis grunted. 'And whales are meant to have smooth skin.'

Umbra caught a quick smirk on his face. She took the whale back with feigned outrage.

'Have you even seen a whale before?' Umbra asked as she put a fish from the sack in their boiling water pot.

'Once,' Varyis said. 'Back when I was a fisherman, long before you were born. I took your mother fishing that day, for some reason. It just happened that we saw it together. She was scared at first, with something like that coming out of the water all of a sudden. But she loved it after she realised it wouldn't hurt us. We stayed with it until sundown. That's the only—' Varyis suddenly paused, then looked intently at Umbra. 'Hold on. How do *you* know what a whale looks like?'

Umbra's eyes widened. She didn't think she had any reason to hide the whale anymore, yet still hesitated. She thought of it still lying at her favourite beach, and could not bear the thought of it being hacked apart and eaten. Now that her people had all those fish to eat, she didn't need to feel guilty about hiding the whale anymore.

'I don't think I do,' she said. She held it out for her father to see again. It didn't look anything like a whale.

Varyis broke into a smile, then he coughed. Then he smiled and grunted again.

Umbra's father had laughed. She had never heard it

before.

That's an awful laugh, Umbra thought to herself with a smile of her own. She cooked their fish dinner in good spirits, and they ate it together in warm silence.

I wonder what mine sounds like.

TWENTY FOUR

Sunset was masked in a thin veil of fog, just like all other sunsets. The orange sun pierced the mist as it kissed the sea and began to set for a new night.

Ashan visited Varyis and Umbra's home with a sack of fresh fish in hand. With all the other fish rotten now, Ashan alone had a valuable food source, yet he did not want to share it too readily. He could think of very few he would wish to share with after the last few days had left him feeling bitter and resentful. He figured that Varyis and Umbra alone were blameless, not present for Ruhan's execution. The decision to share his fish with them was an easy one.

He ran through a whole host of reasons and excuses that only his fish was still fresh and edible on the way, but the truth was that he didn't know, and that would be the only answer he could give.

Varyis was alone when he arrived, and he invited Ashan inside with more enthusiasm than usual. He appeared to be relaxed and happier than he could ever recall, even as he was deteriorating, little more than skin and bones. He and Umbra probably didn't know anything that had happened recently. He wondered if they even knew about Vada.

Varyis was the first to speak up as he noted Ashan's quiet manner, asking what was wrong. Ashan decided not to hold back anything. He told Varyis about the appearance of fish on the coast, of Vada's murder, and of how he had to kill Ruhan with his own hands. He described how the island was rife with paranoia and fear.

Varyis listened with remarkable calmness but with clear pain in both body and heart. He stared at the ground for a long time after Ashan finished. His hands trembled in his lap.

'What a disaster,' he eventually said.

Ashan nodded. Those were the only words that needed to be said.

'Umbra will be devastated about Vada.' Varyis continued.

Ashan nodded again. It had not escaped him that Umbra was soon to learn she had lost a second mother. It was far more than any child ought to experience. Life had truly turned cruel.

'You must be, too,' Ashan said. 'You must have gotten close after how long she cared for you.'

Varyis looked at the ground again with another soft grunt. He seemed to realise the same thing that Ashan had, as he was making his way to the hut—Varyis had no one left to help him. Without Vada, no one could ease his pain until his body eventually failed. Neither Varyis nor Ashan would say it aloud, but Ruhan had unknowingly killed *two* of his kin.

'Don't tell Umbra about any of this if you see her,' Varyis said. 'I'll tell her myself.'

'I won't. She's the only one left who doesn't know. Let's hope no one tells her before you do.'

Varyis furrowed his brow. 'Has this place changed you, too?' Ashan stared blankly at him. 'When did you turn so pessimistic? Look at you all hunched over and sorry-looking. This isn't like you at all. You look like *me.*'

'Can you blame me?' Ashan said. 'I just killed a friend with my own hands. Isn't that a good reason to feel a little sorry for myself?'

Varyis grunted. 'Do you blame yourself? Regret it?'

Ashan fell silent. He'd thought about those very questions himself. He had nothing to say because, truthfully, he had no idea.

'That's not like you either—hesitating like this,' Varyis said. 'I'm used to an Ashan who says and does what he needs to, feelings be damned. Killing your friend must be devastating—I can't even imagine how you feel. Don't let it overwhelm you. If what you see is overwhelming you, close your eyes to it. Stop thinking about what is happening around you and get back to doing what you always do—whatever you can.'

Ashan stared blankly again at Varyis as he spoke. 'That's...different, coming from you. Since when were you a philosopher?'

Varyis grunted again. 'You learn more than you think when you live in four walls. You have all the time in the world to think a little. By the way, were those fish for us?'

Ashan looked down at the sack in his hand that he'd forgotten about. 'I had enough to spare,' he said.

'Thanks, but we have more than enough for ourselves.'

Ashan looked at Varyis again. 'You *have*?'

'Umbra took more than enough from the shore. Our sack was overflowing with fish. It'll still be fresh for a few more days.'

Ashan stood and stared at Varyis, confused and, for a reason he could not place, anxious. *Ours are the only ones still fresh? Why? Why us?*

Ashan suddenly remembered Umbra standing alone on the shore the night he returned from the sea. She had been surrounded by the fish and elated. Only now did he see how bizarre it was. *What were you doing out on the shore that night, Umbra?*

Varyis' coughing brought Ashan back to the present.

'What's wrong now?' he asked.

'Nothing,' Ashan quickly said. 'You still need to have this roof repaired. May as well do it while I'm here.'

He climbed the hut and inspected the hole. It wasn't much work—just a few panels of wood. Enough to keep his hands busy while he could think.

From the roof, he saw two people together on the shore —Umbra and a man with her.

Umbra paced up and down the coast for much of the afternoon and into sundown with anticipation. She walked among strange rocks and shards, with the faint smell of fish in the air. Not a single fish remained on the shore, and her people must have all taken a share already. She hoped that a few days of good meals would lift their spirits.

She felt an elation she hadn't felt in many years, perhaps ever. Her stomach would be satisfied again come dinner time. She felt energetic, and her father was in the best of spirits. She had even heard her father laugh for the first time. Life was good.

Umbra looked out over the sea again, waiting for the sea to stir and the creature to rise from it. She'd anxiously been waiting all day to thank it. Its gift of fish had changed her life so swiftly that it took her until today to realise it.

She waited even until after sunset, but the creature didn't show again. Umbra didn't know how to call out to it or reach it, but she resolved to try each day until she met it again, for its kindness couldn't be enjoyed without gratitude.

Umbra heard the sound of soft footsteps in the evening before she returned home. Adorjan walked toward her. It took her a moment to realise it was him, as his hair was untied and flowed around his shoulders, which seemed to change the shape of his face.

'What are you doing out so late?' Adorjan muttered when they were face-to-face.

There was a different feeling in the air at the sound of Adorjan's voice and the look on his face. It wasn't just his free-flowing hair that seemed to change him—he felt nothing like the Adorjan that Umbra had come to know well and become fond of in their time in the paddies. His voice carried no zeal or affection. His face was bland and unchanging, as though it had been painted on. He reminded Umbra more of Cadeo in that moment.

She unconsciously took one step back.

'Adorjan,' she said. 'What's wrong? Are you okay?'

Adorjan replied with a furrowed brow and intense

stare.

He said with the same unchanged face, 'Vada died.'

Those two words were like a slow knife through Umbra's heart. So absurd were they that she didn't react at all at first.

Then her whole body went cold, and her head ached as her eyes shot open, as the word sank in. *Dead.*

'What...what happened?' she managed to ask.

'She died,' Adorjan repeated, with a cold and dead voice. 'I burned her body. She's gone.'

Those words threatened to bring tears to Umbra's eyes as the reality finally hit her. She'd never see Vada again. She'd never visit her home and stick up for her when she argued with her father. She'd never smell the herbs she always carried with her again. That lady, the one who cared for flowers, the woman who cared for her father, the one who stopped Umbra from cutting her hair and taught her never to lose herself—she was to become another wooden doll overlooking the sea on that creepy hill. Gone.

Umbra felt like breaking down and sobbing, as she had recently learned of the release of pain that came with doing so. But she stopped herself for the sake of the broken-looking man before her. His manner and appearance took on a new meaning. She went from being fearful of him to feeling only pity. No one else would be feeling more pain than Adorjan.

Umbra said the only thing she could think of, the only thing that she could associate with comfort.

'Would...you like to have dinner with us?' Even in her mind, it was a small and perhaps pointless gesture. But it was all she had to give.

Adorjan's face finally changed from empty to confused.

'Dinner?' he echoed. 'What dinner?'

'We still have fish from the shore,' she said. 'Do you want to come over?'

'You still have fish,' Adorjan said. His eyes glazed over as he said the words, then his look intensified as he fell silent. Though he still looked at Umbra, he did not meet her eyes and seemed to look beyond her.

'Adorjan?' Umbra said timidly.

Adorjan blinked. His vacant gaze was gone and replaced with one that was stern and equally unlike him.

'No. Thank you.' That was all he said before he paced off down the shore.

Umbra watched him go, confused but accepting. She felt she had seen Adorjan in deep grief for the first time, and such grief was probably new to him too. His strangeness was probably him finding his way of coping with the grief. *I hope he doesn't lose himself, too.*

As Umbra stood alone and devastated on the shore, she finally allowed herself to grieve. She broke down and wept.

Later that night, Ashan prepared Quy's decrepit old boat to sail once again. There was not much to be done, he knew. The vessel would soon be too far gone, too damaged and tired, to stay afloat anymore. All he could do was patch any holes and rot with fresh wood. He was already a far kinder owner than Quy ever was, doing what he could so that it at least *felt* seaworthy again.

He now cleared the rest of his fish from the deck of the rest of his fish. They were in a state of being freshly dead and refused to age. He piled them into Quy's old fishing net and hung them from rocks on the coast, inside a shallow cave-like hole in the hills. Then, he cleaned the deck again until the smell of fish was mostly gone—a waste of precious time, of course, yet it gave him time to be sure of his conviction. He cleaned for hours, all the while thinking with perfect clarity.

From that moment, Ashan had his eyes and thoughts set on Adorjan. He would be angry and in mourning for a long while yet. He would be unpredictable and even less stable than usual. Between his rage and a paranoid island, Ashan feared Adorjan was turning mad, too.

It was the sight of Adorjan and Umbra on the beach that he thought about. Ashan had been too far away to hear every word being shared between them, but he heard enough. Umbra looked afraid when Adorjan appeared. He saw Adorjan's manner change when Umbra mentioned the fish in her home. He looked stern. Adorjan was already pacing off down the coast and leaving Umbra alone when Ashan had decided he ought to interject. Whatever he said to her made her cry.

This place had changed. It would keep on changing. To go as far as berating a little girl, Adorjan showed what Ashan believed the others quietly felt but would never admit to—desperation, like starving wild animals. Reason and unity would quickly fade away in such a state, and base instincts to survive would be all that remained. Many of the most dangerous wild animals are peaceful when their stomachs are full and their homes are safe. All of them become killers when their lives and homes are under threat. Then, peace and unity become like abstract concepts in their minds.

Ashan was convinced, beyond doubt, that that was

what the people's minds were becoming—that of a starved animal. And in this passage of time, Ashan found that he was becoming so, too.

He turned to desperation, just like everyone else.

The desolate paddies were like a stranger to Thi, without the sun blazing harshly through a clear sky and the satisfying feeling of wet soil on her feet. Though she had worked in this place for many days and years, she looked at it as though it were the first time she'd ever been there. Despite that, she felt the same way here as she always did —nowhere else existed, and no other time mattered but right here and now. Serenity.

It was a timely reminder that Thi was alive, and she embraced it while it lasted.

Thi's characteristic smile crept onto her face, as easily as it always did. *What a wonderful life I had,* she reflected. *How wonderful to be a servant of nature, to use my hands to feed my kin, to toil and labour with joy each day. How wonderful it was when life was simple and predictable. What a worthy life to have lived.*

There were signs of desperate work on the paddies, with parts of it unearthed. Those parts were dry and dead. Someone had fought against the fate nature had for this place, and she respected it. *There's meaning to be found even in futility, I suppose.*

Thi looked down at the paddies once more from the tree branch that she had climbed on. It had not been so hard to accept the reality of what was happening in her home, for she had become adept at acceptance as she grew older.

She saw the wisdom in Cadeo's instruction and decisions. Ruhan would not be the last to lose his mind in the pursuit of survival, and it was wise to discourage others from following his footsteps.

But in truth, Cadeo's wisdom left Thi at the end of her rope. She had no sanctuary left, no one to share her pain with without creating more fear and disunity—not even Lihn, whom she so dearly loved. When Lihn had refused to take the fish on the coast, Thi saw that she was afraid, even if she would never say it. It would be cruel to burden her with more doubts and worries. Thi had lost her closest confidant.

She feared that her days might end in the way Ruhan's did, with some atrocity followed by futile remorse. It seemed an inevitable end to living in fear and pain.

More than anything, that colossal creature in the storm robbed Thi of any hope that peaceful and happy days would ever return. She'd seen it while fleeing to her hut, as the sea rose and swallowed the beach. She had to deny that it was anything but a deception of her eyes, but then Vada was killed. She thought that perhaps she was not the only one to see that thing on that day, and that it was also what drove Ruhan mad.

She prayed that she would be the last person that being would turn insane.

Thi looked out once more over the masked view of the familiar hills, the paddies and the trees around them. She smiled one more time. *Thirty-seven wonderful years. It was more than many others.*

She wrapped the rope around her throat.

She closed her eyes.

She stepped off the tree branch.

Her fall was brought to a firm stop by the rope.

Shadows masked her swaying body as the last of the sun disappeared.

TWENTY FIVE

Adorjan dreamed of a never-ending downpour and a colossal face made of clouds and shadows. He stood both on land and at sea at once, battered everywhere by the storm. The water relentlessly rose until there was no land left to stand on. His people drowned around him, calling out to him.

Adorjan. Adorjan, please.

No matter how hard he tried, he couldn't reach any of them. Each sank to the depths, and he heard his name screamed out in many voices as they disappeared. All the while, a man formed of clouds looked down on them and laughed.

Adorjan woke up from that nightmare in the early morning to the sound of his name. Kien knelt beside him in his aunt's hut and shook his shoulder.

'Adorjan,' she repeated. She was tearful, eyes bloodshot

and out of breath. 'Adorjan. Please…please, come.'

She took his hand and kept hold of him while Adorjan silently followed her, disoriented and frustrated.

'I'm sorry,' she said along the way. 'I didn't know… what to do.'

Adorjan nodded and said nothing.

He was led through the hills, along the familiar trek toward the rice paddies. Kien stopped before them and broke down in tears.

'I'm sorry,' she repeated. She pointed deeper into the paddies and managed only to say 'please…'.

Adorjan followed her direction. Only a few strides further, he saw the source of Kien's despair.

A body limply hung beside the nursery paddy from a fishing rope wrapped around its neck. Drenched in the trees' shadows, it appeared as just a silhouette. Adorjan saw that it was Thi as he drew closer.

Another death, Adorjan thought. *There'll be another burning soon.*

She had lost weight before she died, and she had already been a slim woman. Her skin was much paler than when she had last worked in the paddies, and her long, locked hair had gone brittle. She had already begun looking like a corpse while she was still alive.

Yet, on her aged face, she was smiling. Adorjan believed she found it easier to smile than to have no expression at all. He was incredulous that she still smiled and would always do so.

You were in so much pain that you wanted to die, yet you died smiling.

It was a thought Adorjan couldn't begin to comprehend.

Umbra ate breakfast silently with her father. The fish was still as fresh as the day she found them. She boiled it with seaweed and some salt. Their rice was finally finished, and the fish was all they had left.

She struggled with breaking the silence, knowing how hurt her father would be to find out about Vada's death. In the middle of the night, she had decided that she would tell her father in the morning, but it was difficult to speak now. It was painful to wound someone with words.

Varyis sighed and gingerly laid down his almost empty bowl by his feet.

'Umbra, there's something you need to know,' he said. 'Ashan came by here yesterday while you were out. A lot has been happening on the island, a lot that you don't know. He told me...I'm sorry. Vada has passed away.'

Umbra felt relief—her spirits unexpectedly lifted. She almost smiled.

'You already knew,' she said more than she asked.

Varyis squinted. '*You* knew?'

'Adorjan told me.' She thought about the state he was in and how inconsolable he was. She thought about him waking up this morning without Vada with him. 'He was so sad.'

'I see,' Varyis said. 'How do *you* feel?'

Umbra looked up at him again, taken aback. 'Me?'

'You were fond of Vada, weren't you? You won't remember when your mother died, so this must be your first time losing someone you love so much. How do you feel?'

How do I feel? She had not been asked that question in

many years. It was difficult for her to answer.

'I wish…I saw her more while she was still here. But I feel like smiling when I think about her, and it feels like she is still here with me. I just…feel strange. I know I won't see her again, but it just doesn't feel real.'

'Mm,' Varyis nodded. 'That's what *grief* feels like. Our feelings aren't meant to make sense when we lose someone. Death never feels real.'

'Isn't it wrong, though?' Umbra asked. 'Adorjan must be feeling worse than me. It feels wrong to feel so sad myself.'

'Well, I'm sad, too. I'll miss her coming over. I'll miss her getting on my case about brooding or whatever nonsense she wanted to say. Don't feel guilty for missing someone you care about. Never do.'

Umbra listened and pondered this for a moment. Then, she dared to ask a question she feared was out of line.

'Did you miss mother, too?'

Varyis' eyes went wide, but he didn't seem angry— only surprised. Then, his face and voice softened.

'Yes, I did,' he said. 'I still do. Always.'

Umbra nodded. She welcomed the silence that followed and finished her breakfast.

The islanders stood around Thi's body and watched as Adorjan took her down and set her on her back beside the paddies. Her characteristic smile remained. She looked at peace, like she was in a deep sleep. The marks of the rope around her neck were the only sign of her passing.

Cadeo was struck by how the sound of silence could take different forms. In times of relative prosperity, silence was intimate and warm, especially during hardship and mourning. All were embraced by a shared blanket of silence that eased their sorrow. He remembered the tone of it changing when Quy had passed. Though the silence was heavier, it still brought with it a gift of togetherness as Quy's figure was set, and there was still a celebration of his life along with the mourning. That felt so very long ago now.

The present silence in the paddies was different. There was no warm embrace to be felt—only cold despair.

Cadeo wished that no one else had to see Thi in this state, but after Kien searched the island for him and called his name so loudly, it was unavoidable that the others would follow them here. Now, Nghi, Kien, Adorjan and Lihn were all there at the dead paddies to see Thi.

'We're dying,' Lihn said, finally breaking the heavy silence. 'We're just dying, and there is nothing to be done.'

She said out loud what Cadeo and the others likely thought to themselves. It was impossible to deny the truth of her words. This was the slow, painful death of a whole people, with hope of survival drifting ever further away. *There are so few of us left now,* Cadeo thought as he looked around at his people.

'Maybe Thi was right to do this,' Lihn continued. Her voice was flat and lifeless. 'No food to eat, no paddies, no end to this fog, fish going rotten on the shore. Ruhan was right, too—something evil has come for us. Something that must hate us to torment us like this. Perhaps dying on our own terms is better than waiting for it in agony.'

Cadeo looked up at Lihn in instinctive, fleeting outrage. *How dare you speak of throwing your life away,* he thought. *How dare you spread such a thought to your people, to deprive them of hope?*

But he said nothing, for he had no retort. His outrage faded as he realised that he was coming to believe her words, too. And he saw how deep her pain must have been to say such words.

Thi would be survived by Lihn, who was close enough to her to be called blood. But Lihn didn't cry now. She stood before the body of her best friend, drained of what Cadeo could only describe as her spirit. He felt nothing but empathy for her and knew the feeling of being inconsolable very well. He would pray for her, and that time would heal her, too. *That's all I can do, as ever—wait.*

He felt the absence of all the people they had lost. Each had a richness, a quality that shone only brighter in their passing. Quy had his dependability and near-naive, contagious optimism. Gratus had a blend of near infinite wisdom and softness that made her a sanctuary to all. Vada was both playful and stern, a guiding light in every life she touched. Ruhan had a quiet confidence and efficiency that made all feel safe and secure, knowing that whatever was broken could be rebuilt. Thi was unassuming and meek, proof that contentment, happiness, and peace were possible in this place.

Such personal reflection and loving memory of his people was the best Cadeo could do for them while all else crumbled.

'We can't just keep going like this,' a voice said. All turned to the source—Adorjan. He looked as stern as he had since Vada's passing. 'Look how many have died. Look how we starve and wait for our deaths to come. Will we just keep on waiting after this?'

'What else is there to do?' Nghi said. 'No one here's

blind, Adorjan. We all see what is happening. We all feel it and know how little hope we have left. Nature will have its way with us, and we are powerless against it.'

'I'm not content with that,' Adorjan said. 'No one should be.'

Nghi grew agitated. 'We're not. What will you do about it, then? What can any of us do?'

Adorjan looked dead into Nghi's eyes, unmoved. Cadeo felt uneasy in the sureness that was unlike him.

'The storms, the dead fish, the destroyed paddies— none of this is the will of nature. So, it all must have a cause. Rather than waiting to die, we should find out what it is and stop it.'

'What are you trying to say, Adorjan?' Kien asked. 'What cause?'

'Umbra,' Adorjan said. A chill went through Cadeo at the sudden sound of her name. 'We should start with Umbra.'

'*Umbra,*' Kien echoed.

'Adorjan,' Cadeo said, sternly. 'What is the meaning of this? Do you truly intend to accuse a mere child?'

'I have good reason to,' Adorjan said, unrelenting. 'Go to her hut and you will find fresh fish. The same fish we took from the coast days ago. Ours rotted, but Umbra's didn't. Strange, isn't it, that only she was spared from this evil? We need only see for ourselves and demand that she explain herself.'

The people looked at each other again and murmured among themselves, mostly grunting in accord.

'We've nothing to lose,' Kien aptly said.

Adorjan's words immediately raised their spirits in some small way.

Yet with the subtle change in the air from heavy grief to a morsel of hope, Cadeo felt anything but optimistic. *A mere child, Adorjan. What do you mean to do?*

Cadeo was powerless to prevent what followed, his people pulled along by the potency of Adorjan's sureness. He and his people descended from the rice fields and made for the coast, toward Varyis and Umbra's hut.

'Not all of us are needed just to check for fish,' Cadeo said as they neared the hut.

'Everyone needs to see the fish with their own eyes,' Adorjan said.

'And it takes only one of us to bring the sack outside. At the very least, let us not impose on them more than we have to.'

'I'll go in alone, then,' Adorjan said.

'No, not you,' Cadeo said firmly. He spoke again before Adorjan could protest. 'A woman would put a little girl and her elderly father at ease more than you would. Kien, would you mind?'

Kien approached the hut alone. She first called out, then entered when there was no reply.

She appeared outside again very quickly and empty-handed, looking distraught.

'They're not in here,' she said. 'Neither of them. There's no fish either.'

Adorjan stormed into the hut when Kien had barely gotten her words out. Cadeo and the others were on his heels.

Adorjan stood in the middle of the hut when Cadeo entered. As Kien had said, there was no sign of Varyis or Umbra, nor any fish. Cadeo had very rarely come here, having little cause to do so, but he had never seen Varyis' floor-bed without him on it. He was certain that his condition had worsened to the extent that he could not walk anymore, and he was unable to care for himself in his state. It was no secret that Varyis did not have much life left in him.

The hut smelled of both freshly dead fish and soup. Though the cooking pot was gone, it was clear that fresh fish had been cooked here very recently—fish that should have gone rotten.

Soon after the islanders left the hut, Adorjan declared a search for Umbra and her father.

There were no objections. The hunt for the two of them began.

Ashan pondered over the sudden, aggressive storms that appeared the last time he set sail, which had rocked the boat and capsized him. He remembered how the creature of shadows appeared with an intense glare and the *sound* that tore away Ashan's consciousness as he sank.

His inexplicable survival had gnawed at Ashan ever since then. By all reason, he should have a corpse at the bottom of the sea.

He often thought about the night he and Adorjan saved Umbra. The question of how she had come to fall from the sky was yet unanswered, even by her.

Ashan could not ignore the correlations—he and Umbra were both saved in a manner they couldn't explain. Each had fish that stayed fresh for days, while all other fish rotted. That creature made of shadows had to be at the core. Umbra must have encountered it herself, and it must have looked upon her favourably, as it had him. There was a connection he couldn't place yet.

For as long as Ashan spent thinking about that creature, its motives and its nature, he always came to just one conclusion that mattered—if the creature was the cause of all that had happened, only *it* could bring them to an end.

Ashan now sailed in Quy's boat to the same place at sea where he should have lost his life. All he could think to do now was to appear before the creature again and see what came of an appeal on behalf of his people. He was now certain that his eyes weren't deceiving him—the fog was fading away. He sailed through a typical sea mist, but the water was clear to see, and the sun blazed on him unhindered, just how it used to.

He wished he could sail again as in the days before the famine, when storms, wind, and heavy rain were his only perils, and each voyage ended with a net full of fish to take home as a prize. He wished to sail in his boat alongside Quy once more, where they would spend hours fishing, talking and relaxing under the sun, each day full of simple joys and rewards. He so deeply longed for those days.

Now, he sailed alone, this time conscious that it could be for the last time. It was a miracle that he had even lived until now, and he was thankful for it, but he could not help but feel that he was tempting fate by facing this creature again.

Fate, Ashan repeated in his head with a scoff. *When did I start thinking about stuff like that? How much have I changed?*

He looked back on his island home one more time. It looked peaceful, still and serene from so far away, like a painting that had risen from the water. Though he had seen this sight so many times before, he'd never seen it in this light—with any sense of yearning.

He'd spent most of his life wanting to be away from that place, and it only ever brought him pain. He remembered the disgust he felt as a child when his mother died and his father used a bone from her body to forge a monstrosity of a tattoo on his back. His father had claimed it would keep her with him in spirit. Ashan refused to have tattoos for either his mother or father, who died soon afterwards. Thinking back, his hatred of tradition and superstition only took root when it invaded his home and he saw his father's sick obsession with it. Since then, Ashan slept, ate and lived on the water. It was the only place he felt at ease. Treacherous and unpredictable though the water was, it always felt like home.

The water would be a fitting place for me to die, too. I wouldn't regret it. So why am I so afraid right now?

Ashan rowed until the sky swiftly shifted from day to night.

Furious sea waves struck Quy's craft. He held onto the boat's bow as it was thrown about. Frequent and vibrant bolts of lightning lit the empty sky.

The waves rose so high that he was almost hurled from the boat once more. He stumbled to the back and took hold of the rudder.

He put fear and thoughts of the unknown out of his mind, focused only on what he could see with his eyes and feel with his skin. Before him was a sea storm and aggressive waves. No matter the cause, the rain and sea and winds obeyed the whim of nature, just like the many storms he had weathered in his life. He was to tame his craft and survive that which nature had put before him. Nothing more.

And so, he rowed with the instincts of a seasoned

sailor. He felt the rhythm of the waves— the same melody they always moved to, whether gentle or furious. He guided the boat until it moved as part of that same melody. It rose and fell, just as the water did. Even such an aggressive storm became predictable and tameable when he listened closely enough.

Bolts of lightning kept raining down. The creature was nowhere to be seen, nothing unworldly or unnatural.

'Hey!' Ashan shouted as loudly as he could. 'Hey!'

He shouted and waited. It was to no avail. No man appeared standing in the water, no green eyes glared at him. The only answer he got was the constant cracks of thunder.

Ashan weathered the storm for as long as the craft was able, until the wood began to groan and his repairs were becoming undone. He cursed the boat's state, with no choice but to yield.

'I'll be back again,' he screamed out. 'I'll do this as many times as I have to, until you show yourself!'

No one replied. Ashan resigned.

He let go of the rudder and took the oar out of the water. The sea had full hold of the vessel again.

He made for and clung to the bow again. It was an unpleasant feeling to trust the water to take him home without his guidance. It helped to close his eyes.

A while passed. Then, in an instant, the waves stilled, and he was hit by daylight.

The same island he so despised was before him when he opened his eyes.

For a full day, Cadeo's people searched for Umbra and her

father. The search began with homes and the island's caves, then from the hills to the paddies. The search became more intense with time, as his people became convinced that they were hiding, and that Adorjan's words had been true. In a mere day, they came to believe that Umbra deserved to be under suspicion, that something was deeply wrong with her, and she was the only hope they had right now to end their impending peril.

The strangeness and absurdity of this change were not lost on Cadeo. He did not doubt that their search would be pointless once Umbra was found and his people realised there was nothing to be done or gained for it. Still, he was convinced that he had to allow them to discover this for themselves and to see that such baseless obsessions and flights of hope were not becoming of them.

Meanwhile, he had to watch his people stumble around in their weak and starving states, growing ever more irritable and desperate as the day went on. He watched them grow hungrier, saw them become less receptive to each other's words and become single-minded in a wholly pointless pursuit. He was furious about it. *Adorjan must answer for this.*

Cadeo saw him a little before the beginning of sundown. Cadeo had decided to make for Burial Hill. It was a place that was unaffected by the storm, undamaged by wind and with wooden figures that stood firmly where they had first been set. That place was unchanging and dependable, and he felt he needed to be there to ground him, to remember that the world had not fallen apart yet. He saw Adorjan walking down the hills from the paddies on his way there. He had a certain bounce and vigour to his step that Cadeo found jarring.

He beckoned Adorjan. 'What are you thinking, child?' he asked, his tone a careful blend of warmth and firmness. 'Why would you set everyone against Umbra? Do you see what this has done to your people, how they are now obsessed with a fruitless search and false hope?'

Adorjan blinked, and his face betrayed a hint of surprise. '*False?*'

'Yes, false. What do you expect to accomplish by finding Umbra? By questioning a child about fish that did not rot? And what will happen to our people when they realise their search was all for nothing, and they had only grown hungrier for it?'

'It will *not* be for nothing,' Adorjan said.

'Then tell me—what is the point of all this?'

Adorjan's stare intensified, and he wore a face that Cadeo did not recognise—a face that took him aback and even abated his anger for a bit. Adorjan looked exhausted and broken, yet resolute and certain.

'Promise me first that you will just *listen*,' Adorjan said. 'Whether you think I'm right or not, you have to believe I am telling you what I have seen with my own eyes. Promise me, Cadeo.'

Cadeo promised with little hesitation.

'I've seen things since we found those dead fish at sea that no one would believe,' Adorjan started. 'I can't even believe them myself. I chose not to tell you or anyone else, but now that my aunt is dead and Thi has killed herself, everyone is already panicking. We've already lost hope, so I don't need to worry about not being believed anymore.

'I saw something during the storm at sea on the night we saved Umbra from drowning. It was a massive shadow in the shape of a man, tall as the clouds. It was...

horrifying. It's always in my dreams now. Even when I'm awake, I...*feel* it here, all around us. It's like my own shadow...but Ashan didn't see it on that day. I've done my best to put it out of my mind, but nothing I try works. It's always with me. Then, I saw it again in the storm days ago. Aunt Vada saw it too. We only saw it for a moment before it was gone, but there's no doubt to me now that that *thing* is real. It has to be the reason for this famine, the storms, the dead fish, the ruined paddies—all of it.

'And Umbra...I don't know why or how, but she's connected to that creature. Umbra has been either at the centre of everything it has done or absent. She fell from the sky during that storm at sea and claimed not to know why. She was missing during a storm that was strong enough to destroy huts and our paddies, yet she appeared the very next day unharmed. And now these fish...All the fish we took have gone rotten, so how is it that Umbra's fish is still fresh? Umbra and that creature are connected, Cadeo. Maybe the fish were meant only for her. I don't know, but she is at the heart of all this.'

Cadeo listened to every word intently and patiently. Adorjan, the poor man, had gone insane. That was beyond question. His words, his tone, his temperament—they were all clear signs that Adorjan had lost his mind. Cadeo could not blame him for it. All he had gone through would break anyone. He was reminded of Saepe before he jumped from Burial Hill. Grief had broken Cadeo, too, until his duty brought him back.

Yet, the words of this madman could not be dismissed. In fact, Cadeo wondered if he shared in some of his madness, as he found himself doubting very few of his words. What he described was too close to sightings during the last famine, when his people claimed to see cloud-tall creatures and were haunted by nightmares. Whether this *creature* was real or not was irrelevant. Cadeo believed that Adorjan had indeed seen it.

'This is so much to put on one child's shoulders,' Cadeo finally said. 'And that is still so much hope to give our people that may come to nothing. Do you not see how broken we will all become if this all becomes fruitless?'

'Cadeo,' Adorjan said. 'What other hope do we have? We are already doomed to starve and die. You are the only one left of us who lived through the last famine. Yet, you don't know how or why it ended, do you?'

Cadeo felt a jolt through his heart. Disturbing thoughts he had worked for so many years to repress were brought to the surface again. He dropped his head, lost in the memories resounding in him. He felt the sensation of a boat swaying on a stormy sea that he had long forgotten, and heard the word *father* being screamed out to him. He felt the echoes of a time when his heart broke and was never repaired.

How did the last famine end, he heard in Ashan's voice.

You're the only one left, he heard in Adorjan's voice.

Do you still believe yourself to be the leader of this place, he heard in Gratus' voice.

Cadeo let go of his restraint.

He fell to his knees before Adorjan at the foot of the Burial Hill and wept bitterly, for the past and for the future that he was finally accepting would come to be.

Cadeo's heart broke again. He finally unleashed the truth that had plagued him all his life. *How did the last famine end?*

And he told Adorjan everything.

262

TWENTY SIX

It was not lost on Adorjan that the last time he had looked out over the sea like this was when he stood beside his aunt, and they saw that monstrosity of a creature together. After hearing Cadeo's story about what had transpired in the last famine, he only hated the beast all the more. In its dark head, he couldn't imagine anything there but malice and evil to play with lives in such a way and impose pain on what seemed like its whim.

As Adorjan looked out on the same scene again, the sky, the clouds, and the sea didn't look the same anymore. Nature itself seemed evil for how it had deprived him and his people of any solace. *No longer*, he assured himself, not for the first time.

The boat Adorjan was waiting for finally appeared from the horizon, heading toward the southern shore. He headed down from Burial Hill to meet the boat as it anchored. He made it to the beach before Ashan had stepped off with his fishing harpoon in hand.

Adorjan swallowed the anger that rose from his stomach. The sight of Ashan was sickening.

'Ashan,' he called up to him. 'Please, take me back out to sea. Now.'

Ashan looked back at Adorjan with his eyebrows furrowed. Adorjan did his utmost to look as pleading and pitiful as possible. Ashan, by comparison, looked imposing and sure. *Always.*

'Tell me why,' Ashan said.

'*Why,*' Adorjan echoed, feigning incredulity. 'The same reason you've been sailing yourself, I imagine. It's not to catch fish, is it? Don't you think of that night? Doesn't it eat at you to not know what happened or why? You can't deny it—that storm and calm water was not natural. The way night turned into daytime wasn't natural. I plan to find out what is happening here. Don't you?

'Mhm. And why *now*?'

'If not now, then when? Do you expect me to wait until our people starve to death or go insane?'

'*Before they go insane,*' Ashan echoed with a strange smile. He smiled so rarely it usually looked sinister or sarcastic, but this time it was neither. Adorjan couldn't read Ashan at all. It was now that he realised how far away they had become. Ashan was like a stranger, someone who didn't belong in this place and would never be a part of his people. Adorjan was fine with that.

Ashan sighed, and his face hardened again.

'And what if you don't like what you find?' he asked. 'What if you can't do anything about all of this, and you'll starve and go insane regardless? What happens then?'

Adorjan looked at Ashan inquisitively and accusingly. *What do you know about all this*, Adorjan wished to say. *What have you seen? What are you hiding?*

'Nothing *happens*,' he said instead, suspecting this was the answer Ashan was looking for. 'The same thing that is happening now. But at least we'll know we did all we could.'

Ashan grunted and hauled up the anchor from the sand, beckoning Adorjan aboard with clear reluctance.

'No herbs this time,' he said.

Adorjan helped him push the boat off the sand and into the sea. Then, they were soon sailing away from the shore.

Sea mist coiled around the boat like a stalking predator. Adorjan watched the horizon they headed towards with awe. Sunlight rippled on the water and made art before them. It was beautiful.

A gentle stream of music suddenly began to follow them on their way—a deeply familiar melody. Ashan paused mid-stroke. Though they were too far from the shore to see where the music played, they knew it was Cadeo playing the same song he always did—the melody to guide fishermen home.

Ashan looked Adorjan in the eyes again. 'Cadeo knows we're sailing?'

Adorjan shrugged, seeing no reason to lie. 'I told him we would. Shouldn't he know?'

Ashan looked out to the shore again and grunted, turning back to row. 'I could've done without that music.'

The boat continued to make for the horizon with only the sound of waves and music keeping the two of them company for a time.

Ashan stopped rowing Quy's boat as they reached the end of the island's cove and the open sea. They were far enough from the shore that they could barely hear Cadeo's music over the soft clapping waves. Ashan stopped on the water before the day could inexplicably change into night again, where he was certain that the creature resided.

He set his oar down and faced Adorjan expectantly. That he had ulterior motives for this voyage was obvious from the moment Ashan saw him coming to meet him on the coast. He had never had any enthusiasm for the sea or for fishing. He didn't have it in him to face the sea again after he so nearly died last time, unless he had a good, self-serving reason.

Ashan could guess what that reason was. He was sure that the people would have noticed Umbra and Varyis' absence by now, and that they would be hysterically searching for them. Being at sea at the same time they disappeared would inevitably have made the others suspicious of him. He guessed that that was why Adorjan so desperately wanted to go to sea again—to get him alone to question and blame.

Ashan was guarded. After stopping him from killing Ruhan, Adorjan may well have hated him. Even now, he saw that same anger in his eyes that he'd seen on the day Vada died. After such a tragedy, Adorjan couldn't possibly be the same man he once was. Ashan simply didn't know who was sitting before him anymore.

'Well,' Ashan said. 'What're you expecting to find out here?'

'Do you remember the shadow I saw that night in the storm?' Adorjan asked without hesitation.

Ashan sat at the boat's helm. 'You mean the man who was as tall as the clouds and had big glowing eyes? The one that vanished the moment you saw him? As I recall, you'd been smoking that day, too.'

'It was real,' Adorjan said. 'Aunt Vada saw it during the storm that killed Gratus. I saw it again, too. I know it wasn't the herbs now, and that thing really exists. Whatever's been happening here for all this time has to be its fault. The dead fish, the storms, the fog—everything. In fact, I'd bet you've seen it by now, too. Why else would you keep going out to sea with no fish to catch? And I bet that's why you were at sea again today. Tell me I'm wrong.'

Ashan folded his arms. With such sureness and directness, he truly was listening to a stranger. *Vada's death has changed you so much.*

'What's your point?' Ashan asked.

Ashan had his arms folded in front of Adorjan in his usual haughty and arrogant manner. Adorjan felt his anger spilling from him—in his eyes, his skin, his every breath. He could neither hide nor stop it. It felt like a disease, a sickness taking over his body, brought on by the mere sight of Ashan.

Adorjan realised something as the two of them spoke, something that he should have realised long ago if it were true. *You don't belong here, or anywhere else. You have no people or home. You're alone because you're despicable. I hate you. When did that begin?*

Adorjan forced himself to speak, each word tasting viler than the last.

'My *point* is that if that creature is the cause, it's all that can end this. But we clearly can't fight something like that, and we can't even speak or reason with it. All we can do is learn what ties it to us, what has it so enraged at us. And sever that tie.'

'So?' Ashan said.

Adorjan stood. 'You hid Umbra, didn't you?'

Ashan didn't hesitate. 'Of course. Who else would or could have?'

'Where is she?'

Ashan stood and scoffed at Adorjan's brazenness. '*That's* the tie you're talking about—a little girl? The only child on the island? *She's* the tie to be severed?'

Adorjan refused to be swayed. 'You must have thought the same thing. Why else would you hide her before I even told you any of this? Why would you think we'd be after Umbra at all?'

'I wouldn't have hidden her if I believed any of that nonsense,' Ashan said. 'I know you all well enough to know that you'd all believe that. You'd be happy to believe it if you thought it would save you. Are you so far gone that you would place the blame for everything we have lost on Umbra?'

'We see what is happening in front of our faces, Ashan! It doesn't matter whether you or I wish it were so—Umbra is at the heart of all of this. We would be idiots to ignore it. Is it better for us to keep on starving and waiting to die? Until Umbra is the only one left alive?'

'I'm not letting an innocent child come to harm just because you've scared yourselves with your own delusions.'

Adorjan appeared taken aback. He only grew more

enraged. 'Harming her? I said nothing about harming her. What do you take me for?'

'Don't take me for an idiot.'

Adorjan fell silent for a moment. Not with shame or hesitation, Ashan imagined, but with his head clouded by anger. Ashan had been right, he realised. He never wanted to be right to think so little of his people, that they would ever consider harming a child for their own sakes.

What kind of monsters have you become?

Cadeo's melody kept on playing from the coast. It was gentle on the ears as it echoed atop the empty water.

'What are you expecting to happen?' Ashan said. 'You think you'll get your hands on her and the fish will suddenly come back to life, and the rice paddies will suddenly be ready for harvest again? Tell me, Adorjan— what happens when you do what you will with Umbra and nothing changes? What happens if everything you have told me amounts to nothing? *When* your only hope fails, what will happen to this place, and to *you*?'

Ashan saw something akin to a smile creep onto Adorjan's face. Not one of joy or even malice, but an empty and pointless smile. His face was empty.

'The same thing that is happening already,' Adorjan said. Anger was hardly in his voice anymore. 'We starve and soon die. We would lose to that creature, and perhaps we would deserve it. No one here is innocent. No one. Not me, not Cadeo, not you. Not the child. But if Umbra's caused all of this, she's the worst of us.'

Those words changed Ashan. He let go of his hope of reaching this man. He wasn't the boy he'd known his whole life, someone who had strived to be dependable even when he failed. There was none of that boy left.

This was someone with sureness of mind and heart, someone who was revolting for it.

'This is the man you are now, huh?' Ashan said out loud. 'I preferred it when you were smoking those herbs all day. You were pitiful, but maybe they were keeping you sane. Maybe they kept you a good man. Now, you're just…weak.'

'Where's Umbra, Ashan?' Adorjan repeated, unmoved.

Ashan turned his back. He couldn't stomach looking at Adorjan for a second longer.

He picked up his oar and began to row back toward the island. He let his silence be his answer.

But he soon stopped as he saw something move in the water. It was only for a split second, but he couldn't mistake what it was. He leaned over the side of the boat and saw it beneath them—a lone mackerel fish, alive in the water.

'Come here,' he called to Adorjan. 'Bring the net.'

Adorjan gave up reasoning with Ashan. He hadn't changed, not now, and nor would he ever. He was the same arrogant, headstrong, distant man. He had always been unreachable—headstrong and unrelenting.

Adorjan stood behind Ashan as he looked into the sea.

Never had Adorjan believed Ashan saw him or anyone else as anything but a hindrance. His hate for their customs was unfounded and constantly turned the others against him, which he seemed to relish for his whole life. There was no hope for the man.

Adorjan picked up Ashan's harpoon.

Ashan had left himself with no one to care for him, no one to guide him in life, no one to lean on. He was the epitome of a lonely, miserable man whom life itself had shunned. It was a sad fate to live as someone no one would mourn for. Adorjan actually felt a tinge of pity for him between his overwhelming hatred.

Adorjan stood over Ashan.

He had no cause for doubts or guilt anymore. This man would only stop his people from unifying and finding peace again. No one would miss him, and no one would blame Adorjan. It was all for his people's sake. It was all duty.

Adorjan thrust the harpoon into Ashan's back.

He had never felt such fierce elation.

Adorjan stabbed Ashan again as his body fell onto the boat's hull.

Then again. And again.

He didn't stop, even when Ashan's body turned lifeless.

Never once did Ashan cry out. Never did he even make a sound.

All the while, Adorjan never stopped screaming.

Then, his elation was spent. He dropped the harpoon and looked upon the work of his hands.

'It's just duty,' he whispered.

He was alone on the waves in Quy's boat, covered in red once more.

As Cadeo's music beckoned Adorjan home, a lone fish followed in his wake before slipping once more into the depths.

TWENTY SEVEN

Cadeo began to doze off on the shore with his mind on the past, even as his hands continued to play.

From the very first note he struck, he knew that he wouldn't play well. It was his usual shoreline melody— one he should have been able to play instinctively, flawlessly. Yet, it was like a random mess of sounds, patched together like a tattered garb. His feeble body failed to imbue the song with any vigour. He struggled to even hold onto the sticks with each strike. Though he had become accustomed to distracting himself from his hunger, it was becoming impossible to ignore that he was starving and that death wasn't far away.

The melody grew more erratic the longer he played, yet it was not unpleasant to his ears. It had a certain rawness to it—a substance he could not recall ever hearing in his music before. It felt natural for his mind to wander as his hands did.

He thought most about the memories he had shared with Adorjan, the ones he had suppressed with some success for many years. Now that those memories had been shared, Cadeo found them easier to ruminate over. It was like they had lost their hold on him, or he on them.

It was the last time he was at sea in what was now Quy's boat.

He had sailed against his better judgement that day, yet believed he had no option at the time. The island was at the heart of the great famine. His people had endured hunger and paranoia for months, and all were at the end of their ropes. They had learned that Arinya had been killed, and the island had lost its warm-hearted leader—its only guiding light.

All that was left after her was rage, pain and inevitable death. Cadeo decided anything was better than such a fate.

When he told his family that they were to set out to sea and find another home, Gratus took little convincing. Adra and Amado had been too feeble in their hunger to protest. Cadeo carried them to his boat that very night and set sail. He had faith in his sailing after decades of practice, so he sailed with no small amount of arrogance and sureness.

The sea changed the moment they left the island cove. A storm brewed as if from nowhere, heavy rain fell, and strong winds roused aggressive tides.

It was the most incredible phenomenon Cadeo had ever witnessed, but it did not deter him. Rather, it drove him even harder to get away from that place, despite the protest of Gratus and his children, who pleaded in his boat.

The sea soon grew too angry for even Cadeo to keep

the boat on a straight course, but still he persisted. Gratus began to cry out at the children.

They were leaning over the side of the boat, watching something in the water. Cadeo dropped his oar and leapt to them, screaming for them to get away from the water—all too late.

He vividly remembered the panic as the boat struck another wave, and his children fell into the sea.

He could still hear Gratus shriek in utter panic, still feel his heart erupting as his children called out to him from the water.

He reached his hand overboard. But there was no one reaching back.

Their voices were gone. They vanished as though the sea had pulled them into a void. Cadeo dove in after them and was pulled about by the water as he looked frantically for them. It was to no avail.

He was quickly pulled far from the boat, unable to swim against the strong waves. Gratus still screamed out for Adra and Amado from aboard. There was never a response but the screaming thunder from the sky.

Then a strange and terrible sensation struck them both —a sound crept into their heads and forced agony into them.

It was intrusive, relentless, like a disease consuming them.

It felt like Cadeo's brain was melting, and the world around him with it. The pain seeped far beyond his flesh and into his very being. It made seconds feel like hours.

All the while, the storm abated and made way for a clear sky. The wind settled and left the sea to return to gentle and calm tides. Even the fog that had so long lingered on and around their island dissipated.

Cadeo and Gratus were suddenly in the middle of a perfectly normal sea at night.

Still, the sound crept further into their heads, and it turned into a scream. It was all Cadeo could do to stay afloat until he made it to the boat and climbed aboard.

Then, as the sound grew unbearable, he passed out with his head in his hands.

Cadeo and Gratus had woken up together in the boat while still on the sea under a freshly risen sun. Their children were nowhere in sight, nor indeed would they ever see them again.

They had waited hours there. Cadeo swam and dove countless times searching for them. They screamed their names at the top of their voices until they had no voices left at all.

Between them was an eternally silent acceptance that their children were gone.

Their people found their sanity again in the weeks that followed, with the sudden return of fish at sea and weather for harvesting.

It was to be the last time Cadeo set foot on a fishing boat. He would instead spend his days guiding other fishermen home with music.

His mind was still as burdened and broken all these years later. *I failed my family. I killed our children with my arrogance in the face of the sea. I am no worthy father.* Such thoughts and self-hatred gave Cadeo many a sleepless night and caused him to wake up screaming during the nights that sleep did find him.

But one thought, one realisation, was more horrifying than all others for being so nonsensical yet undeniable. It caused Cadeo such distress that he buried this one the deepest in his memory, until the present day, when he finally poured his heart out to Adorjan—the thought he did not dare to share for fear of what it would mean for his people, for fear of what kind of monster had set its eyes on this island.

The famine, the fog, and the storms all ended the day my children died at sea.

Cadeo saw the boat on the water through his tear-soaked eyes.

Bitterness and nostalgia filled him as he watched the boat approach—the same vessel he had sailed in for a decade. From the coast, it already looked old and frail. Quy embodied a willing person, yet was also a negligent one.

Cadeo had always been fond of his work ethic and willing nature, since he worked harder than most and never begrudgingly. Quy reminded him of himself when he was his age—a skilful sailor and fisherman, full of vigour and a desire to serve. Quy was very much how Ruhan used to be.

To remember Quy now was to remember the last time this island home was at peace and its people were not tormented. He was grateful that Quy could forever serve his people, even in death, now as a memory of those happy days that felt so long ago.

The boat barely managed to keep to a straight course. Even on calm water, it floated erratically and with no grace. It looked like it was being guided by someone who had never set sail before.

That realisation made Cadeo feel uneasy. It was all he needed to see to know that something significant must have transpired out there, for Adorjan to be rowing. One of Ashan's few merits was his love for the sea and sailing—he'd never allow anyone else to row while he was aboard.

Indeed, as the vessel drew closer, Cadeo saw Adorjan holding the oar—the man who was remarkably adept at caring for fields and nurturing rice, yet had never held an oar in his life.

Ashan was nowhere in sight.

Cadeo set eyes on Adorjan. He suppressed whatever sound tried to burst from his lips, as he saw that he was covered in blood.

Cadeo was not yet used to the sight of blood feeling so horrific. His people were not unfamiliar with blood and bones through their tattooing customs and closeness with death. They had come to see the body and everything in it for what it was—a vessel for life until it was depleted. Blood was only a part of that vessel.

Yet to see it now, splattered over clothes and skin and turning a darker shade of red than it was natural, was repulsive. It was not natural. It was beyond words.

I've done something terrible. Those words came flooding back to Cadeo in Ruhan's voice. He remembered how Ruhan had broken down in tears, and his face was filled with guilt and regret.

Adorjan did nothing of the sort. His face was like a blank canvas, devoid of anything at all. He barely acknowledged Cadeo beyond when he stepped onto the sand. A harpoon in his hand glistened with red.

For only a moment, Cadeo caught a look in his eyes that made his heart sink and his horror grow. Adorjan was afraid. There was fear for what he had just done. Yet, there was no remorse or sadness, nor doubt. He looked certain and relentless.

He walked past Cadeo without a word spoken and made for the hills.

Cadeo was left looking at the boat that had set itself in the sand. He gingerly approached it and looked inside.

The hull was blood-soaked.

Ashan was gone.

Cadeo's head dropped in his shame, remorse and pain.

Perhaps Adorjan had lied about only convincing Ashan to tell him where Umbra was. Or he may have killed Ashan impulsively, enraged and grieved as he was. But none of that mattered. Cadeo had failed both of them by ignoring what had been right in front of his face. Adorjan and Ashan *were* perhaps friends once, but it was impossible after Vada died, when Ashan stopped Adorjan from avenging her. Cadeo was even willing to grant that wish.

Now, because Cadeo allowed that anger to go unchecked, another murder had happened on this island. This was his own fault as much as Adorjan's.

And, with no hint of righteousness, Cadeo understood Adorjan now, too. This was desperation in its final form.

Cadeo breathed deeply and looked up to the sky. There were no clouds in sight.

There is no return anymore, he accepted. *What will be will be, for good or ill. And I must bear my share of blame for what has happened in this place. And what will now come to pass. The people's survival is all that matters now.*

He felt a sickening dread and sorrow, yet was imbued with renewed resolve as he stood on the shore and looked out over the water.

He waited for the future to come for him with a quiet and pleading prayer.

After today, let my people's hands take no more lives.

Nota stared at a half-finished painting on the canvas spread across the wall in her cave.

This piece began as a simple depiction of a fish in water. She'd started it after the fresh fish were found on the shore, but the art had grown larger and more grandiose than she expected. It progressed from realistic to abstract over the days she worked on it. Now, only half the fish's body was fresh and vibrant. The rest decayed, with its skeleton exposed under the rotten scales. She'd found new inspiration when her share of fish rotted in her cave, then again when the fish on the shore had been found decomposed.

It was a stunning piece. The island flowers were living well after all the recent rain and sun, and their petals made for vibrant inks. The colours on the canvas blended and clashed with each other at the same time, a mess of strokes working in harmony to create a beautiful and tragic whole.

But Nota couldn't bring herself to finish it. Now, each stroke felt wrong, every new colour like an outcast on the canvas. It felt alive—determined to remain unfinished, messy. She had the makings of her greatest work that evolved as it willed to and brought itself this far, but it refused to be finished. It was maddening.

She tried to bring the brush to the canvas again, coated in a different colour—a delicate and subtle yellow made from the petals of apricot blossoms. But the painting only drifted further from being finished with each dab.

Nota groaned and threw the brush across the cave floor. She paced around it. *I still have no art in me,* she admitted. *I haven't for a while now.*

These thoughts had come the day she did Cadeo's tattoo. Though she had done hundreds before it, that one had unsettled her. She was sympathetic to him, and she'd thought it was a kindness to remind him he had to find his own meaning in her tattoos. But in hindsight, that had been an excuse, just as her outburst to Adorjan had been an excuse. With her own words, she had torn meaning away from her art, abandoning the burden of instilling purpose in her own work. It was all because Ashan had been right —*delusion isn't healing.*

It took Cadeo sitting in her cave, having his flesh stained by Gratus' bones and asking for meaning, for Nota to see this place, and herself, in Ashan's eyes. *She* was a creator of delusion. She was to blame for her people's dependency on her talents, while she never cared for the purpose they placed on her heart.

Knowing all this, Nota couldn't bring herself to paint another tattoo.

She wondered, for the first time, what would become of the canvas once it was filled out, what purpose it would serve after she was dead and gone. So much of the art was empty, made without intent, dead from the moment they were born.

Nota decided then that art without purpose was futile, that she had to paint solely out of her own desire. Proof of that was all over her cave—years of art imbued with purpose. Paintings on her canvas were so strange and unworldly that even she couldn't fathom their inspiration.

Abstract wooden figures on the floor that were inexplicably disturbing and alluring all at once, some of which had made Ashan blush and given her endless delight. All were pieces worth toiling for. That purpose would be all she strived for.

So she painted again, for the first time not for her people, not from idle inspiration, but only to reflect what she felt in the moment.

But the piece refused to be finished. She thought that her ability to create may have finally abandoned her. It was a scary realisation that made it all the harder to paint.

She was close to abandoning her efforts for the day when a darkness was cast across the floor of her cave. A figure stood in the cave's entrance against the last of the day's sunlight seeping in. It looked like it was made of shadows.

It was Adorjan.

She first saw his face. Never had she seen his face so drained of emotion, reflecting so little yet stirring dread in her. He didn't even look like Adorjan anymore, but like something inhuman that wore his flesh like a garment. Then she saw his clothes, covered in red.

She could smell the blood on him before he even entered the cave. It was oppressive and blinding, like a foul fog.

'What...?' She managed to stutter through her tight throat. She began to tear up, not yet understanding why. It was only evident that something terrible had happened. And something terrible was soon to happen again. 'What have you done?'

Adorjan spoke with the same hollowness that his face reflected.

'Ashan took me out to sea.'

His words were poison, sinking into her, killing her from within.

Tears silently trailed down her face.

Ashan was right, Nota thought through her despair. *They really are blaming Umbra. Madness has taken hold of this place. He was more right than he realised.*

She'd never be able to tell Ashan how right he was. She'd never get to tease him again, to laugh at his stoic mask. He'd never sleep in her cave again.

Nota broke as the realisation hit her.

'I know him well,' Adorjan said. 'He wouldn't take me out to sea if it meant leaving Umbra and Varyis alone and helpless—unless someone else already knew where they were and would help him keep them hidden from us. I know you two were...close. There's no one else Ashan would entrust this to. You would do this, if not for Umbra, for Ashan.'

Adorjan stood before Nota and glared right into her. His eyes betrayed nothing at all.

She only now saw that he held onto a harpoon freshly glazed with blood.

He said, 'Where's Umbra?'

TWENTY EIGHT

Varyis and Umbra sat together under the shadow of Burial Hill. Together, they watched the setting sun.

Umbra spent much of the day telling him all about this beach—how she came here most days after her work in the fields, how she would watch the sun setting just like they now were, and how the beach was always lonely.

She spoke at great length and with zeal. She seemed to have changed so much recently, and no more so than when they first set foot on this beach. She spoke with the nostalgia of someone three times her age, as though she reminisced over a bygone time. Varyis got the distinct impression more had happened on this beach than she was now sharing. But he would let her have her secrets. He was just happy to hear her speak like this—like an ordinary little girl.

All the while, though, pain gnawed at his body. He hid

the fatigue that threatened to overcome him, losing himself instead in this moment.

The last of the sunlight presently faded away.

Varyis couldn't remember the last time that he watched a sunset like this—certainly not since he was healthy enough to work outdoors and to walk on his own. He had forgotten how soothing it was, how nothing else in the world mattered for the few minutes that the horizon warmly glowed.

Umbra drifted in and out of sleep beside him, exhausted after what felt like straight hours of talking.

It had been the strangest of days. Never could he have imagined fleeing his home and settling for a night spent under the stars. Ashan warned them their home wasn't safe, and they didn't question it.

He couldn't imagine why Umbra would be in any danger at all, but he knew better than to doubt it. He'd sensed this place had changed greatly, even before Ashan told him about Vada's death and Ruhan's execution. Nothing was unlikely here anymore, and nothing was too absurd if it meant ensuring Umbra's safety. He and Umbra agreed that they would wait patiently until Ashan or Nota's return before they went home again.

'Father?' Umbra presently said, still stirring in a half-sleep.

Varyis was happy to hear her voice again, his heart felt warm every time she said that word—*father*. But he was also a little tired. He felt the short voyage to this beach took everything that he had left out of him. It was a struggle to even grunt in reply.

'I like this beach,' Umbra said. 'I like it at night too. It's different from the daytime. When the stars come out here and I'm watching the sea, I feel...small. Like, I wonder how big the sky is, and how far the water goes. Maybe I could wander the sea, forever.'

Something about those words deeply touched Varyis in a way he could not comprehend. Maybe it was the idea of wandering somewhere that wasn't here, away from what he had been a cruel life. Or perhaps it was the idea of feeling small, even insignificant. Either way, those simple words, spoken with a child's perfect simplicity, had Varyis seeing his daughter in a new light—they were more alike than he had ever realised. She wasn't as far away from him as he had come to fear over time.

'I understand,' Varyis said. His words would probably mean nothing to Umbra, but in Varyis' mind, they felt profoundly important to say aloud. 'I understand.' He said one more time. 'Umbra?'

'Hmm?'

'I'm sorry,' Varyis said. His lips barely obeyed him anymore, and it hurt to speak, feeble and broken as his body had become. His voice was like a raspy whisper. He could barely understand his own words as he grew lethargic, hardly awake or asleep. 'This illness...it's no excuse to be a terrible father. It's no excuse for...failing to make a home for you. I'm sorry, Umbra.'

It didn't seem Umbra had heard a word. She breathed softly and peacefully. It was okay by Varyis. They were words he realised should have been said years ago—for far too long, they had festered in him and weighed him down. They were not so powerful or painful now that they had been spoken. He only wished they hadn't been born of regret.

As though speaking from a dream, Umbra said—'I'm

home now, Father.'

Varyis felt light, freer than he ever had. He'd tasted a miracle medicine for his very spirit, and all his ailments drifted away.

He didn't have the strength to speak again, but he managed to smile.

It stayed on his face as he allowed his eyes to close and his body to rest.

He felt the tremors slow and the pain in his core fade as his body finally gave in to that which tormented him for so many years.

At last, carried by a soft wind and the relentless melody of slow tides, he fell into the deepest of sleeps—

A sleep with no dreams.

TWENTY NINE

No longer did Adorjan hesitate. No longer was he weighed down by doubts and burdened by inadequacies. No matter what Ashan had said, Adorjan didn't miss the man he used to be—he barely remembered him anymore.

He finally understood his aunt's final lesson to him on Burial Hill, and was determined to take it to heart. She would have been proud of the man he was becoming.

I'm not a flower on the hill anymore, Auntie.

He knew the others on the island saw that change in him, too. Nota and Cadeo had both had the same fear in their eyes when they saw him, a reflection of the weakness that Adorjan once felt in himself.

He was glad that they felt it, for it was fear that made Nota tell him everything.

Now, he guided the boat gracelessly over the sea until it touched the shore under Burial Hill.

He took the harpoon into his hands.

It was the first time his feet had touched this sand. It was softer than the rest on the island, like walking on clouds. The beach was surrounded by the rocks of the hills and faced west, where the sun set over the sea. He liked this beach already. He would return here often when the famine was over. It would be a fine place to clear his head and relax after working on the paddies.

At first, all he saw was sand and the belly of Burial Hill. Then, two figures at its base—a girl, and her father beside her, motionless.

Varyis slept. Umbra's eyes shot wide at the sight of Adorjan.

His feet kept moving through the sand toward them with a rope in hand.

Umbra tried to shake her father awake to no avail.

She shook him harder and called out, '*Father.*'

He didn't even stir.

Adorjan kept moving forward.

He saw a father and a daughter before him, terrified and powerless. He saw a man too weak to protect anything at all. He saw a little girl who had no one to defend her.

His heart was torn in two. It was agonising.

Yet, Adorjan was becoming adept at burying pain.

He dragged Umbra away from her father through the sand. It barely took any strength at all.

Umbra pleaded and begged, her cries growing louder as they neared the boat.

He fought against her as she kicked and lashed out to bind her in the rope. Then, he set her down in the boat.

He blindfolded Umbra with a torn piece of a fish sack.

He could barely see her through the tears set in his

eyes. They wouldn't stop falling.

I refuse to cry, Adorjan kept telling himself. *Never again will I cry.*

He stepped back in the sand and walked through it to meet Varyis face-to-face again.

Umbra still screamed from the boat, but Varyis was silent and still asleep, a smile set on his face.

It took everything Adorjan had to stand above him. It took killing every part of himself that screamed at him to stop.

There's no going back anymore.

'Varyis,' Adorjan said. 'I'm sorry it's come to this. Truly.'

Varyis didn't respond. He didn't even stir in his sleep.

Adorjan knelt beside him.

'A parent shouldn't ever lose a child,' Adorjan said softly. 'It wouldn't be right to let you—'

Adorjan silenced himself. His heart tore again as he realised the man before him had not heard a single word, that he would not wake from his sleep, and that his smile would never leave his face.

He's dead.

Nature had run its course and robbed Adorjan of his duty. Something like relief coursed through him, and the harpoon fell from his fingers.

He screamed at the sky as loudly as he could, freed from one more burden.

Then he fell silent, and Umbra along with him.

He made back for the boat, where she lay and whimpered. Fear emanated from her, even with her eyes covered. *To lose your father now...life has been cruel to you. I wish it weren't you.*

Adorjan decided it would be cruel to let her hold onto false hope.

'Your father is gone,' he said. The words left his mouth with no softness, for he had no more left to imbue them with. 'I'm sorry.'

Adorjan rowed away from the shore again. The short voyage was heavy with silence.

Umbra said nothing. She made no sound at all.

Cadeo was joined in his dire watch of the sea from the coast by his people.

First, it was Nghi who explained that he had come at the request of Adorjan. Then it was Lihn and Kien, who told him the same. Only Nota never appeared on the coast that night.

They looked more like corpses than living people. Their search of the hills had taken a toll on them, pushing them beyond their limits in their starvation. They had pushed their starving bodies to the limit, and it pained Cadeo all the more knowing their search had been in vain.

Ashan had been cunning to have hidden Umbra in a place that only a boat can reach, as the last fisherman left with the only boat. Cadeo didn't know how Adorjan found out what he had done, but Cadeo was certain Umbra would never have been found through searching alone. His people had searched, had further starved themselves, had expended their energy for no reason at all. There was simply no other option left—this all had to be worth it.

He did not want his people present for what would soon happen, to share in the blame any more than they had to. He did not want them to even know what would take place on this night.

But Adorjan had chosen to make the entire island party to this. Cadeo knew him well enough to imagine what he was thinking. He had seen how diligently Adorjan oversaw the work in the rice paddies, how he ensured each person had their share of labour and how each person was praised for their part. Such a man probably believed in sharing blame as well. He would want his people to be guilty for their own survival, too.

Though Cadeo was deeply at odds with this, he found that he respected the principle. *Perhaps there is some wisdom in that,* he reconciled. *They cannot be sheltered any longer if they are to survive this. Perhaps they ought to see how much their lives will cost.*

His contemplation was swiftly cut short by the sound of a scream. It was Adorjan's voice. Cadeo grew tense, for it was not a scream of pain or fear, but one that bordered on elation. He was ever more afraid of what else the night could have in store.

His people hardly reacted. They kept watching over the sea or bowed their heads toward the sand, as though they had heard nothing.

This is truly happening, Cadeo thought sadly. *We have all changed, become too accustomed to tragedy. Even I am not as sickened as I should be.*

He could not think of any reason for such a scream, beyond another heinous act. Only Umbra and her father were not present here. It all hinted that more tragedy had befallen them. But Cadeo could not bring himself to think so little of Adorjan, even now that blood was on his hands. He could not imagine killing family in front of their own.

And with anything but elation.

After some time spent waiting in dread, the boat appeared again, with Adorjan rowing at the helm.

Any hopes Cadeo had that Umbra would not be there, that she would be spared for a while longer, were in vain. She was at Adorjan's feet as the boat hit the shore, bound in ropes and set on her stomach like some sort of prey. Her tiny body was covered in sand, and her unkempt hair sprawled out over her back. She hid her face against the boat's hull.

She looked utterly powerless and pathetic.

Cadeo instinctively looked at his people, who eyed one another. They all shared the same look—incredulity, horror, disgust. Every emotion one could feel at a tragedy soon to occur.

All watched silently as Adorjan hauled Umbra out of the boat.

Adorjan set Umbra down in the sand on her knees.

He could feel the eyes of all his people on them both. He had arranged for his people to gather here with this moment expected, where he would be met with confusion, disgust and outrage.

So many great burdens willingly shouldered in recent days, all for these people. They all had to be present and see for themselves how far he had gone, and how far he was about to go, for their survival. For all that work and pain to have gone unnoticed would have been the worst of injustices. Their judgement now meant nothing to him. *None of you will be innocent after today.*

Umbra knelt in front of him, still and distant as though she were already dead.

Her long hair flowed in a sudden, soft gust of wind.

Adorjan stood over her with the harpoon in hand.

He kept looking at her, his feet frozen in the sand and his hand squeezing the harpoon tighter.

Ashan's words crept into his mind.

What happens when you do what you will with Umbra and nothing changes...when your only hope fails, what will happen to this place, and to you?

Adorjan wouldn't waver. He was convinced of his rightness, certain that everything he had done was born from pure intentions and love.

His hand hurt from how hard he gripped.

You've come too far already, he told himself. *There's nowhere to go but onwards,* he told himself.

He could not spur himself on, could do nothing but look at Umbra, for she was only a little girl.

Adorjan began to shake.

He looked down at Ashan's drying blood on his clothes, at the hands that had been prepared to kill Varyis.

What have I been doing?

Conviction didn't matter at all anymore.

What do I do now?

The strength that righteousness had given to him fled, like a beast freed from its cage.

There's nowhere to go but onwards...I don't know what to do.

It began to rain. Cadeo and his people watched Adorjan silently standing over Umbra in the sand. Cadeo saw Adorjan's feet frozen in place, how he looked down at his hands and the dried blood on his clothes.

Cadeo saw him do so for a long time, and understood what was unfolding—hesitation, doubt and regret.

He was grateful beyond words that he finally saw this hint of the humanity and empathy that had been Adorjan's greatest asset since he was a child.

He cannot do it, Cadeo realised with some relief. *He has found that there are some things he is not willing to do, no matter the cost. We have not all gone completely insane.*

It was a moment of immense pride that, despite everything, this place had still given birth to people with purity in their hearts that could not be taken away. That was never going to change.

It also strengthened Cadeo's conviction.

He stepped toward Adorjan and Umbra with all the energy of an old, starving man.

Adorjan looked up and saw him approach. He looked pleading and lost, like a scared child.

Cadeo turned and faced his people. They looked frightened too, riddled with dread and defeat. *Everyone here is so young,* Cadeo realised. *It is an island of children. Really, who else could have been a shepherd for them but me, Gratus?*

He would not postpone the inevitable. There was no other way forward. At no other time had he been so certain as now, with Umbra finally before him, bound and helpless. His people would once more be subject to the whim of whatever natural or unnatural force had found this island.

He spoke to his people in as loud a voice as he could.

'Umbra has to die,' he said. The words felt unfathomably foul leaving his lips. They were like a poison cloud. 'She will die, so that we may survive.'

What followed was as Cadeo had foreseen—there was silence, then protestations.

His people asked why.

They said this could not possibly happen.

They called him a monster for ever thinking of such a thing.

They protested that they never agreed to this when they searched for Umbra.

They said they would never accept the death of a child, not even for their own lives.

All the while, Cadeo patiently listened to every word, without reaction and unmoved. He stood firmly and accepted his people's vitriol and outrage. He looked at them with pity, for he was convinced of what was truly in their hearts despite their protest. *You are all afraid and angry at your own helplessness. I understand that there is more comfort in being a protester than a bystander. But--*

Adorjan finally spoke up before Cadeo could.

'This has to be done,' he said. Though he spoke softly and with a voice that emanated defeat, his voice brought an abrupt end to all protestations. 'You all know it too. Any one of you could step in and stop this. But you won't. None of you will, because you know you'd doom the rest of us to die.'

None moved.

Though they were outraged, sickened and incredulous, none took a step forward.

Umbra knelt in the sand alone, silent and distant, her head bowed.

'I don't want to do this either,' Adorjan said. 'But someone has to.'

'*I* will do it,' Cadeo said. They were difficult words to

say—a pronouncement before his people meant there was no return. Yet, it was freeing to have them leave his body. He felt calmer. *It seems that there is also comfort to be found in proclamation, when one accepts that there is no path left but the one they are walking.*

Adorjan's eyes widened. 'No, Cadeo,' he said. You can't ask me to allow you--'

Cadeo raised a hand. 'I am not asking, Adorjan. I *will* do it. You are still young and have many years ahead of you. Do not burden yourself with any more regrets than you have to. They are not easy to live with. Not at all.'

'No,' Adorjan said, with no hint of sureness. 'I won't regret anything. It's my duty...for my people.'

'Child,' Cadeo quietly said. 'All that has happened is not your burden alone. It is okay to falter now.'

Adorjan softened. His face and eyes showed understanding, then were filled with relief as Cadeo's words took hold in him.

He set the harpoon down in the sand. The blood on its tip was dry.

'I'm sorry,' he said, his head bowed.

Cadeo shook his head. 'Please, go and join your people.'

'Cadeo,' Adorjan said. 'Thank you...for all of this. Thank you.'

Cadeo could not respond. Such thanks made this burden feel all the heavier, for it felt more appropriate that what he was soon to do be completely thankless.

Adorjan and his people sat away from the shore.

Cadeo and Umbra were alone on the sand.

The light rain had turned into a downpour. The wind roused and grew stronger.

'Umbra,' Cadeo said. She did not react to his voice. 'Just know that we do not do this because we want to, but because we must. This will always have been your home, and we always will have been your--' Cadeo stopped, disgusted with himself.

He had spoken the same words to Ruhan before his death. They were so practised, devoid of real empathy, like he recited an old song. *How have I become so accustomed to death?*

He looked at Umbra again, at her frail little body bound in ropes.

This is just a child *before me. A child who knows she will soon perish. She must be going mad with fear. She has every right to despise me.*

Cadeo forced his old body down into the sand and sat beside Umbra.

'Umbra,' Cadeo said, his voice in an undertone. 'Listen to me, child. This island is not the home you once knew. It is not a place where a child should be forced to live, with people like us. In this place…there is only pain and dread. You will…you will soon be freed of that. You will leave us all behind here. But…all this pain will be gone and forgotten one day, like a wave on the shore. Perhaps we are just another wave…dying in the sand.'

Umbra stirred a little to his words. She moved her head.

He could not let her die in darkness—it felt far too cruel.

He reached for her blindfold, his hand trembling. He pulled it away, and he saw her completely. Her face would be set into Cadeo's memory. It would stay with him in his dreams and through every waking moment for what remained of his life. It was the very picture of innocence, of perfect blamelessness. It was indescribable and beautiful.

I...am no longer human.

Cadeo could not stop himself from shedding a tear.

In a way, this tear was the last gift of empathy and love that Cadeo had left to give to her. He did not shy from it.

'The next time you close your eyes, this place will be gone,' Cadeo said. 'And we will not even be a memory to you.'

Cadeo turned to his people and looked each in the eye. He looked as intently as he could with the tear still running down his face.

If you must see this, do not forget this moment, he said through his glare. *Do not forget the price for your survival. Do not let harm come to one of us ever again.*

His people said nothing in response. None averted their eyes.

None but Adorjan, who buried his face in his hands.

Cadeo helped Umbra to her feet.

Together, they walked into the water.

The rain grew heavier still.

The water touched Cadeo's knees. It was still and calm.

He looked upon the girl in his arms one last time.

She looked back at him and caused Cadeo heartache once more.

She looked calm, even at ease. She looked serene and as peaceful as the water itself.

Cadeo felt another tear fall down his face, then another. He could not stop the tears. *This is acceptance,* he realised. *You...are the strongest of all of us.*

'Umbra. Close your eyes.'

She did so.

Cadeo breathed deeply and silently prayed.

He prayed for forgiveness, not for himself, but for his people, that they could be blameless.

He prayed that this monstrous act would not be in vain.

Cadeo forced Umbra under the water.

He held her there.

Umbra did not move.

There was no struggle, no fight.

It was as though Cadeo held nothing at all.

He wept until he could hardly breathe.

Umbra began to squirm.

Cadeo wept louder and harder.

'I'm sorry,' he whispered. 'I'm sorry.'

She struggled more.

Her bound body was helpless before even his feeble strength.

He heard voices calling out to him from far beyond his reach.

They screamed *Father.*

'I'm so sorry.'

Father.

Cadeo could not take it.

He longed to let Umbra out of his arms and pull her to the surface. He longed to embrace her, to swear no harm would come to her. To spare her from an undeserving and cruel fate.

But Umbra was gone.

Truly gone.

Cadeo suddenly felt nothing but the water in his hands.

He looked down through his tear-soaked eyes, but

there was only darkness at the bottom of the sea.

Umbra had vanished from his hands.

The heavy downpour faded with her.

The wind died down until it was gone.

Did I just kill…?

He lost all faculty for thought or reason as he stood completely alone in the water.

He looked down at his empty hands, with only enough sense left to know that something unfathomable and completely unnatural had taken place once more.

I…am worse than a monster.

'It…' Cadeo found himself saying. 'It is done.'

No sooner had the words left his lips than the sea before him began to ripple.

A shadow was cast over him—one that grew as something rose from the water.

And it kept rising, lording over him.

It was the shadow of a man.

It was blacker even than the night sky.

Its eyes glowed in a vivid green light as bright as the full moon.

It looked down into Cadeo.

Terror hollowed him, like an idol of the dead.

THIRTY

Embraced by darkness, Umbra felt words in her that formed an old tale—one of a boy who lived a life plagued with luxury and excess.

His given name meant little to most, while his family name demanded respect and awe with its every utterance. He resided in a place where the sun was ever shining, and sporadic rain nourished endless crops and sweet fruit. In life, he was left in want of very little, for his stomach was always full, and his home was like a fortress against the elements.

But for all his life, he craved that which was immaterial inside the beautiful walls and courtyards of his home on the edge of the sea.

He was in want of a present father, but his father spent his days far from home, creating philosophies and guides for living, consulting those whose power and influence spread beyond his country's shores.

He was in want of a loving and considerate mother, but his mother spent her nights indulging in drinks that numbed her senses and the pleasant company of men who were not her groom.

Though he was surrounded by servants and wealthy neighbours, the boy grew up alone.

His sole solace came by way of his father's couriers in the form of gold coins and gems of immeasurable value. His mother would spend the coins in service to her debauched lifestyle, but she allowed the boy to keep the gems as his own.

Each was unique, yet equally stunning. Some were vibrant red, like a rose in bloom—some were a deeper blue than an early morning sky.

He came to cherish them as the echoes of his desire for a present father. They became his closest friends, his confidants and his guiding lights through his youth.

As an adolescent, he studied in the same philosophical arts as his father—a duty which grew from an obligation to his family name into a passion. He was fascinated with lofty words and adored dismantling them into simplicity.

His sole allure as he grew in age and knowledge became exploring life's meanings. Through studies and quiet contemplation, he came to realise that being born into excess set him on an empty path devoid of meaning.

There was no meaning in the base pleasures of his mother nor in the longing for acclaim and prominence of his father. Neither path was virtuous.

The boy often left his estate in search of meaning, venturing far from his servants and wealthy neighbours. He met those whom he had not realised existed—farmers living off what the land grew for them, with lives stripped of extravagance.

He saw in them lives that were worth living. He dressed with the simplicity of the farmers, never again adorning himself in gold or silver, and learned to work on their land.

They often spoke about gods with awe and love, and thanked unseen forces that they could eat each day. They called it prayer.

It was an alien concept to the boy, for his wealthy neighbours only uttered the word god in disdain and ridicule. His studies had taught him that gods were concepts to be challenged rather than awed, doubted rather than thanked.

The farmers' faith kept the boy feeling like a stranger among them, kept him from calling them his own people.

All but one young girl.

She was not well studied or keen to learn in the way he was. She had no fascination for theory and no interest in debates. Yet, the boy learned far more about life as they spoke. She was content with whatever each day brought her, with the simple meals that awaited her at the end of each day. Her joy and mildness were infectious. She gained the boy's respect. He would look at her as a mentor on his new pursuit of a simple life. They grew close over months until they were inseparable.

The boy abandoned his studies of philosophy. The fields and the workers on them became his teachers.

Though his home still stood firm and his family's wealth would long endure, his only connection to riches became the gems of his father that he always kept with him for fear of his mother's greed.

He understood what it meant to not be alone, having found people to call kin. Those farmers taught the boy another lesson without words, merely by living with one another and treating all with kindness—one could not be virtuous without sharing what they found value in. With each harvest, they shared. Each fertile land, they shared. Each meal, they shared. None kept anything valuable to themselves.

As he approached the age of manhood, the boy tried to share these lessons with his wealthy neighbours, to teach the value of a simple life and the emptiness of wealth. But he found that it fell on deaf ears. Most cared only for the philosophies of those prominent in name, and the teachings of a child were immaterial. They followed philosophies that advised dominance and prominence above all.

However, this endeavour taught the boy another lesson that left him disillusioned with his new path.

One of his wealthy neighbours was outraged upon learning that he was spending his days away from home and in the fields with the common people. The boy thought the outrage had come from the farmer's lack of wealth, as it had done for his other neighbours who reacted similarly.

But this neighbour instead called him a hypocrite for claiming the philosophies he taught to be his own. The neighbour claimed that the boy was merely a vessel for the philosopher rather than their creator, just like every other prominent philosopher the boy came to loathe.

The neighbour asked the boy how he differed from clever birds that only echoed the words of their masters.

The boy meditated on this and could not deny the truth in their words. He had been a vessel for his father's teachings and those of his enemies, which he diligently studied. Challenging and denying them was not enough to make his own.

He had been a vessel for the common people's ways, especially those of his mentor girl's. Bringing them to the wealthy was not enough to make them his own.

He learned that he had nothing at all to call his own. For all his life, he had received rather than created, taken rather than given.

On that day of harsh learning, the boy fled his home.

He walked for hours away from his estate and from the people's farmland until he was alone in a forest on the hills that split his home from his father's city. He spent days there, surviving with the knowledge and skills he learned from the farmers. He was hot during the days, cold during the nights, dependent on trees for shelter during downpours and wary of the creatures that roamed the forest.

He came to respect the earth itself in a new light upon being rendered helpless before it. He was in awe, coming to regard the earth as his home more than the stones and mortar that formed his estate. For even they were born of the earth.

Then came a day when the ground shook.

The quake came with no warning. Trees fell. Mud and debris rushed down from the peak of the hills like a raging river. The creatures fled into their burrows in terror.

The boy was helpless and alone. He had nowhere to flee to, nowhere to hide from the ground tilting under his feet.

The safety of his estate was far out of reach. There was no one to hear his voice crying for help.

The forest was flooded by the mudslide. He was surrounded by darkness as the earth buried him.

He dug with his hands with all his strength as he struggled to breathe.

He knew not whether it was for minutes or hours, but much time passed. He drifted in and out of consciousness until the darkness that trapped him merged both states. He did not know whether he was still alive or dead.

Dying was not a fear of his, but it was far too early. Death ought not to find him now that he had begun to understand what it meant to live.

He kept digging, kept drifting between sleep and wakefulness, until sunlight broke through the ground once more.

He found his way to the surface again, which no longer quaked.

He found a new awe for nature and gratefulness to it.

For the first time, he offered a prayer of thanks, not knowing or caring what was there to hear it.

That day, the boy found his own philosophy, one born from awe rather than the words of others—

He had no meaning to search out.

No power to attain.

No teaching to create virtue.

Goodness itself was meaning.

His humility before nature—before the sky, the ground and the water—was his first step on the path to goodness.

Without humility and virtue, he was not living a life of his own.

Nature would be the god that he could not comprehend, but was eternally thankful to.

The boy began to create meaning.

And so, he made the long walk back to the place he once called home, to his estate and the servant who surely awaited his return.

He saw reminders of nature's power on the way in the form of craters in the earth.

But the boy also saw strange visions on his walk.

He saw a green light above the clouds, like a crater in the sky. Then, from the sea, something vast figure rose—a man-shaped figure made of darkness.

So real were these visions that the boy trembled.

He watched the figure as it descended into the water, and the green light faded with it.

He wondered if he was sleeping still, if he was still buried in that mud and if these were visions before death reached him. Or if they were visions bestowed upon him after his recent revelations. Or if it was some manner of madness that plagued him after his burial.

He hurried to his estate.

He found his wealthy village now destroyed. The buildings had fallen much in the same way as the trees had after the quake. There were signs that the sea had drowned this place and left destruction in its wake.

The farmland was now like a wasteland, all the farmers' labour rendered futile.

The village was now drowning in fog and looked nothing like the place he once knew.

There was nobody left here. No one at all.

His mother was not in their wealthy estate.

His mentor girl was not working in the fields.

No one, rich or poor, alive or dead, was here but the boy himself.

It was as though they had never existed.

He spent days in that place, but none ever returned. The fog never faded.

On the fourth day, the boy saw the vision once more, that of the creature made of darkness.

It ascended from the sea near his estate. It stood on the same shore as the boy and approached, drifting atop the sand like a mist.

The boy was not frightened and had no instincts to flee. Alone in his broken home, he was defeated. Before this creature, he was in reverence.

He sensed emotions emanating from it.

It was angry.

It was sad.

It appeared…powerful.

309

It spoke in words that the boy could not understand with his ears but comprehended with his heart.

He was bestowed with peace in his spirit as the creature drew closer still.

The boy saw nothing but the darkness that made the creature tangible.

It consumed him in body and essence.

The boy felt power.

He felt what was once incomprehensible and always would be.

Darkness became his sole reality.

He wandered far from his home over time, with no destination or purpose.

He carried with him memories of home and the people he once knew. Some gave him comfort in his voyage, and some made the concept he once called his heart *ache.*

Over time, those memories faded too.

His sole connection to the place he had called home *was the beautiful gems of immeasurable value. He could not remember why he still carried them with him, only knowing that he could never part with them.*

Those gems remained beyond value and attached to the boy's very essence, no matter how much time passed.

Concepts of nature, gods and philosophy became immaterial to him with time.

Darkness and endless power became all-encompassing as all that existed during the boy's wandering.

There was nothing to inspire awe in him anymore.

The creature's mouth opened widely. There was a faint echo of the green light of its eyes shining from within it.

Something was born out of it.

It slowly poured from its mouth and into its hands.

It was a child's body.

The creature set it down in the sand, as though setting a baby down to sleep, where it lay perfectly still.

Umbra lay before Cadeo.

Around her were strange, beautiful stones. They shone like tiny stars.

Cadeo did not have the sentience to react nor to fathom the sight before him. He was overcome with lethargy.

He looked up at the creature again.

The creature looked down into Cadeo again.

It *screamed.*

It was not a voice heard with ears.

It crippled Cadeo's mind and spirit.

It seeped into his and his people's very beings.

It was agony.

Everything went dark as the world seemed to disappear.

THIRTY ONE

Before Umbra was an endless calm sea beneath a pure and pale fog-ridden sky. Her body felt lighter than a feather.

She was almost alone. None of her people were with her on the shore. There was not a sound—no birds, no insects, no wind stirring the sand.

Everything there was different. The huts, the sand, the hills and the trees on them all looked the same, yet they felt devoid of an essence she could only describe as *colour*. A colour not seen with her eyes but felt in the air.

The island, everything on it, and everything around it were colourless. Dead.

The creature was all that kept her company in this place. It *stood* beside her and watched over the sea with her. Its pitch-black body was a stark contrast against the whiteness that surrounded them.

Its eyes shone in their strange green tone as it looked

down on Umbra.

Behold the heart of what the mortals call life.

Though the creature spoke tenderly, its voice was like thunder against the striking silence it broke through.

Its voice seeped into Umbra. It was vibrant, like it pulled her into a painting of many tones. The words felt warm like a small flame, yet they were filled with sorrow. They were alive in her. They made her feel sad as well.

She had echoes of fear left in her from the hands that held her down in the water and the feeling of her life leaving her body.

She had the cloud of grief for her father in her, the slow acceptance that he was gone. It had hurt more than she could have imagined, even after all the years watching his slow decline and preparing her heart for this day.

But she also felt remnants of the serenity she felt as the end approached, with Cadeo's words giving her her only solace—

The next time you close your eyes, this place will be gone.

She wondered, as she looked around a place that didn't feel like her own, if her wish had been granted.

Down by her feet, she saw gems scattered in the pale sand. There was no sun to let them shine, but they were beautiful. She felt a nostalgia that wasn't her own.

She didn't wish to touch them again.

'They're beautiful,' she said to the creature. 'You shouldn't give them away.'

The creature's voice changed into one with a deeper tone of sadness.

I understand. Then, I shall carry these with

me again, as I always have.

'Where are we?' Umbra asked. It was only her eyes that told her it was her home, and every other part of her being that told her otherwise. 'Did I die?'

Alas, that is for none but you to decide, as is the nature of all homes. Their names are not akin to their being but are rather owned and bestowed. Your question itself, perhaps, alludes to the answer merely by being asked.

Umbra listened closely to the creature's voice. It was a new way of hearing that was difficult to do with intent. The words seeped in and forced understanding into her.

But even after hearing, she had no more answers. She didn't know if this was still her home or why she was in this place. Yet, with the creature's voice in her, she didn't care for the answers. It felt like this was where she belonged at this moment.

Though it was a place of isolation, she felt safer than she ever had.

The creature spoke again, as if in response to her thoughts.

...it is dangerous to think of yourself as saved by nature of simply being least of all by any other's hand least of all by my hand. Tell me, do you hate your fellows for what they have done to you?

It spoke in the form of a question that Umbra had never pondered. One of the words was clearer than all the rest, a word she had never uttered—*hate*.

So harsh a word it was that she didn't even want to bring it to her lips.

She eventually spoke with conviction when she answered. She hoped that conviction meant she spoke the truth.

'No...I don't hate them. I can't. I think they were sad when they did that to me. Cadeo was crying, too. I don't understand why I had to die, but maybe I...I deserve it. I must have. My people would never hurt me if I didn't. I can't hate them if this was all my fault.

The creature listened. Its face was completely devoid of features but for its glowing eyes, but to Umbra, it looked sad.

Such humility is a beauty beyond the innocence of a child, but it is a sign of a rich heart. My heart is cold, for I could not look upon them with such pity.

Umbra asked a question of her own. She was scared to ask it, because she did not know whether she could bear more loss.

'What happened to them? To my people?'

...they still live. They are neither awake nor asleep, neither here nor elsewhere. For you are the one who has been displaced, and they have been left behind.

She couldn't comprehend all the words that flowed into her, nor all the feelings they brought with them. But they carried relief with them. That was enough for her.

You have my pity. For you are guilty of

nought, but have suffered much for it.

Umbra felt a tingle in her heart at the creature's words. Had she not been so overwhelmed by tranquillity, she might have shed tears.

'Thank you,' fell out of Umbra's lips.

For what reason do you honour me with your thanks?

'I'm not sure,' she admitted. 'But it just feels right to thank you. It's…nice to be pitied.'

She spoke earnestly, though her voice was not enthused.

The creature looked out to sea again. The waves made no sound as they gently stroked the coast.

It spoke again.

Are you happy like this? Would you stay here and call this place your home? Or would you have your people awaken, that you may return to what you once called home?

The question was clear and weighted with burden. Umbra looked at her island home again, this time with inquisitive eyes and a deliberative mind.

She saw this place for exactly what it was—a piece of land in the middle of the vast sea, riddled with trees, foliage, and teeming with life. That was *all* she saw.

She realised now all that she had lost, all that had been taken from her. Though there was no hate in her heart, she couldn't call those who lived here *her* people anymore. Life wasn't the same anymore, and it never would be again.

And without her father, this place was no home at all.

Umbra found her answer.

'I don't want to be here at all,' she said. 'I want to be anywhere else. There's nothing here for me. It's not my home anymore.'

The creature made a strange sound. It was not a word, but rather akin to a groan or sigh.

It fell silent for a long time before it spoke again.

There is courage in facing the unknown and willing yourself to step into it... Then I may bestow upon you an alternative. Do you wish to wander—free of home, free of time, with nowhere to call your own?

Umbra didn't have to ponder for long. She questioned what it meant to *wander*. But she found that it didn't matter. After the many nights she spent imagining roaming the seas freely, she now craved a life of wandering with every ounce of her being.

She craved to be rid of this place and the pain it had brought to her.

She longed for Cadeo's final words to her to be a reality —*we will not even be a memory to you.*

Those had been kind words. They had shown her a longing she didn't realise she had.

Umbra nodded.

The creature knelt beside her. It embraced her.

Its body felt warm. She felt the sensation through her body and blood.

It felt unnatural—like a union with that which ought not to have existed at all.

It felt like medicine for her heart.

Then savour this fleeting moment. Look

about you with all your eyes, hear with all your ears, feel with all your skin. For everything will soon change, and these sensations will never come for you again.

Umbra looked at the island, the huts, and the hills one more time.

She took one more look at the endless sea of calm waters that had brought her peace for countless nights.

She gifted herself with one more happy feeling—the last memory of her father, embracing him with the warmth of the setting sun on her skin, as they watched day turn into night together.

I'll miss this place.

Then that feeling faded away.

Everything in her, born from flesh and blood, faded away.

Her essence became that of a shadow—formless and infinite.

Umbra felt herself grow.

She felt herself become endless, an entity as free and weightless as the wind.

She was consumed by blackness, yet the world was so bright and vivid to all her senses.

Umbra felt her very being become unfathomable, even to herself.

THIRTY TWO

A new day was born on the island. It was new, yet vaguely familiar—like a dream interrupted too soon, one of clear skies, sunlight, and no trace of fog. It was a morning greeted by birds joined in song.

Cadeo's eyes opened anew.

He could feel a profound change in the air and earth, the tangible shift from a dying island to one born anew. It was a perfectly ordinary day.

His people awoke along with him, and all sat together on the beach.

Before them was the beautiful, vibrant blue sea and the peaks of distant islands on the horizon.

Something was scattered in the sand with them—hordes of freshly dead fish, innumerable. The smell of them filled the air and was like nectar to their lungs.

It was all like a waking dream. Cadeo could not yet dare believe he was not still sleeping, suffering a cruel dream he could not wake from.

But the fish felt very real in his fingers, so very fresh and alluring. He held it as if it were as precious as a newborn child.

Nghi took a fish into his hands. It was large with a subtle orange ripple along its scales.

Then he bit into it. He buried his face into it and feasted on it.

His people saw and did the same. They took whatever fish they could set their hands on and ate without restraint.

There were sighs, groans, tears, screams—all filled with relief and elation.

Cadeo joined them, devouring a small fish by his feet. It was warm and slimy on his tongue, cold and with bones that tore his mouth. He had never tasted anything so good.

Never did any of them wonder whether the fish would again rot before their time, for all could sense the same change in the air.

All sensed that nature had become dependable again.

Sunlight broke into Nota's cave and woke her.

She gasped, first with shock, then with relief, as the terrible scream and pain in her body that forced her into an unnatural sleep were gone. She still lay curled up in the same place by her canvas.

On it was the painting of the fish. It remained in the same state—half-fresh and half-rotten, its scales turning into ash. It remained unfinished, rejecting every stroke of Nota's brush and repelling every new colour set on it.

There was a strange stench in the air, as there had been for days. As her hunger deepened, Nota had begun to smell that which wasn't there—fresh-cooked rice, boiled salted seaweed, fruits, fish. All were pleasant scents, torturous figments of her imagination.

But this scent was different. It was bland, colourless, and did not arouse her senses in any way. It felt realer.

Nota turned her head and saw her cooking pot boiling atop a fire.

She crawled to it with great effort to find a mess of fresh fish and weeds inside.

She filled her bowl and ate it without restraint. The fish was hot enough to burn her lips and tongue, but she could not stop eating. She filled her bowl again the moment it was empty. Her stomach ached from how quickly she ate it.

Even after she had her fill, there was more left in the pot. A sack full of more fish had been left in her cave, too.

This is real, she finally realised with her stomach now full. *I'm really eating again.*

Nota spent the rest of that day dozing in and out of sleep, and eating again each time she woke.

She found enough strength on the following day to find her feet and leave her cave.

She learned from Lihn that all the fish had been found on the shore, and that Adorjan would soon have to set out to sea to find out if the fish were indeed alive.

Lihn didn't detail what had transpired before waking on the shore, nor did any others that Nota spoke to that day. No matter how much Nota insisted on knowing, the most she heard was from Nghi, who said—'They're gone. Let them rest.'

She already knew what she needed to. Umbra and Varyis were gone. All her people had been fed as well as she had. The island was rid of the fog.

After Ashan's words claiming that their people would turn on one another for the chance at survival, it wasn't difficult for Nota to imagine what her people refused to say out loud.

Relentless guilt found her once again for the part she had played. *Ashan went as far as dying for their sake. I'm despicable, to have betrayed Umbra for my own sake. Why would I deserve to live more than him?*

She pondered this in the days that followed and concluded that she was again afraid, not of blame, but of the idea that her people had been right all along.

What if we're only alive because Umbra isn't? Then Ashan has died for nothing. Was he wrong to go so far in protecting her? But how can it be wrong to protect a little girl from harm? Such were the questions that Nota obsessed over in the day and would keep her awake for many nights to come.

Such questions still weighed on her when Cadeo visited her in her cave, as she had expected.

He asked Nota to carve the burial figures for Umbra and Varyis, which served as a final confirmation of their demise.

'Would you mind?' Cadeo had said. It was the first she had seen of him since the morning she ate again. He seemed different—gentler and emanating a humility. He looked and sounded like an old man to her, for the first time. 'You need not hurry. I know it will be a lot of work to do...both.

'And one for Ashan,' Nota added with some spite. *You're not about to disregard him. Not ever.* 'He'll need one too, no?'

Cadeo paused, then nodded with a sad smile. 'Please,' he softly said.

Nota saw that perhaps Cadeo had avoided mentioning Ashan to spare her feelings. She wouldn't have expected such courtesy and awareness from him either.

'Please do not take them to the hill,' Cadeo added. 'I will come to collect them myself when they are ready.'

Nota worked on the figures for three days.

All the while, doubts were resonating in her head—the same feelings of making art without purpose, of feeding into her people's delusions just because she was asked to. She feared that she had learned nothing, not from Ashan, not from the famine, not from her inability to paint.

But in truth, she worked diligently on the figures because it felt right to. She wanted to, and she would have even without being bid to. *This is all I have to commemorate the dead right now,* she accepted. *It's all any of us have. That's as good a reason as any.*

Ashan's figure was easy to craft in his likeness. Nota had seen him so often and taken note of his every and most intimate detail, more than she even realised. His rough, locked hair, his unblemished skin, his brooding face, the unrelenting intensity in his eyes—making it all immortal as wood felt natural. Nota allowed herself to cry as she worked on him, to lose herself in memories that inspired the art. Some were sensationalised, she knew, but she could not help but obsess over the parts of him that still brought warmth to her heart, even now. His finished burial figure gave Nota closure she had not expected. Looking at him now, she realised that, above all, she would miss his abrasiveness, his insensitivity, and his stubbornness. But her sorrow hurt far less with the memory of his righteousness and conviction.

Varyis' figure was more difficult than she had expected, much to her shame, for she had seen very little of him in recent years. *Actually, I haven't seen him at all,* she realised. *Not since he became bed-bound.* She made his figure as she remembered Varyis from when she was younger—as a zealous fisherman, a tall and imposing figure. He didn't smile often, much like Ashan, and he used to scare her when she was a child. She trusted that the way she remembered Varyis would be the way her people would like to remember him, too.

Umbra's was the most difficult, both as a test of her skill and of her strength of heart. She had to start her figure from scratch, as she could never bring herself to prepare for even a child's death before her time. So she had to remember Umbra's every detail and temperament.

She hadn't known much about Umbra either, not her personality or her temperament. Nota had never seen Umbra laugh or smile, yet it felt wrong somehow for that to be the characteristic to immortalise her.

Nota spent a whole day pondering how best to craft this figure.

She finally decided to immortalise her with the quality she herself would remember her for the rest of her days— the one that she didn't see in her, that failed to capture her as Nota saw her, but one that would ensure she would never forget the price of her life.

Umbra's figure immortalised pure child-like innocence.

Time meant very little. Adorjan could barely perceive its

passing.

He sat, paced and lay in Aunt Vada's hut for days. He lost count of how many times he had cried. He lost count of the many times he'd seen the sun rise and fall, the many hours he spent staring at the roof. But he did so until he could think of nothing but his hunger.

Someone had left a sack of fish for him outside at some point on the first day. He couldn't bring himself to eat any, nor could he eat them when they were found on the shore, as the thought alone made him feel sick.

He decided against preserving them in salt and threw them out before they rotted. He had since spent every moment in his aunt's hut.

Now his hunger was unbearable, and his stomach felt like it was eating itself. It was all deserved.

Adorjan spent an unknown number of days absorbed in endless remorse and regret.

There was no escaping it, he knew. Nowhere to hide, nowhere to retreat to, no sanctuary from it. He had long since accepted it and the ruthlessness it crippled him with. It was a burden from which he had no right to be freed.

Lihn appeared in the hut one morning soon after sunrise, waking him from another sleepless night.

'If you have time to sleep here, you have time to fish,' she had said. 'Nghi is making salt right now. Don't let his work be for nothing.'

Adorjan had only said, 'I'm not a fisherman, and I don't fish,' in return.

Lihn said, 'You are now and you will now,' before storming out.

Adorjan slowly came to understand her frustration during the next hour, and he lay in that same spot. *The fish will have already started rotting, since we have no salt. Soon, we'll have no food again. We need fresh fish.*

He then realised that only he could fish again. Only he had the strength and relative skill to set sail. Though he was no fisherman, he had to be for his people to eat again.

That was enough to get Adorjan to eat once more, to give him the strength for labour. He boiled the fish in water without salt and ate a meal with no flavour. So tasteless it was that there was no pleasure in the feast.

He ate until his stomach was full, then made the long walk down to the last fishing boat. On the shore, he did what he had seen Ashan and Quy do countless times. He removed the boat's anchor from the sand and pushed it out onto the water until it was carried by the waves.

Adorjan's arms ached after just a few strokes with the oar, and he wondered how Ashan and Quy managed to do this every week, or indeed how he had managed to row the boat anywhere himself. Still, rowed until he was beyond the island's cove.

Then he kept rowing. No changes came—no sudden storms at sea and no fog. No shadows on the horizon. Out there was only water and blue sky as far as the eye could see.

And there were fish in the water. Some swam in groups as they passed by the boat, some leapt out of the water, and some stayed deep underwater and could barely be seen.

The famine had passed. Adorjan could now be certain.

He revelled in the relief for a moment, until he realised that he had no idea what to do next. Never had he sailed with Ashan or Quy to see how they fished. All he knew of the art was that the net had to be set in the water and held to the boat by a rope.

Adorjan threw the net out while holding the rope, but it snapped shut the moment it touched the water, like a predator's jaw.

Ah, so I have to throw the net where the fish are gathered, he thought. *The rope is for closing the net around them.*

So, he cast out the net again and waited for a group of fish to pass above it. Then, he snapped it shut once more and pulled it on board. Only two small fish had been caught, each too small to make even a single meal.

Adorjan had newfound awe for Ashan and Quy's skill and patience.

This must be why there are two nets, he also realised. *One for catching the fish and one for holding them.*

He emptied the fish from one net to the other, then cast the net out again. This time, caught none.

He found the work was a strange mix of debilitating, tiring and compelling. Each time he cast the net, he came to understand more about the sea and the life in it, how it was not to be tamed but to be endured, surrendered to. Each lesson spurred him on to try again and again.

Adorjan wasn't conscious of time passing by while he was on the water. All that mattered was catching more fish than before.

He stopped only when it became too dark to see the fish in the water. He slumped onto his back, having not stopped fishing since he started. He marvelled at the fruits of his labour—a few fish writhing in the net. It was enough to keep his people fed for a few days if they were frugal.

He couldn't hide his disappointment from himself. *I don't want them to have to be frugal. Tomorrow, I'll catch twice as many.*

Then Adorjan suddenly realised how far the boat had carried him—beyond the island's cove into dark waters.

He looked over the sea from where he came, but couldn't see his home island anymore. He saw nothing but dark water and stars, utterly lost and starting to panic.

But he was soon offered relief, as a familiar song was carried to him with the wind. He didn't wait any longer, and he rowed the boat with the melody as his guide. It was no small miracle that the water was as calm as it was and allowed a smooth journey back.

Though the moon was much higher and the stars were much brighter by the time he did so, he eventually got close enough to see the island again. He made it back to the shore, utterly exhausted.

Cadeo, Nghi and Lihn waited there to meet him. They were angry in their worry for him being out so long after sunset.

Adorjan apologised by presenting the few fish he had caught.

Nghi took the fish into his sack of salt and set out to deliver them to the others.

Cadeo told Adorjan to go home to sleep, and he didn't need much convincing. He slept the moment his body touched his aunt's floor-bed and slept well until deep into the next morning.

Adorjan had one of the fish he caught for breakfast. Perhaps it was the freshness of the catch, but it tasted good even without much salt or herbs.

He decided to follow what used to be his daily routine and made for what used to be the rice paddies.

It was quiet there, and he was completely alone. The paddies were still in as sorry a state as when he was last there, even more so after being abandoned for many days.

He sat among the plants that were still buried in mud.

Sorry to have left you alone, he said in his heart. *But now, we can take care of you again. We'll build you back up, and it will be another harvest before long. You'll see.*

There would be much work to do in treating the paddies and nurturing the rice to grow well. Since the paddies had been healthy for so many decades, Adorjan never had to build one from scratch before. He didn't even know how to start. But he was also relishing the thought. After the labour at sea during the day before, he yearned for nothing more than to put his hands to work again.

The earth will know. The soil and the rice will know. They will teach us the way.

The paddies bestowed Adorjan with a gift while he sat there. It took a while for him to notice, lost in thought as he was, but he was gifted with *joy* when he finally did, the first he had felt in longer than he could remember.

He crawled toward what he saw and reached out with his hand, scarcely believing his eyes.

There, in the small patch Adorjan had worked for so many days to treat, stood a single healthy rice plant.

THIRTY THREE

Cadeo played his t'rung on the island shore.

It was just a cluster of hollow bamboo held together by rope, yet it still played as clear and pure a melody as ever.

Today, he played by instinct and feel. It was a song of notes that slowly rose in pitch while remaining low in tone. It sounded strange to him, giving him images of a wild lone creature on its hunt, of an unseen moon that had not yet risen, of the unknown sea depths. He was glad to find his music was still able to stir feelings in him that could not be described with words alone.

How strange the last few days had been. His people worked endlessly with fresh energy and determination, hardly speaking as they did so and seemingly working with an intangible synergy. Cadeo felt that it was made of the unspoken guilt that hung over all, that now lurked everywhere on the island as the fog had.

None spoke of what had transpired, of what had led to their survival. He felt that there was a chance that they never would, that they would try to force it into a forgotten memory with time. There were some merits to that.

Better to live in a way that one can move on with living, lest one becomes stagnant under the weight of guilt, Cadeo thought. *I tried my best, but I could not take that weight off my people's shoulders, and they have been forced to carry it still.*

Soon, with the setting of the burial figures, his people were to allow those feelings to fade. They would place the burden of their guilt upon those who were already gone. Cadeo had been tempted to allow that tradition to come to pass again, even asking Nota to make the figures again, just this one time to avoid burdening his people further, but he could not deny that such a temptation was born from cowardice.

Cadeo thought that other traditions and practices may die in the near future. Though she had not said so aloud, he could feel Nota's hesitation in her work—inking her people's skin, immortalising them through art. He thought it would be cruel to have her do so again after all this. He also thought that, in time, none would lament the loss of those customs. He himself could have no qualms about letting them die, for they had already lost their meaning in his eyes, perhaps long ago.

But this tradition of crafting the dead's likeness in wood would not die, Cadeo was sure. It did not need to be bound in superstition to be valuable. Instead, it would need to be bestowed with a new meaning.

Three new figures stood side by side before Cadeo, watching over the sea—Umbra, Varyis and Ashan.

Cadeo himself was truthfully in agony when he first saw them in Nota's cave, and that pain lasted until now. *Death as a price for life,* he bitterly thought. *Death at the hands of their own people, no less. Our lives could not possibly be worth this. We must come to accept this sooner or later if we are to give their deaths any meaning at all. We must earn our lives.*

He kept on playing, even as the sun set. *This truly is exhausting. I cannot keep up with this for long... it would be wonderful to teach this art to someone while I still can.*

Only now, Cadeo realised he had never considered who he would pass this skill to. Ruhan did not have the temperament or gentleness to create melodies. Quy did not have the diligence or motivation to learn such a skill. Ashan did not have the patience or the desire to be taught by him. Adorjan had his own crafts to cultivate—the most important of all.

Cadeo thought of Nota, of her love for art, the diligence she worked with, the wisdom and care she had shown through her words. There was no one better suited than she. *She will need wisdom and care in these times. Perhaps that is how I can best help her, by teaching her one craft to replace the other.*

Cadeo became exhausted. He let go of the sticks in his hands and allowed the music to fade away into the wind. He would not play any longer.

You are not a leader, he heard in Gratus' voice. The memory made him smile. *Indeed, I am not a leader, but am something else. I am just one of my people, no greater or worse.*

His hair swayed in the wind—that which he had called proof of his wisdom. It was long enough for its tips to lie on the ground when it hung freely. Half of it was the dark brown colour from his youth, which was still as vivid as it was in his memories.

It was beautiful to Cadeo, and always would be, but no longer a source of pride—only an extension of himself.

The other half was grey and white, brittle.

I don't have long left. I shan't waste my time feigning leadership or wisdom. My people will need purpose to return to their lives again. This shall be my purpose for the rest of my days —to lighten the load they will have to carry for far longer than I will.

Cadeo took hold of Umbra, Varyis and Ashan's idols. He stepped out into the water with them.

He still did not feel at ease with this. There would be protestations from his people—that he acted in secret, that he had broken the traditions they shared without their input. Part of him worried that this would be seen as disrespectful to the dead, that his people would not come to see this in the way he did.

But Cadeo was not striving for their approval, nor their thanks or understanding.

The best way to honour the past is to let it go when it burdens us.

That was the realisation that gave him the strength to let the burial figures go.

They were taken hold of by the sea, and they drifted away from the shore. They floated gently, as though they were clouds in a soft breeze. Cadeo watched them go until they were lost in the darkness of the water.

He allowed himself to smile. He was determined to smile still, even when he was not alone.

For despite all the pain and regret he would carry until his last breath, Cadeo chose to be grateful for life.

Alexander Linton was born in South London, England. His work includes the genres of fantasy, science fiction, historical fiction, horror and psychological fiction.

He is a traveller, and he writes his novels, comics, short stories and video games all over the world.